PRAISE FOR GIRLFRIENDING

"A novel that is so charming and warm and smart and about friendship and love and middle-age and I want to give it to all my middle-aged friends going through divorces and life reckonings."

—CURTIS SITTENFELD, author of *Prep* and *Romantic Comedy*

"I swallowed *Girlfriending* down in one big, thrilled gulp, not having realized how thirsty I was for exactly this calmly mesmerizing and fresh book about midlife. Also? It made me want to be a better person, somehow, even though it's sexy, page-turning fiction (i.e. not self-help). I am a huge Susanna Daniel fan and will be for life."

—CATHERINE NEWMAN, author of *Sandwich* and *Wreck*

"*Girlfriending* is a novel to read in a passionate rush, immediately start again in a more savoring way, and then press into the hands of everyone you know. This beautifully-written tale of marriage, divorce, love, sex, and everything else brims with compassion, shimmers with truth. Destined to be the dog-eared bible for those going through midlife queer awakenings (and their girlfriends, who will undoubtedly steal it). Susanna Daniel is a treasure."

—AMY SHEARN, author of *Animal Instinct*

"A magic trick of a story about a life that's been knocked over and broken open, full of vulnerability, generosity and desire. This novel literally makes me a happier person."

—MICHELLE WILDGEN, author of *Wine People* and *You're Not You*

"What does it look like for a middle-aged and semi-newly-out 'lesbian adolescent' to go on ten first dates? In Susanna Daniel's hands the answer is tender, very funny and as messy as real life. A loving and complicated portrait of a woman negotiating the intricacies of finding a girlfriend and of rediscovering herself, one romantic rendezvous at a time."

—LUCAS SCHAEFER, author of *The Slip*

"Ravishing, racy, and tender. *Girlfriending* is a joyful, full-throated experience."

—FLYNN BERRY, author of *Northern Spy*

"Daniel delivers a pitch-perfect story with this sensitively rendered novel about a late-in-life lesbian awakening… Daniel's evocative prose and expertly plotted tale combine heat and heart, viewed through the experiences of a woman coming into her own power."

—BOOKLIFE

"Told in vivid prose and includes sage observations about life and human connection… A charming and insightful exploration of reinvention and connection."

—KIRKUS REVIEWS

GIRLFRIENDING

A Novel

by Susanna Daniel

THIRD RAIL PRESS

For Curtis

ALSO BY SUSANNA DANIEL

Stiltsville
Sea Creatures

GIRLFRIENDING

To the west, to the west, I need anchors.
To the west, to the west, I need strong hands
To pull me up over the mountains
Before I love you again.

—Chris Pureka

ZERO

DURING THE NINE WEEKS that I knew Z, we sent each other one hundred texts a day.

Once, she sent a text that said *You are sooooooo amazing,* and once she sent a text that said *I can't believe how lucky I am to have met you,* and once she sent a text that said *I am nowhere near your neighborhood . . .,* and once she sent a text asking if I'd walk the Camino de Santiago with her one day, and I said yes, then looked up the Camino de Santiago. *I cannot wait to walk the Camino de Santiago with you,* I wrote, and she gave that message a heart.

Excitement = fun + fear, I remind my children, but sometimes the portions get wonky.

Once, Z and I laughed so hard I stopped the car in the middle of the street to keep from crashing. Once in bed we laughed so hard that I smeared snot all over her beautiful belly. Once she said she loved how I cry when I laugh, and it was the first time in my life I didn't wipe away those laughing tears in mild embarrassment. Once, we lay naked together and I told her things about myself I didn't like, things I'd done that I wasn't proud of. There was something between us that was safe and thrilling and very precious, a mixture that was as unfamiliar to me as was the speed of it all. I'd fallen before, but never like this: hard and fast and feet-first, unafraid.

To end it, she sent a late-night text: *I've been thinking a lot and I've decided you're not right for me.* I asked to speak by phone or in person, assuming that we could come to some sad but humane parting of ways. She didn't respond. My best friend Amanda tells me that, technically speaking, this isn't ghosting. Whatever it is, it makes me feel inhuman. An inconvenience, a nuisance. Left alone on a scorched island, haunted by memories of all that lush splendor.

In middle age, it's sacrilege to wish for a failing memory. I will not do it.

ONE

I'M FORTY-SEVEN YEARS OLD, swimming naked in a cold lake in my midsize Midwestern city, when I get my first-ever black eye. When the woman's elbow meets my ocular bone, I feel the blow in my sinuses and the sky darkens woozily. I swallow a mouthful of lake water flavored by blood and sneeze painfully several times. Nova Weston, a stranger whose name I will not know for a year, treads water with me as dozens of women swim past us, round a buoy, and splash back toward shore.

"Oh my word, oh my word," she says. "I'm so sorry!"

"I'm OK!" I say through my watery shock.

It's October, sunny and windy, and the rough water shoves us around. Her lips are lavender and her eyes are green. There's a dark mole in a crease of her neck and plenty of silver in her wet hair. She's my age, maybe a little older. Over her freckled shoulders, the modest skyline glints in the morning sunlight.

"Let's go," I say, coughing into a wave.

The stranger puts her face in the water. My nose stings and I have trouble syncing my limbs. I slap the base of the buoy, start back the way we came, and catch sight of Amanda in the distance. She's waiting on the boat ramp, holding my backpack, her light blond hair blowing. The organizers of the annual Goddess Plunge—my participation fee will go to a local food bank—unfurled a red carpet down the ramp, and now the swiftest goddesses lurch shakily toward their people. After I crawl onto land and find it in myself to stand, Amanda appears at my side with a towel and a paper cup of apple cider. "Holy moly," she says about the blood, which trickles between my breasts.

"But no sharks!" I say. I down the cider, which is tepid.

Amanda pulls me out of the fray, sits me down, trades my towel for a sweatshirt, and presses the towel to my nose.

"Ouch." I swallow a mouthful of warm blood, then vomit bloody bits of granola onto the grass.

"It's not broken," says Amanda, rubbing my back.

The possibility had not occurred to me. I inhale and air flows wetly. "I need my underwear."

Amanda fishes through my backpack and hands them to me, and I put them on and lie back in the grass. My teeth knock against each other and my head aches. Then the sunlight dims and there stands Nova Weston, wearing overalls and eyeglasses.

During the minute we spent treading water together, I glimpsed her nipples: small, dark coins.

"I did this," she says to Amanda.

"It was an accident," I say. "I'm fine."

"She's fine!" says Amanda cheerfully. When I asked her months ago to join me at this event, I'd hoped we'd swim together. She'd laughed a long time before offering to be my ride.

Nova's lips have regained some of their color. "There's a medic around here somewhere," she says.

"Was someone hurt?" I say, and both women look at me. "Oh. Anyone else?"

"Someone's wearing a warming blanket, but I don't know. What size t-shirt are you?"

This stranger is very cute in a bookwormy way—I like her eyes and the squarish shape of her chin—so I feel shy about answering, but then again I'm lying half-naked beside my own bloody vomit. "Large," I say, and she springs up, saying she'll be right back.

Amanda examines my face. "The bleeding stopped," she says.

"Pants?"

She hands them over and I wriggle them on. I hobble to stand. "How do I look?"

"That eye will be swollen shut in half an hour. Otherwise, so cute."

My stranger returns with an ice pack and a black t-shirt, across the bosom of which is a drawing of three women lounging against our city's skyline in togas and tiaras. This image does not feel true to my experience. "I'm really, really sorry," she says, backing away. "I shouldn't be allowed to swim in crowds."

"Please don't worry," I say. It hurts to smile.

Amanda gives me her arm and I hold the ice pack to my face as we weave through the crowd. We step into her car and the world goes quiet. She hands me her phone. On the screen is a photo of me on the red carpet, waving at the camera, my breasts bouncing blurrily. It is not a flattering picture—I'm wearing many chins and there's something lopsided about my eyes—but I look unapologetically gleeful. I still feel gleeful, though my skull hurts.

No phones allowed at the event, for obvious reasons. "I sneaked it," says Amanda. She pulls away from the beach and the lake slides by my window. Shadows of elm trees reach toward the lake's dark, choppy center. Life is passing, and fast.

A DAY LATER, still emboldened by the swim, I'm sitting in my car outside the diner where I'm meeting Amanda and our friend Gwen for breakfast when I absentmindedly open social media on my phone. I don't have a conscious desire to seek out or avoid posts from Z, but when her face appears on my screen, my heart clenches and my breath holds itself. Three selfies, dinner out with friends. She looks so happy. I want to say her face is beautiful, and this is true, but it's not the right word. What is the word for something you want to hold in your palms and admire? What's the word for something you want to study in every light, at every angle?

A minute ago I was calm, and now I am sweating from my hairline, so I make a move I've been deliberating for weeks: I force my fingers to my little keyboard and remove Z from my followers and myself from hers, check that I've done it correctly, then take deep breaths. There's a shaft of strong morning sunlight coming in through the windshield, and I close my eyes and show it my face.

Inside, Amanda is unstrapping her bike helmet and unwinding her scarf, and Gwen is sitting with a cup of tea and her needlepoint. Each of them welcomes me with a side hug and I slide into the booth. "I just disconnected from Z online," I say. "What have I done?"

Gwen puts down her needlepoint and covers my hand with her own. "Good," she says. "That one has worn a groove in your brain."

"Did she get an alert?" says Amanda, who is not on social media.

"No."

"Are you sure?"

"Yes. She won't know unless she checks."

"I approve, but why?"

"I want to stop thinking she's someone I know. She's not. She doesn't want to be."

"You were pushed out of a plane," says Gwen, speaking

metaphorically. "You're going to need some help getting back up. How do you feel about psychics?"

Last month, Gwen gave me a tarot reading. My card was the Knight of Swords, which means I have something urgent to say and it's important I get it out. The people I'm drawn to—lesbians, witches, social workers—tend toward astrology and mediums. What a thing, to believe the universe owns stock in your personal life.

"Skeptical," I say to Gwen. "But I'll try anything."

Did Z push me out of a plane? It's as apt an analogy as any, except the plane was safe and warm and wonderful. The hard ground was the hard ground.

Gwen and Amanda use Z's real name, which I can say only with effort. She is Z because my ex-husband of three years is X, and my first-ever girlfriend, who left me for a semi-pro mountain bicyclist, is Y. And after Z?

I can't take another ending.

Amanda and Gwen both vacillate between unhappyish and miserable in their long marriages. Amanda's husband talks to her like she's an alien who landed in his home, as if her essential needs—connection, equality, passion, shared goals, mutual respect—are strange, inconvenient chores. The bottom line is that he's not very nice to her and they don't love each other in an active way, yet he believes everything is fine and wants nothing to change.

Gwen's husband spends all their money on vintage records and marijuana and has never once loaded the dishwasher.

X and I have two kids who just started middle and high school. We keep things on pretty good terms, all told. A little friction, a lot of warmth. We pledged from the start of our separation to make it through with love and kindness. One reason we've succeeded is that, despite three years separated, we've been too lazy to make it legal. It's only one piece of the whole shebang—we worked out the custody and financial stuff right away—but I can't pretend it's not essential. In this, we're the opposite of the couples I've known, most of whom lead with the legal part and let the really important stuff follow. What results is bruising and disillusioning and chaotic, a private emotional mess sorted by spectators and handed back in a scorching, steely bundle. What if we all just cooled our jets for a while, then came up with an agreement based on what we've learned instead of what we've predicted? Because anger is cleaner, and cleaner is easier.

Gwen completes a stitch, then tell us that she's consulted a psychic named Mila a few times. She says, "If you're open to it, there's a chance she could help."

"Send me the link?" I say.

It's true that I'll try anything, but at the same time I have no desire to consult a psychic or an astrologer or anyone else, including the therapist who saw me through the end of my marriage. My brother is an internet-famous relationship guru, and he's told me half a dozen times that what's happening with me—the sadness, the anger, the confusion, the perseverating, the inability to conceive of my own future happiness—is grief. Grief disorders the brain, he tells me. Grief takes time.

We order, and then Amanda folds her hands on the table like she's in a meeting and says to me, "You need a plan."

It's not the first time she's said it, but this time I'm listening. "What kind of plan?"

Gwen, who is a nurse with the school district—years ago, she pulled a nail out of my younger son's foot and we've been friends ever since—is nodding in agreement. "Steps. Milestones. Rewards," she says. "Like AA."

"Dates," says Amanda. "You need to go on dates. Lots of them."

I haven't so much as glanced at the apps in weeks. What's the point?

"How many, do you think?" says Gwen to Amanda.

"A thousand," says Amanda, nodding sympathetically at me. "Or ten?"

I allow myself to imagine this. Ten dates, ten women, ten potential goodnight kisses. My heart might be broken, but the rest of me works. Why not?

"You've given Z enough of your power," Amanda says.

Amanda always had a sixth sense about my attraction to women. More than once, before I was out to myself, she'd mention an acquaintance and say something like, "I can see you with her." If she'd expressed even the faintest surprise when I finally did come out, would I have hesitated or stumbled? Instead, I've aimed toward women with an exuberance and surety typically associated with youth. But really, it's the exuberance and surety of a woman who has spent most of her life worrying too much about other people's opinions, wondering too often if all she knew was all there was.

On one level, I know I've given Z enough, truly I do. Not because she's unworthy, but because I deserve to move on. And I would like to record Amanda's words and lie down in a dark room and let them play in my ears on repeat for hours, until I'm healed, then get up and walk into the sunlight and never think of Z again. I'd like to reclaim the helm of my heart and brain.

Gwen says, "Let's define your goals."

"To go on ten first dates?" I say.

"Yes, but with the purpose of accomplishing what?" says Gwen.

I thought about this a lot in the weeks after Z, when I was floundering to define the potential I felt I'd lost. "Eventually, I want a lasting relationship that builds steadily over time," I say. "So I guess I want to meet someone who can make that happen with me."

"OK. What else?"

I want to forget Z. I want more experience in bed with women. I want to have some fun. I want to forget Z.

"I want to move slow," I say.

"Emotionally, you mean?" says Amanda. "Not physically."

"Right." Physically, I'm good to go.

"Dating ten women to get over Z is like eating celery to fix a full stomach," Gwen says. "But I've done that, so I can't judge."

"Did it work?" I say.

"Yes, but I can't tell you why."

The food arrives, and I shimmy out of my coat and dig in.

"Two things happened in my house this week," Amanda announces around a mouthful of omelet. "One is that I learned that Lionel has been cheating on his science quizzes. He told me himself."

Lionel is Amanda's gifted, autistic son. He's twelve years old and in eighth grade, having skipped kindergarten and fifth. He owns two snakes, two turtles, and one bearded dragon, and though his bedroom smells like dank, salty earth, I visit often to get the latest news. He doesn't name his animals, but he keeps careful records of their eating and waste, and once he told me that the python tied itself into a knot for three days. "What evolutionary purpose does that serve?" I asked him, and he said, "I'll find out," and made a note in his journal.

"And two," Amanda says, "Marcus told me he no longer wants a sexual relationship. With me, I mean."

I pull in my coffee and sit up straight.

Since X and I split, women tell me things they didn't before. I see now that part of my loneliness in my marriage came from living inside a bubble populated mostly by other people who chose the same bubble. When you're in the bubble, it's difficult to admit that there might be happiness outside of it. My friendships back then were happy-marriage-based friendships. We complained about our partners only on the he-forgot-our-anniversary level. Every so often a morsel might slip: *He cheated last year but it's over now, we're back on track. I almost left because of his drinking, but he stopped and we're back on track.* Being on track is the golden rule inside the bubble. When I deliberately went off track, several of my then-friends asked me if I was having a nervous breakdown.

We never talk about Amanda's marriage on the he-forgot-our-anniversary level. Her husband, Marcus, is a VP at the healthcare software company that put our town on the biotech map, and she's parlayed her midwife practice into the only birthing center in a hundred miles. From the outside, they are a power couple. It's not possible to know the guts of a marriage, but I do know he expects food on the table every night, and that he regularly guilts Amanda into returning even moderately priced items while he recently spent thousands on a bike that he rarely rides. Amanda makes good money running the center, but she'll never make what he makes, and this leads to the problematic math that results in her working full-time while also managing their home and child and sorting their unwieldy calendar and making their meals and packing his clothes for trips and everything else. There's no priority that ranks above Marcus's work. Their home, like most, is a capitalistic biome.

Amanda's chin is trembling. I could shuffle to her side of the booth, but something tells me she doesn't need soothing. She needs strategy. How do we survive our own lives? Like literally how, using which tips and tricks and weapons and armor? Meditation or journaling or gratitude practice? Affairs or drinking or shoplifting?

"What does he mean, exactly?" I say.

Amanda does this wonderful thing with her hands when she's telling a story, a series of karate chops, like her hands have a stutter. "I asked—again—if we should talk about the fact that we haven't had sex in months, and this time instead of saying he's tired or whatever, he said, 'I'm sorry, but I think that part of my life is behind me.' Then he shrugged."

"Wow," I say.

"Is it weird to say I'm relieved?" says Amanda. "And even hornier than usual? I slept in the guest room."

"*You* slept in the guest room?" Gwen and I both say. Of course she did. Marcus probably slept like a baby in their king.

Here's something else I know about Amanda's marriage: She and Marcus talk to each other all the time, and when she processes out loud about work or their kiddo or her fears, he asks questions and she opens up to him like she does to me. He and I share the same precious key to her. He gives too much advice and doesn't follow up, but there's no question that in a certain light, they have the stuff of a successful couple, the trust that invites shared vulnerability. But I've never had that, so maybe I'm wrong to think it means something.

I happen to know that they've had sex once this year, a fifty percent decrease from last year. She doesn't love him anymore, and she doesn't think about whether he still loves her. She's over marriage, she says. It's snake oil and the gig is up. Still, twice a week they sit together on their back deck, chatting about the day and making weekend plans.

Gwen says, "If he doesn't want sex and you do, why is his stance more legitimate than yours?"

"Right," I say.

"I don't know," says Amanda. She stares into her water. She looks tired. Her fingernails are bare and short and her hands are visibly dry. I want to take them in mine and warm them up. It's not strictly true that I'm a little in love with her, but would I marry her if she asked, or could we spend our last acts in adjoining condos? Happily.

"Is this something you're willing to live with?" says Gwen.

"For the rest of your one wild and precious et cetera?" I

say.

Amanda's hands go to her lap and she gives the barest shrug. "We'll see," she says.

AFTER BRUNCH, Amanda and I say goodbye to Gwen and drive in separate cars to get our dogs for a lap around the dog park. It's my off week, kid-wise—they return to me tomorrow—so my time is my own. The park is ninety fenced acres of restored prairie, two hills to get the blood pumping, many wooded trails. My dog checks to make sure Amanda's dog is following, then sets out at full speed, then stops abruptly to sniff a smattering of rotting crabapples, then takes off again.

Several acres of this prairie burned last summer, and hundreds of bright green seedlings rise from the charred expanse. This is one of my favorite places.

Which is one reason I wasn't expecting it when, a year ago, my first-ever girlfriend Y brought me here to tell me she was going away for the weekend with a woman named Layla, who'd told Y she hadn't lived until she'd ridden a gravel bike. Y and I had been dating exclusively for nine months. In the next breath, Y said we needed to *reify* our heretofore monogamous relationship, stat. Clarity was not Y's strong suit. I said, "Are you saying you want to be poly?" X had been ardently polyamorous since our split, a choice that I interpret as the natural result of his hardwired self-sufficiency. I didn't want to be poly with Y or anyone else, but I also didn't want to lose Y, almost entirely because I didn't want to lose my nascent lesbianism. Y looked at me pityingly and said, "The thing is, Layla isn't sure she wants to be poly."

Dating women has felt so right in every way, except for a few instances of blithe, unacknowledged cruelty, which have surprised me.

Amanda bellowed me back to life after Y. "Y sucks. Take

what she gave you and leave the rest," she said. It was a month before I could return to this park that I love, and another before I acknowledged Y and I were a terrible pairing, that I lived in constant fear of disappointing her by being myself, and I was relieved to be free of her.

I breathe heavily while we trudge up the hill. It's sunny, pleasant, and crisp, and the maple leaves plastered against the path look like craft-store versions of themselves. I ask Amanda if she'll continue sleeping in the basement or return to their dormant marital bed. "I like the basement," she says. "I can fart whenever I want."

"Bloom where you plant your farts," I say, and she laughs. She's an easy laugh, one of the many things I love about her.

She and Marcus tried for a second child, but it didn't happen. From what I've observed, having one child comes with more pressure but heightened closeness. I'm grateful I had a second, not only because my younger kiddo is a delight, but because I don't know if I could handle the intimacy and diligence of that three-pronged family structure. Especially when it becomes two-pronged.

"We're still sure he's not sleeping with someone else?" I say to Amanda. It's not the first time I've said it, and it won't be the last. But it's not sex and love he wants out of life, which is the problem in a nutshell.

"There's a coworker he's mentioned a few times." She shrugs. "It doesn't feel like this is about someone else."

"No, it doesn't."

"He's just not into me anymore."

"I resist that explanation."

"I'm not aging well," she says. "It's the light hair."

"You're aging beautifully. And anyway, it's not you."

This is one of the hardest things to believe, I know.

She bites her lip and leans into the hill. Then she says, "He thinks I'm not pretty enough to be his wife."

Back when I was still dating men after my marriage ended, which I did briefly in an obliging way before realizing—hallelujah!—I was not obliged at all, I met an online date on a street corner, and he looked me up and down and said, "I'm tired of women lying about their weight on their profiles." My photos were recent, a mix of face pics and body pics—had I misrepresented myself?

I've never had a conversation with a woman where suddenly I didn't know my own body and mind. If this isn't reason enough to stop dating men, I'm not sure what is. Also, the curve of a breast makes my mouth water, and three times after having sex with a woman for the first time, I've dozed against her without thinking twice about whether her arm might fall asleep.

Later on that same Last Man date (can you believe it went on from there?) the guy—whose name I honestly don't recall; ditto his unexceptional face—told me he'd been 1L at Harvard when Barack Obama was 3L, and then he said, "One el means—" and I held up my hand and told him I lived on planet Earth, and anyhow there's adequate context.

How will you know if someone went to Harvard Law? The same way you'll know that he thinks you're a fat liar!

There's some evidence that Marcus is a textbook narcissist, but there's also evidence that he's not. When Lionel was diagnosed, he didn't beat his chest or demand a second opinion. He told Amanda to make Lionel's favorite meal, and he came home from work with balloons and pints of ice cream and they sat down as a family and had a celebration—this was Marcus's word—of their son.

Of the many things I believe about men, I don't believe they're fundamentally shallow or cold or fickle. But it's been a long time since Marcus seemed excited by life or by Amanda. It would be a lie to pretend he isn't a beautiful man, getting more beautiful with every crow's foot and silver hair. And charming, when he's in the right mood. He preens; I've seen it. Before they go out, he claps a hand to the back of his neck and checks out both sides of his jaw in the mirror. Once in a blue moon, Amanda wears lipstick and puts on low heels. Otherwise, she wears the same pair of sneakers every day and buys a new pair every six months. Her look consists of low-slung black pants or dark jeans, subdued dark blouses, the occasional funky barrette.

Like Marcus, I don't remind Amanda she's beautiful often enough. She has freckles everywhere, even on the backs of her pale hands, and fine, naturally strawberry-blond hair that curls at the ends, and years ago she started wearing her bangs in that very short way that looks hip, though she complains that they don't lay right if she doesn't use a straight iron. She has keen green eyes and a heart-shaped face and ten different laughs, including a snorty giggle that is all her own. She's a little androgynous in a badass way. If I saw her on the street, I would be into not just her looks but also her swagger, which verges on imperiousness.

We take a break from analyzing her husband so Amanda can tell me about Lionel's new occupational therapist, a trans man who's teaching Lionel to ride a skateboard to work on balance. I mostly listen while doing some math in my head to figure out how much I can put toward my IRA this month. In a pause, she says, "My knees have started popping when I go up the stairs."

"But not when you go down?" I say.

"They ache when I go down."

We keep a running list of activities that make us feel old. Lifting weights, stadium concerts, early flights, loud restaurants, weddings. Going to the dentist is a big one for me. Teeth are all about irreversible decay. My father's teeth are worn yellow nubs, more round than rectangular, and every time I catch sight of them, I think about him dying. He turned eighty last month.

Tomorrow, Amanda will leave town with Marcus—he's presenting at a conference a thousand miles south, and Lionel is staying with a neighbor. She doesn't travel much with Marcus these days and the timing is bad, but it's too late now.

We part at the park gate, and I think only fleetingly of being dumped here. The pain of Y has long since been eclipsed by the much greater pain of Z. Amanda says that breakups are like sprained ankles—you don't know how bad it's going to be until a little time passes, and either it can bear some weight or it hurts so badly that you head straight into an opioid addiction.

Amanda says, "I love you!" and I say, "I love you!" But we don't hug because the dogs at the ends of our leashes are pulling us in different directions.

THREE DAYS BEFORE SHE DUMPED ME, I picked Z up from work at lunchtime and drove to a swimming pond outside the city. It was June and the sky was clear, but we were the only ones there. We swam to a floating dock and hauled ourselves up the ladder and lay on the sun-warm wood. She propped herself up to look me in the eye.

"I have a few questions," she said, touching the neckline of my swimsuit with a fingertip.

"Go for it," I said.

"I'm afraid I won't always be able to be myself with you," she said.

"Are you yourself now?"

"Yes, more or less. More and more."

I shielded her face from the sun with my palm and her blue eyes relaxed. How I adored even the slightest of her smiles. Her lips. The smudge of pink on her cheeks. Her front teeth and her back ones. "I'm not interested in whoever you think you need to be. Leave her home."

"That works for me."

"What else?"

"What happens after the blush is off the rose?"

"If I liked you for the blush not the rose, that'd be pretty naive. I know blushes fade. Mine will fade, too."

But I had the curious feeling that it already had. Did she think I was prone to speculating about the distant future? (I was not.) Maybe she was beset at all times by women offering her the moon, and I was just one more smitten suitress.

"Will you always bake me cookies when I'm sad, or was that just an early-days thing?"

"I'll bake you cookies for the rest of your life."

"Good answer," she said slowly, like each word was its own sentence.

She ran a finger over my lips and I parted them to let her in. This went on for a while.

She said, "Will we rely on each other without suffocating each other? Will we get busy in our lives and neglect each other? That's two questions, sorry."

"Being together will make our lives calmer, more joyful, more meaningful, sunnier and snowier, even tastier."

"How?"

"A hundred ways. I'll pick up paper towels when you're out and bring you coffee when you're having trouble waking up, and listen to you recount your dreams, because I know you need to get them out."

"I'll only recount the juicy ones. What else?"

"I'll drive when you're tired and turn down the volume when you have a headache and give you advice when you want it and keep my mouth shut when you don't. I'll listen to songs you love and love them too, and when you snap at me, I'll make funny faces at you until you laugh."

"What will I do for you?"

I thought, but it didn't take long. "Ask me about my day, please. Like regularly, even daily if it's not asking too much."

"It's not. That's too easy."

"Really? No one else has ever seemed to think so!"

This made her laugh a little. Directly into my ear, she whispered, "I'm in."

We were starting to sweat in the sun. I cupped her thigh and she held me at the base of my spine. We kissed and then dozed, facing each other. After we woke, we raced back to shore. She won. That night on video chat, we showed each other our weird sunburns: her left side and my right side, two halves of two wholes.

LAST YEAR, alarmed by reports of rapidly rising housing costs, I scraped together enough to buy a renovated ranch in a modest, nondescript neighborhood, and most mornings, if work isn't too heavy, I walk the dog with my headphones in my ears, exploring its uninspiring crannies. There's a weedy basketball court in one direction, a bowl-shaped park in another, and within walking distance are a gas station, a pretty good Mexican place, a library, and a Korean tailor. Half the homes on my block fly American flags, and one has a sign on the door that says GONE TO HOME DEPOT. My neighbors on one side are a gay Black couple who occasionally text me late at night to tell me my garage door is open. On the other side is an older hetero white couple who take long walks every day. They start out together, but by the time they return, she is half a block behind him, holding one hip.

With these walks, I'm learning my neighborhood at the level of the cracks in the sidewalks, the interesting bulbs on the tree trunks, the tidy front porches. Today, above the many-colored treeline, there is a full morning moon.

Can you see the moon? I text Amanda.

Wait.

I wait.

Yes, it's there. Oh my!

I know!

I send a group text to my brother and his husband in California and my father in Miami, time zones be damned: *Check out the moon this morning?* To my dead mother, I think, *Look at the moon!*

I am not alone.

For a few months now, food has tasted better, richer, more interesting. I gain pounds, I lose pounds. I do a lot of sweaty hot yoga and use deodorant regularly for the first time in my life. Only in the past couple of years have I released the tight mental chokehold I'd always kept on the size of my body. Feast, famine, punishment, reward, pleasure, pain. Part of this sea change is because I date women now, and through this new lens I've come to love the fleshiness of bodies, the contours and curves, the humid pockets and idiosyncratic turn-ons. My own included.

In the 1980s, before I started puberty, my glamorous babysitter explained to me that if a girl stands with her feet together, there should be a diamond-shaped space between the tops of her thighs. In silhouette, light would penetrate here, like starshine from her pubis. I'm pretty enough in a conventional way—I'm complimented most often on my eyes and my smile, second-most on my hourglass shape, and somewhat often on my ankles, though I've sprained them so often they're no longer slender—but it's safe to say light has never once shone between my upper thighs.

It's been 42 days since my last period. The one before that was a week early, and the one before that was 24 days late. So far, perimenopause feels less like a fading than a last hurrah, less a whimper than a bang. Every period is emotionally and physically overpowering, heavier in blood and aches and the blues than ever. I buy a box of tampons thinking it will be my last, and then two months later I'm buying another.

After one of the two times we slept together, I caught Z glancing at my body and couldn't read her expression. "Pink," she said about my bra as I fastened it. Was this approval or disapproval or something else? For what it's worth—zilch! bupkis!—I adored every inch of her, every mole and freckle and dimple and stretch mark, the curves of her ears, her sturdy ankles, her ladykiller grin. The pleasing topography of her breasts under her ironic t-shirts, her clean trim fingernails, the whites of her eyes when she rolled them at herself, the way her lids reddened when she started to cry, the aging skin at her neck. "You are so beautiful," I told her more than once, when words failed me.

Z resurrected my faith in Big Love.

Once, I asked Z about her hardest-ever breakup and she told me—Clara, who moved to take care of her aging parents—and I thought, petulantly and nonsensically, *I want to be your hardest-ever breakup.* But I didn't. She had a teeming stable of exes and I did not care to join them. With Z, I could see the vanishing distance, not a plateau but a series of gentle hills, a canopy of bright sunlight interrupted by clouds. Shining starlight, intermittent fog, flashes of hard rain, every sunrise, a last sunset.

After she disappeared, I told Amanda that I'll never again have with anyone the connection that came so naturally with Z. Amanda frowned and said, "You think?"

"Maybe someday I'll find ninety-three percent of it," I said.

"The seven percent will be more than made up for by the fact that the new woman will acknowledge your existence," said Amanda.

THE SMALL CITY WHERE I LIVE has a relatively big reputation, nationally speaking. People compare it to Austin and San Francisco, talk about the liberal politics and queer community and good food and healthcare. I think for a long time I stopped short of falling in love with the place because of this reputation, which does not totally bear out. For years there was only one restaurant that served truly spicy food, and there are a lot more regressives here than we like to admit, and just as many strip malls as in my Florida youth, as many chain and big box stores, as much blank charmlessness. But once I abandoned the idea of what the city was reputed to be, I found that I like what it actually is: a low-key, restful place, light on traffic and violence, and heavy on rivers and lakes and bike trails and woods. The limited options suit me nicely.

When I came out, the real fun began.

A few things we're long on here are craft fairs, live music, and quirky events for adults. People go on and on about raising kids here, the great schools, but I'm most delighted by how much there is to do for me, a single middle-aged woman. Which is to say that when it comes to making plans, the tail usually wags the dog for me. I know I want to go somewhere or do something, then I invite someone to go with me.

Which is how, on a Saturday evening in early November, for the first of my ten dates, I end up driving myself and a woman named Nadine to the industrial-chic community center on the cool side of town for an event called ADULTING 101. For $10 a ticket, we're promised the opportunity to learn: how to brew beer (eyeroll), change a tire (I haven't done this in a decade), split wood (cool), parallel park (I already know how to parallel park), administer CPR (can't hurt), tango (eyeroll), and properly dice vegetables (don't get me started).

Nadine, whom I met on the apps, is short and blond and curvy, with a touch of punk—heavy black boots and slouchy jeans and a black hoodie—and she doesn't meet my eyes as she settles into the passenger seat of my car. She opens and closes the makeup mirror and buckles herself in and says, "Don't axe murder me."

I pull away from her condo, saying, "*And they never saw her again . . .,*" and she laughs.

Nadine has two cats and is desperately in love with one of them; I know this from her social media. She has a beautiful rack but plays it down. She wears her hair in a low messy bun and heavily applied blue eyeshadow, which gives her a retro look. We're the same age, but she has the aura of someone with a past life, and before we're across town I've gotten the brass tacks of her story: She's sober and works as a surgical tech after twenty-plus years of restaurant work. (I don't drink, either. After I left X, I found myself checking the clock once too often, poured out my wine, and never looked back.) In addition to the cats, there was a dog she adored, who died last year. She loves horror movies and Lisa Marie Presley. She's originally from Georgia but doesn't speak to her family, which reads as a sore spot she has no intention of exploring with me.

I have a thing for self-made people, and there's also the matter of her stellar bosom, but after we park and head inside, she says to me, "I don't kiss on the first date," and I say, "So just oral sex, then," and she gives a stingy chuckle.

Inside, we stand in line for a long time to buy cans of non-alcoholic beer. I ask Nadine questions and she shrugs a lot and speaks quietly. When she asks me a question, she uses a voice that's meant to be intentionally self-conscious, like we're in an interview: Where are you *from*? What do you *do*?

In a pause, she says, "I don't date. Not that I can't date, I just don't."

"Why?"

"I've been preoccupied with other things."

"So is this your debut? I'm flattered!"

I mean this to be jokey, and she takes it that way. She has a shy smile and a fidgety manner that I find charming. I'm not nervous, but only because I've slipped into my brave first-date suit and nothing can touch me in it. Which works both ways, of course. I have no idea how I come off besides confident, mildly funny, and very attentive. These are the traits my alter ego brings to the table; they are of me but not me. The last time I ditched my alter ego was with Z, when we were alone and naked and ourselves together.

Nadine is hard to read, but by the time we're halfway through our drinks, she's decided she wants to split wood, so we get in line behind a young couple wearing matching mustard-colored beanies.

"So you have kids," says Nadine.

"Two."

"I like kids," she says.

I smile.

"No, really. I do."

"I believe you. I mostly like kids. I like mine a lot. And a few others."

"When was your last relationship?"

I tell her about Y and I don't tell her about Z. When I get to the part where Y tells me her new lover isn't sure she wants to be poly, Nadine smirks. "Classy," she says.

At least she told me in person, I think. I'm not to the point where I'm thinking generously about Y, but I can feel that time coming, and I suppose I will welcome it. Y was not my person, but my experience with her taught me what I don't want: serial monogamy. I like dating, I like sex, and when the situation calls for it, I like emotional intimacy. But I'm not looking to tumble from one girlfriend to the next. I want to build something that lasts a long, long time, or else keep it light.

"And you?" I ask Nadine.

"No comment," she says.

When it's our turn, Nadine gestures for me to go first, so I hand her my beer and put on safety goggles and make a show of stretching. The axe is heavier than I think it will be. The dude in charge of the booth—the crowd here is mostly women, but the booths are mostly run by men—places a piece of wood on a stout stool, then has me practice swinging a few times. If the axe slides out of my hands while it's over my head, it will hit a wall, not people, so I give it all I've got and the wood splits. I go again and miss the wood entirely. Again, and it splits again.

"Killer!" says the dude after I hand him my axe.

Things go downhill from there. At the tire-changing booth, Nadine stubs her toe and starts walking with a limp, and then at the knife skills station—I have basic cooking skills and no desire to improve them—I glance up from mincing a shallot to find the instructor frowning at my hands, then feel the knife slice through a thin layer of knuckle. He wraps it up and sends me off, and now I'm holding my hand above my heart and Nadine is still limping. We skip the tango.

I get us both another fake beer. Amanda told me that for each of my ten first dates, she's going to give me a mantra to repeat when I'm feeling wobbly. Wobbly, for me, happens when I can't think of anything to say. So now, as Nadine calmly looks everywhere but at me, I say my mantra to myself: *This is my lesbian adolescence. It won't kill me to feel uncomfortable.*

Nadine says, "I need to know how you feel about horror films."

I name some scary movies I've liked, and she says, "So you like scary if it's also artsy."

"I'd watch a non-artsy scary movie with you. But I tend to scream a lot. It annoys my children."

"It won't annoy me."

"Will you hold me if it's too much?"

"Maybe for a minute." She shrugs. "I think you can handle it."

"Every time I watch something scary, I regret it the whole time, but then afterward I feel great."

"Endorphins," says Nadine. "I don't get them anymore. I hardly ever feel scared. Watching movies."

"What about when you're not watching movies?"

"All the damn time."

We inch forward in the line for what is, gratefully, our final experience of the evening—the CPR booth—and Nadine tells me about work. This morning, a grouchy older patient told her he was tired of giving out his birth date every time he came to the doctor, and she said to him, "Sir, I can't say I relate, because no one ever asks me about my birth date!" So he asked her and she told him, and he wasn't grumpy after that.

"You love your work," I say.

"I do."

This is a huge turn-on for me. So many of us have rag-dolled into our professional lives, which is completely understandable, but I've cobbled my income together from bits of skill and talent and love, and I get so much daily satisfaction from my work that it's hard to imagine living otherwise.

The event is starting to thin out, and by the time we've reached the front of the line, there are only two couples behind us, all younger women. Nadine goes first, practicing on a dummy, and then the instructor, a young Black guy with fingernails painted dark green, has me lie on a mat with my arms at my sides. Nadine kneels next to me and her hoodie gapes.

"I have a good view from here," I tell her.

She doesn't adjust. "Look all you want, but I might not revive you."

She puts her hands between my breasts, and the instructor moves them lower and straightens her arms. He tells her to pretend to press twice per second.

"Open your eyes," says the instructor.

I open them.

"Open your mouth."

I open it.

When Nadine first presses on my chest I hardly feel it, and the instructor says, "You can press a little harder." I hold my breath for the next one, and she manages to push some air from me.

"Are you holding your breath? Don't do that," says the instructor.

She comes down again.

"Straighten your arms," says the instructor.

She does, then pretend-pumps several times.

We switch places. I'm aware of how I look from below, all jowls and chins. The zipper to her hoodie is beneath my palm, and I can't quite say how this happens, but when I straighten my arms and pretend to press down, my right knee torques to one side, and I end up falling over in an attempt to avoid crushing Nadine, who winces and curls into a fetal position. The instructor kneels over her, and after helping her sit up, announces that I bruised her rib.

"I don't think it's broken, though," he says.

"I broke her rib? I broke her rib?" I say.

The instructor helps her up and she leans on me for a short walk to a couple of empty chairs. When we sit, she hunches over herself for half a minute, shuddering, and I think she's crying but really she's laughing. "You bruised my rib!"

"I'm a klutz! I'm sorry!"

"You paid for the drinks. It's only right."

"Your place or mine?" I say.

We hobble to the car and I help her into the passenger

seat. She giggles most of the way back to her condo. When we get there, she says, "Let's do it again!" I can't tell if she's jokingly serious or completely joking. Was this a good date or a terrible one? My sliced finger throbs.

I don't get out of the car because I've pulled up right in front of her door. She's holding herself with her right arm and puts up her left hand for a high five.

"You have my number," she says, and gets out of the car, waving over her shoulder.

I CALL AMANDA ON THE WAY HOME, and she answers groggily.

"Go back to sleep," I say.

"I will," she whispers, "but tell me how it went."

"I sliced a knuckle and bruised her rib." The stubbed toe seems hardly worth a mention.

"So it was a success!"

"Yes! But—"

"Don't say it."

"—she's not my wife."

"What did I just say?"

"I know."

"Did you smooch?"

"No."

"Did you want to?"

"Yes. She's surly but it kind of turned me on."

"Surly?"

"Like she couldn't be bothered to be on the date but was willing to put up with me. I can't read her."

"And that's a turn-on?"

"Not typically."

"Second date?"

"After we both heal."

"Good enough."

THE VIDEOS THAT HAVE MADE MY BROTHER GABE internet-famous feature him sitting on a stool in his sunny kitchen, wearing a concert t-shirt (he owns six Indigo Girls shirts, four Taylor Swift shirts, and three Jackson Browne shirts) and counting down a listicle while his words flash on the screen. *Four Questions to Ask Before Sleeping Together. Nine Ways to Outlast the Honeymoon Stage. Twelve Green Flags That Look Like Red Flags.* Last time I thumbed through his account, I noticed that Abby Wambach and Sandra Bullock recently started following him. I hope everything is OK in their relationships.

Gabe's pit bull, Elton, appears at his side in most of his videos. The divot in Elton's skull flexes while he gnaws a toy.

Sometimes Gabe makes compilation videos of himself with his clients—they've signed paperwork for this, I assume, since my brother's husband is his legal counsel—where they're smiling and thanking him. I told him this reads as cultish to me, but he said it's more like the spot on my website where I list the authors I've helped get published, except instead of books it's happy couples. I used to think he sat down every day to record the day's content, but he told me that he does the whole week every Monday, and after that I could tell that he was changing his t-shirt but not his jeans. This left me a little disillusioned.

Since Gabe started with the listicles, he's doubled his hourly fee, he's booked out for months, and he's been interviewed twice for the Well section of the *New York Times*, which is the part our father is most proud of, since he's not on social media but gets the *Times* delivered every morning.

Once, I tried to explain to my father the significance of what Gabe has made for himself, but this was immediately after I tried to explain what an Airbnb was, and it was all too much. For my father, it's enough to know we're happy-ish.

Which we are, generally. My brother's marriage, which turned six years old this year, is a precious gem. The laughter, the patience, the teamwork. The last time we were all together, my brother, who appears to his followers like the most affable, easygoing person in the world, stalked to his room and slammed the door because we'd all greeted him too exuberantly when he wasn't yet fully awake. "He needs protein," his husband said, getting up to make him eggs. Later that same trip, my brother went on a rant about why, of all the symbols and colors, queers got stuck with rainbows. "Are we *children*?" he said, and his husband said, "I can see how that can be tiresome." I texted Amanda: *My brother is complaining about rainbows!* And she wrote, *Give him a kiss for me!* Because another thing that makes my brother grumpy is kissing him when you're not his husband.

His take on Z is that I've given more credence to her words than her actions. This is less the opinion of a big brother than of a guru who believes that healthy relationships require open and direct communication between parties who are fully whole and at all times emotionally regulated. "Not to mention timing," he always adds.

"So become a perfect person at the perfect time and then you're worthy of love?" I say in response, and he says, "That's not what I'm saying—" and then I redirect the conversation, because where's the part where you take a deep breath and dive in?

I thought we were going to be brave together, I wrote to Z after her last text. I'd thought we would hold hands at the lip of every sinkhole. I'd pull her over one and she'd pull me over the next.

What I wouldn't give for someone to be brave with me.

I KNOW MY BROTHER MINES LESSONS from life for his channel, but I'm still surprised when, while waiting for the school bus to drop my youngest, I open social media to find a new post from him—not a video, exactly, but a series of sentences that appear one after the other against a backdrop of a slow-rolling surf.

The first sentence is:

I hate to break it to you . . .

I wait. The pace is a little slow, in my opinion.

The next sentence is:

. . . but how someone treats you is how they feel about you.

My gut shifts.

You don't have to make excuses or try to interpret them.

Don't I?

If they ignore you, then you don't exist for them.

Then the zinger:

If they treat you like shit, they believe you are shit.

He picks up on the third ring. He's walking his dog and there's a lot of wind on his end. "Hi!" he says.

"Not today, man," I say.

"What does that mean?"

"I just saw your new video."

"I've told you, that's not how it works. What's new to you is not necessarily new."

"The one with the beach. The one where you hate to break it to me."

"Oh yeah, what did you think? Effective?"

"A little too," I say. "Please don't use my situation for your channel."

"What situation? Oh, Z? I didn't."

I wait for a gust of wind to pass. "It feels like you did," I say.

"You're not the first person to be rejected romantically."

"I realize that. And if I were merely rejected romantically, it wouldn't be so hard. It's the rest of it that feels like a personal indictment."

"What's the rest of it?"

"Are you being obtuse intentionally? Why am I having to explain myself here?"

"You're mad because you have to explain yourself? Wait, Elton is pooing," he says.

This version of my brother—rational, lawyerly, professionally patient—is not my favorite.

"No," I say. "I'm frustrated because it feels like you're using my pain to collect views."

"Is that necessarily a bad thing, though?"

"So which is it, did you use my stuff or not?"

He sighs. "Not. And yes, maybe. I always have quite a few clients experiencing the magical thinking that comes with heartbreak."

The term *magical thinking* makes me think of elves bustling through my brain. "Don't therapy me."

"Well, do you want my help or not?"

It's my turn to sigh. "I want your help."

There's a loud whooshing noise and several sharp barks. Elton does not abide city buses. "So how's that going for you?" he says.

We're done with my complaint. My brother is an internet-famous therapist, and everyone is his subject, even me. And where do I get off complaining, as a writer? He never promised to access a world other than his own for his work, and neither did I. What other world would that be, anyway? I don't write fantasy. I don't write legal thrillers. I work from life, and so does he.

"I'm OK when I'm not miserable," I say.

"You're living around it?"

"Most of the time."

"That's the waterline for now. Keep floating."

"You and your metaphors," I say. "I love you and goodbye."

He calls back just as the school bus is squeaking to a halt. My youngest bounds off and returns my wave as I give my brother what he asks for: step-by-step instructions to make yogurt in an Instant Pot. "Got it," he says when I'm done, and we hang up.

WHEN I LEFT X, the family's outdoorsperson, I assumed I would never camp again. But after a year, in a fit of energy, I bought a tent and set out with my children. We camp at least twice a year, including at the tail end of the season, after the leaves change but before they fall.

Now, we're headed to a state park on the nearest Great Lake. Everyone is quiet during the two-hour car ride, wiped out from a long week, but at some point my youngest says something about Texas being next to Florida—these are the two states where my family of origin lives, where the kids have been many times—and my oldest says, "Wrong! Texas is next to California, right Mama?"

"No," I say.

My oldest pitches the tent and my youngest places chairs around the fire pit and I haul our supplies and set out my yoga mat and do several sun salutations while they ask me questions about where things are located. Then we walk to the beach to let the dog run on the dunes. They say we're landlocked here in the middle, but the beach is wide and the water pans to the horizon and the sunset is every bit as pretty as those of my Floridian youth.

I throw a stick for the dog and head after her down the beach. The boys have a football and are using driftwood as a target. I leave them behind. A minute later, I step over the corpse of a large pewter fish with a bluish cast—a steelhead—and twenty yards down I spot another. A third is splayed out in the shadow of a felled tree trunk, and from its dorsal region spills a mound of fresh-looking orange roe. I gather the eggs in both hands and wade into the water to let them wash away. Then my phone rings.

It's Amanda. She's chewing something, probably fruit. "Where are you?" she says.

I show the water to the camera. "Beach," I say.

"I'm coming to you. Can I fit in your tent?"

Amanda's not a camper. The answer is yes, but barely.

"Send your location?"

I send it. "Site 114," I say.

She arrives just before the burgers are ready. She's brought her own beer and chair and sleeping bag. Something's up, but I don't ask. My youngest, who has great comic instincts and iffy self-esteem, a combination that worries me, does his Grumpy Old Man act using a tree branch as a cane. I ask my oldest three times to please stop texting his new girlfriend, then take away his phone. Amanda drinks two beers and tells a story about neighbors who were featured in a magazine article called "How to Create an Enticing Sex Room." This takes some explaining for the kids, though I muddle it because what is a sex room? I set up the beds, then we move to the fire and wrap ourselves in blankets. The sky is very dark and the stars are out. You get out of town to dampen the hustle, but it's never quite gone, and by the time we settle into our chairs, my youngest has dropped two marshmallows in the fire and is balling his fists, and I raise my voice at my oldest to stop badgering me about his damn phone.

In a pause, Amanda says, "Lionel got suspended from school."

"For what?" say both of my children, who are protective of Lionel.

Amanda stares into the fire. "He offered to show his penis to another boy. A younger boy."

"Oh no," I say.

She's worried about this, or something like it, since Lionel started puberty. She knew he'd started because he kept telling her how big his penis had gotten and insisting on showing it to her. The last time I was over he offered to show it to me. I declined in a straightforward way.

"I wish you'd called me," I say now. It's not the right thing to say.

"Can we not?" says Amanda.

This is a sore spot, her reliance on the women in her fancy neighborhood over me. She doesn't want to bother me, she says, and she's done them so many favors of the domestic, dog-sitting, child-minding kind that they owe her. She needs me outside her bubble so she has a place to go. That's all fine, but I want to be useful to her. She's so very useful to me. Right now, I'm not thinking of Z because of the hours I've spent crying on Amanda's shoulder. Or at least I'm not thinking of Z in a primary way. She's always with me, a tireless suckerfish on my heart.

"Is Lionel OK?" I say.

"He's ashamed," she says, then starts to cry.

My youngest goes to Amanda's side and hugs her.

"What are you going to do?" says my oldest.

"Maybe a new school," says Amanda. This has been a potential outcome for a while now. Public school was always a placeholder for Lionel. My kids have done well in public school, though last year my youngest struggled in math, and three weeks before the end of the school year, his teacher said to me, "It's too bad he was never moved into the right math class this year," as if she were a neutral observer. Now, X and I spend hundreds every month on a private tutoring program with a pun for a name.

"It's going to be OK," I say to Amanda.

I goad the boys into cleaning up and scoot my chair close to Amanda's. The oldest starts lecturing the youngest about why *Thor: Love and Thunder* is a better film than *Avengers: Endgame*, and I say, "*In my opinion*," loudly.

Amanda holds up a hand. "Listen," she whispers.

We listen. Somewhere, a man is raging.

The sound is coming from the next campsite over, which we can't see through the woods. A man's voice says very clearly, "*Why do we do this bullshit? You're such a bitch*," and a child's voice says, "*I'm scared*," and a woman's voice murmurs.

We sit still. The shouting rises and falls.

"Stay here," I say to the kids.

Amanda and I put our dogs on their leashes and turn on our headlamps.

My teenager moves to the chair beside his brother. "Don't go," says my youngest.

"We won't be long," I tell them.

"Can we go with you?" says the teenager.

"No," I say. "We'll be right back."

Amanda and I walk until the signpost for the neighbor's campsite is in sight, then turn off our headlamps. The shouting is more distinct from here. Why hasn't anyone else come away from their fires? Amanda calls the park ranger, who tells her to call the police, and after Amanda gives the info, we stand in the dark, looking up at the stars. Headlights appear over a crest. We shuffle onto the shoulder and two police cruisers pass us and pull into the angry man's site. We walk back to the kids.

"What happened?" they say.

"The police came," I say. "You're safe."

I'd like to tell the guy to get in his car and drive away forever. Except for two things: alcohol and guns.

"Bedtime," I say.

My teenager hugs me and heads to the car, where he's made a nest in the trunk. My youngest stands by my chair. "I'll be back," I say to Amanda, who's tapping at her phone in a way that means trouble.

It's getting colder, and I bring the dog inside the tent. My youngest climbs into his sleeping bag and I zip it for him. I read a chapter of a book and kiss his hairline. "You smell like cold sweat," I say. "My favorite."

"You smell like mama," he says.

He doesn't want me to leave, but he doesn't say it.

"I won't be long," I say.

I pull my camp chair close to Amanda's and lay my hand on her arm. She's staring at the fire. "You're lucky," she says to me.

"I know," I say. My neurotypical children, my freedom. I sink low in my chair and close my eyes. "I wish I could be unstrong for like one week. Don't you wish that?"

"Sure, but how?"

Good question. When Marcus told her he no longer wanted a sexual relationship with her, Amanda didn't fall apart. She got her book and her readers and her favorite blanket, and she went down to the basement and took her eight hours from the world's teeth, as one does.

"They offered him the job," she says now.

It takes a blink or two to sink in. You cannot move one thousand miles away, I want to say, but that's not my place right now. I also can't say, Let's take a gander at that state's divorce laws.

She says something about the ways in which Marcus's work will change—more regular hours, more time at home—and I hear his words behind hers. I could tell her Marcus will never work less, will never lift her load, will probably never pull her back to his bed, but she already knows this.

"What are the odds on this?" I say.

"Fifty-fifty," she says. She opens a third beer. She hasn't drunk a third anything for years.

The angry man's truck glides past, followed by both cruisers.

"Good riddance," says Amanda.

I HAVE A SECRET: Since leaving the bubble, I wake up vibrating with joy more often than not, even with the suckerfish on my heart. I'm grateful to wake up each day in this heartbreaking and beautiful world, lugging outsized grief and love in this brief vessel of a body. The sun is just rising and my youngest is snoring as I unzip myself and my dog into the frosty morning and walk to the beach. I take a photo of the golden sun opening over the black water like a beneficent eye.

The suckerfish is resting. I fake out the pain, zig when it zags, by switching channels when Z's face appears in my brain. My brain is a boxer in training, and on a morning like this, as my dog trots into the woods in pursuit of something, then trots out in pursuit of me, my brain is light on its feet, gloves up.

When I return to camp, Amanda hands me a mug of coffee. She's wearing running clothes and her hair is pulled back, her eyes dark with worry. "Go," I say, and she is off.

When I open the hatchback, my oldest's face appears from behind a blanket of blond hair. I place his phone beside him. "Hi, Mama," he says, and I grab the food crate and kiss his forehead.

"Sleep," I say.

My youngest joins me in the chairs, hands stuffed into the pockets of his hoodie. "What time is it? Did I sleep in?"

"You did," I say, though my watch is dead and my phone is who knows where. I make him a mug of very milky and sugary coffee and he gets our books from the tent and we read for a while. Eventually my oldest joins us with his phone. "How'd you sleep?" I say.

He snaps a photo of his own face. "Good," he says, sending the photo off.

Amanda comes back and I make eggs and bacon while the boys strike camp. Then we all go to the beach, and after hemming and hawing for a while, we wade into the cold water, holding hands. Amanda breaks off and dives in, and I follow her. I swim as far as I can without breathing, then rush back to the sand. There's no one else on the beach, so Amanda and I change into dry clothes and point our faces to the new sun. The boys wander away to change in private. There's sand in my underwear and my nipples are ice cold and so are my feet, but I feel fine. The world is splendid.

Except. "I think you're going to go," I say to her.

Amanda grunts.

"I don't want to factor in," I say.

"You factor in," she says.

"Book a consult with a lawyer there," I say. "Get some facts."

"I already did." How long has she known? "The facts are not good."

I squeeze her hand. The boys come back lugging driftwood and then work on building a raft. When they play together I look away, as if my gaze might turn them to bickering stones.

"Let's not go home," says Amanda, because it's getting on time.

"Good plan," I say.

On the way out of the park, I go into the office, where the ranger sits with the local paper. I tell him I wanted to check on the family in site 116, and he says, "They're leaving today. Evicted."

"I thought the guy already left."

"No, he's sleeping it off."

I tell him I saw the guy's truck leaving last night.

"They told him to take a drive. He came back."

They told him to take a *drive*? "I get why he has to leave, but why does she?"

He shrugs. "The cops said they've been married fifteen years. The kids are little."

I look at him.

"She made her bed," he says.

IT'S SLEETING WHEN I VENTURE ACROSS TOWN to meet my second first date. On the way, I pass two cars that have skidded off the road. One is half-wedged under a chain link fence and the other sits in the dead center of a field, headlighting its own tire marks.

Gretchen meets me at a bar downstairs from her apartment, and when she sits down, we look at each other for a minute, smiling. She seems very young, though what is thirty-six to me now? The age I gave birth to my second child and published my second book, a couple of years before I knew I wanted an entirely different life.

"I never know what to say!" she says.

"I'll start," I say. "How was your day?"

Gretchen has the hairstyle they're calling a wolf cut, which is hip and queer and youthful. I know from her profile that she works as a carpenter. She says she had a fine day, mostly framing out windows for a remodel.

I want to know what it's like working in a man's

profession, but when I ask she just shrugs, like she's never thought about it before. "They leave me alone," she says.

The seconds lag. She has an anime character's big, clear-blue eyes and a pianist's long fingers, and during one of the many pauses in our conversation, she finishes her white wine and signals the waiter for another. She's very pretty, but I have the feeling that all her jokes will go over my head and vice versa.

I ask about siblings, pets, music. I have tickets to see a maudlin singer-songwriter later tonight at my favorite local venue, but the real draw is the opener, Chris Pureka (they/them), one of my favorites. I'm thinking I'd rather go alone than drag this young woman whose favorite bands I've never heard of—mostly synthrock and femmecore, she tells me, though this doesn't help—but then she tells me that on her last first date, the woman came into the restaurant, looked around, found Gretchen with her eyes, sat down, and said nothing. After a minute, Gretchen said to the woman, "You don't find me attractive, do you?" and the woman said, "No, sorry," and Gretchen said, "That's OK, you can go," and the woman thanked her and left.

"I don't know if I find someone attractive until I've been around them for a while," I say.

"Do you find me attractive?" she says, dipping into her wine.

I like her forthrightness and also I like this cute thing she does with her mouth, a kind of self-effacing grimace. And for reasons only the moon understands, I'm ready to rock, sexually speaking.

"Yes, I do," I say. "But the age difference."

"Don't worry about it," she says.

As responses go, this one never makes much sense to me.

"I have two not-small children and I haven't gotten my period for seventy-six days," I say.

"I understand," she says. "I like kids."

I pick up the tab and we walk to my car. She touches her own cheek and asks for a kiss. Her stylish hair is soft against my face. I feel an urge. Then she's pulling me toward her by the waist of my jeans and we're making out on the sidewalk.

"Let's get in your car?" she says.

There's no way I'm missing the show, but she's willing to go along. We make out some more after I park at the venue, then go into the dark room holding hands. We're a little late and find seats in the back. I get us drinks—my usual nonalcoholic beer, a white wine for her—and as soon as I sit down, the lights dim and out comes Chris Pureka, alone with a guitar. They greet the small crowd quietly and start to play, and I forget all about Gretchen.

What is it about this musician? I follow them on social media and they post a lot of pictures with their dog, and with a partner or relative who looks very much like them, at least in presentation—slight frame and short hair and delicate features and rosy cheeks, button-down shirts and matching chihuahuas. With Chris Pureka's music, it feels as if there's no scrim between the songs and the artist, as if all their suffering translates directly into these notes and chords. Except when channeled like this, it's not suffering at all—it's communication. It's an offering, and I accept it.

This is my fifth or sixth time seeing them live. Gretchen is here but not here. I'm sorry, I want to tell her, but I know you'll wait because those were good kisses.

After forty minutes, they're saying good night, and the lights come up, and Gretchen hands me her empty glass, so I go back to the bar.

When I sit down again, Gretchen sidles closer to me. I'm not comfortable in small folding chairs, generally, and I tell Gretchen, who is not the right audience for this joke, that I envision a future where everywhere you go, there's a

Barcalounger. Like at the movies. Everywhere, I tell her, even at therapy and the DMV, and there will always be the titillating possibility of sneaking in a cat nap. Maybe, in a world full of Barcaloungers, people will speak softly to each other, step gently around each other's outstretched toes.

Gretchen gazes at me with her anime eyes and says, "Barca-what?"

The lights dim again and the older, maudlin singer-songwriter sits down on stage and tells us right away that he doesn't play songs anymore; he plays meditations. For a long time there's only one soft riff, and then he aims his chin at the mic and opens his mouth.

I have no desire to challenge an artist's assessment of his own creative work, but aren't these *songs*? Isn't a song, like a poem or a story, a fluid and unboxable thing? And if this is a meditation, is it his meditation or mine? Isn't a meditation a closed loop, not an offering?

While I'm thinking in this thorny way about the music, I feel the tip of Gretchen's finger graze my left nipple. When a woman touches my nipple, my body responds. I can't help it and I have no desire to.

She's sitting very close and her arms are crossed, so her roaming hand would be difficult to detect in the dark. I shift to give her better access and press my mouth to the hair behind her ear. A thumb joins the finger. It is a marvel, this body of mine, the way it revs. In this stage of my lesbian adolescence, I'm generally more comfortable giving than receiving—this will change, hooray!—but for the moment I let myself revel. There's something so capable and forthright and playful about her touch. I already know that the sex will be very, very good.

In my ear, she says, "I'm going to take you first."

We leave after the second meditation, and on the drive to her apartment she is pressed against me and the seatbelt sensor is dinging. It's cold out and we rush to the bright green door of her building and up stairs that smell like old lasagna and into her tidy studio with the bed on the floor.

"I like it narrow but deep, with a lot of pressure," she says between kisses, "and I like to be kissed when I come."

"I'm not sure what the first part means," I say.

"I'll show you," she says.

Within a few minutes of crawling onto her mattress, my brain switches into sensory mode, so most of the experience is soft focus and smell, like I'm a newborn. But at some point at least an hour in, I lie back to catch my breath, and we both notice at the same time that she is covered—arms, thighs, jawline—in blood. My blood.

"Don't worry," she says, and goes to her bathroom. The shower turns on.

My thighs, the inside of my wrist, a spot near my belly button. The sheets.

She comes back and we start in again, and the next time we stop, she goes back to her shower. I think of HIV. I think of how hygienic my straight sex life was, even at its margins. I think about Gretchen's cool calm. I'm not particularly worried until after we go another round, at which point my brain clears.

She showers for a third time and I pull on my shirt and underwear. Then she lays beside me and we look around her room together. She made the side and coffee tables from a rough, light wood that looks too soft to hold a screw. She doesn't own a television or books. Her loveseat, the only place to sit beside the mattress, faces a bay window, and over the tops of bare trees is the lake.

She pulls on her skinny jeans and leaves her breasts bare and runs her hands through her hair. A good look on her.

"I'd like some kind of pretty tapestry for my table," she says. "Maybe you can buy me one."

"Sure?" I say, snagging on her words and letting them

blow away.

There's the matter of the sheets and the smell of blood in the air.

"Did you jumpstart my period?" I say.

She shakes her head. "It's not your period, it's just something that happens with older women . . ."

Is it me, or does this convey some depth of experience? The word *friable* comes to mind. Part of me wants to lounge for another hour, but I'm embarrassed about the blood. She's showered three times but otherwise seems wholly at ease.

"I'm going to go," I say, kissing her bare shoulder.

"I'm not going to see you again, am I?" she says.

"I'm not sure," I say. "I need to think."

"Have me over next week, cook me dinner?"

I don't cook much when I don't have my children. And I don't invite dates to the house when I do. If she asked this question, specifically and insanely: "Can you realistically see yourself choosing a recipe, driving to the grocery store, then cooking us a meal?" instead of the question she did ask, my answer would be no.

She walks me to my car and we kiss some more, but I'm ready to go. It's my own self calling me now, my fifteen minutes of car time and the dog who will greet me when I stomp in from the garage and step gratefully out of my boots.

But here's the thing about wanting. People talk all the time about living in the moment, and I understand what they mean, but it's not the moment that gives me trouble; it's the future I need a better bead on. Today, I'm chasing my freedom as fiercely as I'm chasing these first dates, but past-me has chased marriage and babies, has made and lost friends, has dodged change in favor of calm. Isn't it likely that future-me will mourn my empty house as keenly as today-me basks in it? Today-me wants to go on ten first dates while future-me wants a lasting relationship with one specific human. How does one live in the present, let go of the past, and aim toward the future at the same time?

One muddles through, is my only answer. Maybe you have a better one.

THREE

MY MOTHER HAD TWO SISTERS, one younger and one older. I spent holidays and summers with them as a child, and we stayed close through my mother's decline and after her death. My mother's younger sister, who is single and has no children, is aging fast and early, while her older sister, who is widowed with two grown children and five grandchildren, is easing stylishly into her mid-eighties, a fact that must make my ill aunt's deterioration even more painful. Never are single people as single as when they are in physical need.

When my brother and I receive word from our cousins that our younger aunt is in the hospital with hallucinations, we scuttle our schedules to fly down and help our cousins pack her up and move her into an assisted living facility. This will be backbreaking work; she's lived in the same charming bungalow for fifty years, since starting her career as an art teacher in the public schools, and she has a penchant for accumulating things and stowing them in drawers and closets, under beds, in the guest bathtub.

Gabe and I meet in the airport terminal and drive a rental straight to the house, where my cousins are already waist-deep in piles to donate, move, toss. We need to work quickly, but it's not easy to keep from hunting for treasure: a trove of painting and craft supplies; original art from her bohemian days; broken pottery, meant for mosaics; five jewel-colored bowling balls; an original Coca-Cola sign the size of a wall, which hung outside my grandfather's filling station in the 1950s; jars of antique marbles; my mother's twirling baton from high school; photographs of my grandparents, happy; photos of all of us, happy. My aunt lived a rich life until she didn't.

The evening I arrive, while elbow-deep in my aunt's bedroom drawers, I find a jade-colored urn the size of my palm. I bring it out to the living room, where my cousins are packing dishes and my brother is standing on a stool, pulling down a brass chandelier that had been in my great-grandmother's home.

"This is Mom," I say to Gabe, holding up the urn.

"No, it's not," he says for some reason.

"Yes, it is. I remember."

I made my mother's funeral arrangements, and when I was offered the option to keep part of her ashes, I declined—a decision I've regretted since. My aunt did not decline.

"Really?" Gabe said. "Ew."

At the hospital the next day, I show the urn to my aunt, and her eyes widen. When I ask if I can please take the urn home with me, she nods.

"I miss your mom every day," she says.

"Me too," I say.

THE NEXT DAY, I make eleven trips to Goodwill. The attendant looks over my stuff as he helps me haul it into a giant bin. "This is a life," he says more than once. Unused picture frames, full bottles of perfume, compression socks with the tags still on. All four of us work for hours and there's progress, but not enough. There are buyers for her house but the negotiations are ongoing. On our third day of work, my brother reports that his lawyer husband has a suggestion: We work for one more day, but leave the rest to the sellers, who are looking to chop another hunk off the sale price anyway. Before arriving, I would have said no to this suggestion, but now it's a lifeboat in an infinite sea.

Gabe is not sentimental. During our final hours in the house, he's chucking whole drawers into bags while I perch on a file cabinet in a corner, skimming newspaper clippings and Post-It notes and decades-old greeting cards. I keep a plaque bearing my grandmother's full name, which lived on her desk when she worked as a bank manager. This is how she put three girls through college without much help from my grandfather, who was occupied with grand ideas and what was likely bipolar disorder. I also keep a twirling trophy of my mother's, even though the gold figurine has broken off the wooden base. Of my aunt's, I keep a smooth wooden bowl full of polished stones and a collection of wooden spoons she inherited from my great-grandmother. My aunt was the keeper of the family things as well as stories. The things will disappear with the house, and, unless one of us does something about it, the stories will disappear with her.

My cousins are brisk and tireless and kind, natural helpers. One of them, the more tender one, has tears in her eyes when we lock the front door of my aunt's house for the last time. Before we get into our cars, all four of us stand on the brick walkway with our arms around each other and our heads bowed, something we've never done before.

AFTER I'M HOME, Gretchen and I exchange several text messages, mostly about her bedsheets.

Don't worry about it, she says when I ask if I can replace them.

What size is your bed? I ask, because I can't remember. Big enough!

Full, she writes. *But I'm more worried about the mattress pad.*

Online I find a set of cute sheets with little rainbows all over them, and a heavy-duty full-size mattress pad, and have it all sent directly to her place. When they arrive, she sends me a photo of them right out of the box.

We have sex sheets! she writes.

Hoorah! I write, though I'm still not sure I'll ever see her again.

On a walk with the dogs at a park that extends like a finger into the lake, Amanda says, "You don't know if you want to see her again, or you don't know if you will?"

"The first one," I say.

Amanda lets her dog off leash to sniff along the water, but mine trots alongside us like a third wheel. A jogger snaps at us to leash Amanda's dog and Amanda says, "Right away, sir," and keeps walking.

"Does she want to see you again?" she says.

"Yes." She's mentioned seeing each other twice now, plus that night.

"OK, walk me through this. It's been a while, but I think these things are usually a yes or a no for me."

"I can't explain it," I say. "The Fates are in charge."

This is true. I would like to see Gretchen again, sure. But it's OK if I don't.

"I think doing nothing is a choice, yes?" says Amanda.

"Yes," I say. "But."

"But what?"

"I have the strong feeling that I'm in an opening-doors place, not a closing-doors place."

"What does that mean?"

"It means I want all my options open, like a child."

"Because this is your lesbian adolescence?"

"Exactly."

But a few days later, when Gretchen texts to ask point-blank when we can get together again, I know the Fates have spoken.

I'd like to chat on the phone when you're off work, I write. *Can you call me?*

She doesn't reply.

BEFORE MY THIRD FIRST DATE, I have a second date with Nadine, who, to my utter surprise, texts to invite herself over to watch a scary movie with me. *But I have my period, so no funny business*, she says. She pulls into my driveway in a bright blue hatchback papered with bumper stickers, even on the flanks, and my dog barks at her. One of the stickers reads THANK GOD I'M SWEDISH, and as I lead her into the house, I say, "Are you Swedish?" She says no, she just likes the sticker.

I really like how weird she is.

I make us salads from everything in the fridge: romaine, salmon, goat cheese, pistachios, red pepper. When I start to add golden raisins, she asks me not to and I accidentally do it anyway, and she says, "I'm not allergic but I hate them," and I start to fish them out but she tells me to leave them. "I just won't like it very much," she says, shrugging.

We start the movie and hold our salads to our chests. She's wearing the same black hoodie and I make an effort not to look at her breasts. I lay a blanket over her and then reach to get another for myself, and she says, "Can't we share?" So we do.

The movie is gory and makes little sense, and during the parts where a child murders her foster parents using her own dark powers, I watch Nadine's face through my fingers. She wears a passive, serene smile. Without meeting my eyes, she says, "I know you're checking me out."

"You're prettier than the killer orphan," I say.

"I don't mind but don't forget my period."

She finally looks at me, so I kiss her.

We make out for a long time and she lets me fondle her beautiful breasts, but she doesn't touch me except with her lips. Her hands are I don't know where, while my hands are on her.

The first time I kissed Z, in my car at the end of our first date, she held me firmly by the elbow. One day, I will kiss a woman and not think of Z at all.

After the movie is over, I walk Nadine to her car and kiss her again. I have no idea what promises I'm making, but I find myself asking her when her period's over. "It comes and goes these days," she says. I tell her again that I don't mind and she tells me again that she does.

I don't have a mantra for this date because it's not a first, but later, as she drives away, I find myself thinking: *It takes as long as it takes.*

Is it just me who finds herself regularly embattled with time? It was one week after meeting online that Z and I met in person. Another week before we saw each other again. Three more days before our third date. Then she was traveling for work, and when she returned we saw each other a few more times before she disappeared forever. That was five months ago.

Something is wrong, isn't it, when you measure the imbroglio in weeks and the fallout in months? At this pace, I'll be longing for Z on my death bed.

AT X'S HOUSE, which used to be my house, there is a cereal bowl filled with condoms on a shelf in the kids' bathroom. It's right there at eye level when I go looking for a hand towel. I'm here for our weekly transfer dinner. I cook when the kids return to me, he cooks when the kids return to him. We've set it up so there are no hard walls between our homes. What do the kids have to climb to live between us, what do they have to straddle, what stays quiet and what gets said out loud? Nothing, is our goal. They climb nothing, they keep nothing quiet. Still, they understand so much more than we've told them. If not in their brains, in their bones.

I move the condoms to the back of the shelf but keep one in my hand. It's encased in a butterscotch-colored package. I take the condom to the kitchen island and place it in the center of the complicated board game we've been playing since dinner.

"It's a little early," I say to X.

X shakes his head. "Is it?"

We both look at my teenager. "Do you know how to use this?" I say.

"I'm fifteen!" he says.

X and I look at each other. I had sex for the first time at sixteen, he had sex for the first time at nineteen. We think our teenager is saying he's too young, but what if he's not? First you hear that eighty-five percent of kids have seen porn by age eleven, then you hear kids are waiting until college or later. This boy is man-sized, with hair on his legs and everywhere else, a deep voice and size-12 feet. But he is also an awkward, naïve child, and now he's blushing.

"Are you and Lisa on kissing terms?" I ask him. This is his new girlfriend, not his first.

"I can't hear you," he says, rolling the dice.

X catches the dice in one hand. To me, X says, "I taught him how to use it. I'm sorry, I forgot to tell you."

I would have liked to have known about this, but I trust X. When this teenager was ten, he and I sat on my bed and went over it all: wet dreams, sperm and egg, menstruation, oral sex, pornography, consent. He asked a dozen eager questions.

I gave him a toiletry kit with travel-sized deodorant and shampoo.

When I tried to have the same conversation with my youngest, he said, "I already know," and I said, "OK, then tell me why a woman menstruates," and he said, "Because she has an egg that hasn't been fertilized by a sperm and the uterus has to empty out to get ready for a new egg." We didn't have the talk, but I gave him deodorant anyway.

"Once you do it, you can never go back," I say to the teenager now.

"I'm not available for this conversation," he says.

"And if she gets pregnant, in this state, she legally has no choice but to stay pregnant," I say, a fact that makes my molars hurt.

My teen looks at us both. "We haven't even kissed yet."
We both relax.

"Kissing's fun," says X. "You should try it some time."

Our youngest, smirking, says, "What's fun about it?"

Three years ago, when we sat the kids down to tell them I was moving out, our oldest asked if he would have Legos at both houses, and our youngest said, "Wait, are you saying we're not going to live together anymore?" He's a showboat, a ham, a natural comic—and a sage.

"It makes you feel good," says X.

"And it's like you go into a trance," I say.

"And the more you do it, the deeper the trance," says X.

"The sad thing about kissing is that sometimes it's the best part, but once you move on, you never really go back," I say.

"You can go back," X says, because he likes to disagree even when he agrees, "but not with the same person."

"Are you done?" says the teenager.

"I'd like to hear more," says the younger, and his brother tells him to shut up, and then X and I demand an apology, which ends in X taking the teenager's phone and the teenager stomping upstairs and the younger doing nothing to contain his schadenfreude. I ferry dishes to the sink and start to load X's dishwasher. We renovated this kitchen just after our youngest was born, with part of the advance I earned for my second novel. X turns off the water and says, "No offense, but if you load it I'll just have to load it over again."

I leave the kitchen and put on my coat. My youngest comes in for a hug. "Bye, family!" I say loudly and cheerfully. I doubt the teen will hear, he's likely already in headphones. "I love you all!"

I load and unload my own dishwasher nearly every day. Still, my first thought when X chastises me is to think he's probably right, I'm incompetent. My second thought is that inside this moment lives my entire marriage.

IT'S ANOTHER TWO WEEKS BEFORE GRETCHEN TEXTS to say she's ready to talk on the phone. I happen to be at the YMCA on the cool side of town, standing on the sidelines of a notably exciting fifth-grade basketball game. The air smells of chlorine and shoes. When the buzzer sounds at the end of the fourth quarter—and my phone chirps with an incoming text—the teams are tied twenty to twenty. My youngest's team is called the Pickles and their shirts are bright green; he's made three important assists and two baskets. There's some confusion about whether or not the game will go into overtime, but then the clock resets and all the adults sit back down and the referees get back into position. I've been sending X real-time updates. He and his two main girlfriends—Major and Minor, I'll call them—are all seeing music together, which may or may not mean they'll all end up in the same bed. After I let him know about overtime, I text Gretchen to say I'll be free for a few minutes in a few minutes, and she writes, *Gotcha, no rush.*

Being a sports parent is composed of some large percentage

driving around, some percentage tedium—sometimes I listen to podcasts on the sidelines, but I hide my earbuds in my hair so the kids don't notice—and a small percentage down-to-the-wire excitement like this. It's been a long time since my oldest practiced viral dance moves in the outfield. Now he plays the kind of sports where the equipment costs hundreds of dollars and we spend weekends in hotel rooms. It could be worse, and for the most part I comfortably tolerate the way sports shape our schedule. I particularly like the part where I can observe my children without being told to stop staring. When either of my children is pitching or aiming toward the hoop, I get so nervous that it's hard to watch.

Now, my kid makes a final assist with three seconds left on the clock, and his team wins by one basket. The crowd goes wild.

The coach will sequester the team for a post-game pep talk, so I find a quiet-ish spot near the locker room and call Gretchen back. Right away, I tell her I'm on borrowed time. After this, I'll pick up my oldest from a friend's house and go home to make dinner.

"I wanted to wait to talk until I knew what I wanted to say," Gretchen says.

"I respect that. I'm glad to hear from you."

"I figure you want to break up, am I right?"

This wasn't the language I'd use, but I appreciate the need for shorthand.

"Yes," I say. "I don't think there's a romantic future here, but I enjoyed spending time with you."

I sound like a robot, which is not what I want.

"I wanted to get to know you better," she says. "I thought we had something. I really do understand about the kids and the full life. I don't think you believe me, but I do. This is what I wanted to say—I like you, I wanted to see you again."

Did we have something? Maybe, but not enough of it.

"You're great," I say. "And that's a really, really nice thing to hear."

She sighs heavily. "Do you want to keep in touch?" she says.

Sure I do. But I won't. But maybe?

"I'd be happy to keep in touch," I say. "But mostly I want to tell you that I'm going through a lot of change and the time we spent was really fun and new for me. I appreciate you."

She makes a joke about being happy to help, but she doesn't sound resentful. I might be making a mistake, but I don't think so. Am I looking for someone to sit on the sidelines through overtime with me, or someone who will listen indulgently while I recap the final minutes, or someone who won't even ask about the game because she doesn't care and we spend most of our time together in bed? Am I looking for another Z, someone who breaks open my future and has the promise to reshape it with me, or someone who fits neatly and happily on my own sidelines, and I on hers? Am I looking to have more sex with more women—yes—or make a connection that grows over time—also yes? Am I killing time while my heart heals? What am I doing?

Gretchen sounds amused as we say our goodbyes. I end the call as my son's team ends their scrum with a cheer. Go Pickles!

The smile on this kid's face as he weaves toward me. The bright pinks of his cheeks and soft swell of his child-belly, the dark moles above his elbow that no one else in the family shares. He is the one who looks most like me. He looks like my mother, too, though she never met him in this life, and of all the things I regret on her behalf—she never traveled, never made the most of her career, never left her turbulent marriage—this is what I regret the most. There is magic inside this small human who looks like his dead grandmother. There is magic here at the humid YMCA on a Friday evening, bouncing toward me and into my arms, complaining ebulliently of un-metaphorical hunger and thirst.

ON OUR FOURTH DATE, Z and I met on my side of town at a Belgian pub. It was storming. I was sitting at the bar when she came in, and when I turned around to greet her, she said, "I love how happy you are to see me!" And I said, "I am *so* happy to see you!" And then we kissed as deeply as two adults can semi-respectably kiss in public, and then we ate burgers and talked. After dinner, we made out in my car.

It doesn't matter anymore, but there was something about the kissing. It wasn't just that time and space ceased to exist, along with breath, because that happened when we talked, texted, once when we watched TV. It was something else, an egoless wormhole sensation—OK, that's overstating it, but when we kissed, I never wanted to stop.

That night, she pulled away to catch her breath, and sometimes when I think of her now, I think of the look on her face in that moment. I'd like to say it was excitement, but given what happened after, it was more likely fear. What I saw in our future was calm and supportive and genuine and lasting. What did she see?

If I were a person who spooks easily—in dating, not movies—those kisses might have sent me running, too.

After we parted ways that night, I texted her: *I can't believe we made out in a restaurant!* She wrote back, *Those kisses!* and sent three flame emojis.

Before Z, I had a go-to song for kitchen-dancing or house cleaning or driving at night with my windows down, and there's a line in the song that says, *Don't even try and ex-plain how it's so diff-er-ent when we kiss . . .*

It was different when we kissed. I don't listen to that song anymore.

The Belgian pub closed permanently a few months later. Z had erased me by then, and my first thought when I heard the news was to text her. (I did not.) My second thought was that going forward I would be spared the memory-trigger of that evening: the rain, the kissing, the laughter, the look of fear on her breathtaking face.

I DON'T TRY FOR A THIRD FIRST DATE until after the new year. I spend winter break triaging requests from my kids while trying to meet deadlines. My oldest and I binge a very funny show about video game designers and my youngest makes superhero weapons—a storm breaker, a staff, a scythe—from cardboard boxes. I strong-arm them into going on long walks with me and the dog, and every afternoon, we go sledding at the hill near my house and they end up fighting. They make cookies and macaroni and cheese using every pot and pan. I buy an inflatable hot tub and we all spend an hour in it every night, but then it stops working and is snowed under within a week. Then they go back to school and to X, and I take long baths before bed, thumbing at the crossword while a mud mask dries on my face.

Fiona is a sporty, cheerful college professor who lives an hour outside of town, in a wealthy lakeside community that's often compared to a Midwestern Cape Cod, if for no other reason than the surfeit of power boats and deck shoes and white people. We meet on a Saturday morning at a snowy trailhead near Fiona's house. When I comment on her enormous, shiny pickup truck, she tells me it was her gift to herself for her fiftieth birthday, and I bite my tongue over questions about gas mileage. She's written academic books and we bond a little over the trials of writing projects, and she's a good talker, so as usual I learn a lot about her life and she learns nothing about mine. I realize this is as much my fault as anyone else's, but I can't understand how people get to know each other without asking questions.

The trail is steep, and I huff after Fiona as she bounds ahead. There's no future with Fiona, given the geographical distance, not to mention the distance that grows between us every time she summits a hill and I slog up behind her, folded and sweating. But she is very cute in a seventies-summer-camp way. She talks about her job and her estrangement from her religious siblings, and these topics get us all the way to the top, where we sit on a boulder and watch the misty morning.

When we get back to the parking lot, she says, "I never know how to end things."

I think of Nadine and give Fiona a high five. "Want to do it again sometime?" I say. But do *I* want to do it again?

"Sure thing," she says, and climbs into her colossal vehicle.

I'm not halfway through my experiment, and already I've lost the thread. I no longer know what I want except to forget Z or bury her memory under a thousand fresher ones. When I talked to Amanda on the phone this morning, she told me to take it one date at a time. "All you need to do today is get some fresh air," she said, then gave me my mantra, which I repeat to myself as I drive home through the honeyed morning.

There is no blueprint for building a more authentic life, but I will find my way.

FOUR

I LURK IN AN ONLINE LATE-IN-LIFE-LESBIANS GROUP, which is mostly posts about happy couples who met on the apps, accompanied by joint selfies in matching beanies and sports bras. I'm a little jealous, but mostly I feel glad for them.

I'm scrolling in bed one morning, my dog beside me with her limbs in the air, reveling in my hand on her belly, when some combination of key words stops me, and I read an Alaska woman's long post about having connected hard with someone—"She told me she felt so lucky to have found me!"—but one day the object of her affection didn't respond, and hasn't since.

In that moment, I understand why Amanda doesn't consider Z's behavior ghosting: because Z dumped me *before* going silent.

I text Amanda: *Something clicked and now I understand ghosting and you were right.*

She sends back the demented unicorn emoji with hearts for eyes.

Next I read all ninety-seven comments posted in response to the Alaska woman's question. *She told you she was busy,* says one. *You're worth a few seconds of her time, let go,* says another. *Maybe you said something that offended her?* says one tone-deaf individual.

Maybe she was cheating.

Maybe something truly tragic happened and a relationship is no longer in the cards but she doesn't know how to articulate that.

Block her and move on.

A lot of the posts aren't answers but encouragement: *You've got this, don't forget you're a badass, never compromise, you deserve so much more.*

Once, Z told me her niece refused to talk to her about her love life, which she found annoying, and I reminded her that teenagers believe that bearing a moment of discomfort will leave them severely injured if not dead, and she said, "That's so true!"

It is true of teenagers, and it's also true of adults.

But what do I know of another person's discomfort? I know I can bear my own, and that's all I know. I can be so smug with my soothing breakup calls and straightforward communication. But I'm just as ignorant of Z's private motivations as I am of any stranger's. There are more ways to be a human than there are ways to be me. My opinions can only be my own.

NADINE AND I TEXT EVERY FEW DAYS, and she invites me to an event called Cocktails in the Conservatory at the local botanical garden. She offers to drive, and when I step into the front seat of her compact SUV, I bang the side of my head on the roof, then step on an empty bottle in the wheel well and roll my ankle.

"Oh brother," says Nadine.

I feel a little shy with her. Last time we saw each other, we spent all that time necking, to borrow a term from my mother, and now here we are. I'm wearing red lipstick and vegan leather pants and a plaid tie, which I learned to tie by watching a tutorial on the internet. Nadine is wearing black jeans, combat boots, and a black sweater, and her hair is several inches shorter than it was the last time I saw her. When I compliment it, she says she cut it herself because her hairstylist is on maternity leave.

"I cut it, it grows, I cut it, it grows," she says. "I'm not sure which of us will back down first."

Nadine, I'm sorry to report, is one of those drivers whose foot is on the brake when it's not on the gas. We scoot to the other side of town, and I step gratefully out of the car.

The place is packed. We weave through the crowd to get to the bar. Once our NA beers are in hand, we take a flight of stairs and stand at a railing above the crowd.

Nadine says, "Do you date trans women?"

I think she's also asking if I date, am dating, generally. Other people.

"I would, but I haven't," I say. "Do you?"

"Same."

I don't look at the faces in the crowd. One of them might be Z's face. One of them might be the face of the woman who gave me a black eye—my swimming companion, as I think of her. Hers is a face I picture often, with an indecipherable riffle in my heart.

Around us, parakeets flit and trill, and below us koi the size of baby arms wriggle under waterfalls. Here and there, quail dart from the underbellies of plants, dodging shoes. Air plants snake from limbs, pink stamens spike from bromeliads, palms lean like lazy kings. This is the flora of my childhood. Long ago, I brought my babies here in the winter, one in a papoose and one at the end of my arm, all of us sleepy in the humidity.

Nadine tells a story about playing a trick on her coworkers, which involves hobbling a few steps away and peering at the ground like an old man, then hobbling back, and by the time she returns, I'm in stitches, as my mother would put it. I touch Nadine's waist and she slides toward me, and we kiss. I ask her if she has her period again, since we both know there's no predicting these things anymore, and she shakes her head slowly. Her lips are very full and wet. "I packed a toothbrush," she says.

Later I will realize this is meant to be an overture. But, me being me, I mistake it for a bid for conversation.

"Oh!" I say. "Did you want to stay over?"

Her body, all those delicious curves, shifts away.

"That's great, I mean," I say.

She chews her lip. "We've hung out a few times now. I'm not going to sleep with you then just go home," she says firmly. "That's not me."

Having sex and then returning to your own cozy bed sounds swell to me, but suddenly, I'm a jerk. "We hadn't talked about it, that's all," I say. "Of course you're welcome to stay the night."

But she's closed up. She angles away from me and looks down at the crowd. The music is very loud and my hands on the railing are sweating. Sometimes I can handle crowded-event-level stimulation, and sometimes my nervous system activates. I wipe my face on the sleeve of my blazer. I can feel my hair frizzing.

"Do you want to go?" I say to Nadine.

She shakes her head and takes a swig of her beer.

I try again for small talk. I tell her that when I was growing up, I didn't understand why people owned hair dryers, because whenever I used one my hair looked shiny and calm for five minutes, then sprung into a staticky nest. "There's not enough mousse in the world," my mother used to say, taking my messy hair between her palms.

Why am I thinking so much about my mother? I think it must be a way of calling her up, asking her how I'm doing.

How *am* I doing?

Nadine smirks to acknowledge that I've spoken.

"Let's go," I say.

We scoot back across town and she cuts the engine in my driveway. "I'm open to friends with benefits," she says. She doesn't ask me what I'm open to, and I don't say because I don't know.

"You really are welcome to stay over," I say. "I don't think it means the same thing to me that it means to you. But I think I understand."

"Sure," she says, shrugging, and follows me inside.

The sex is good but not great, and it's almost entirely one-sided. I feel like I'm following through on a promise I made under duress, and I feel terrible for feeling this way. After, I get her water for her bedside table and plug in her phone for her and let her choose her pillow. "Your bed is so *hard*," she says, and I kiss her and turn over.

Somehow, I sleep. When I wake up, Nadine is sitting up and thumbing her phone. "Good morning," she says neutrally.

"How did you sleep?" I say.

"I didn't."

"I'm sorry. Do you drink coffee?" I say.

She does. I get up to make it, and by the time it's in mugs, she's in the kitchen wearing her clothes. We sit on the sofa. I have yoga in an hour, but I'm pretty sure she'll be gone by then. I do want her to leave, but I do not want her to leave like this.

"I don't understand why you're upset," I say. "I mean, I understand that you're upset because I didn't assume you'd stay the night, but for me that's something we'd talk about first."

"It's fine. We wouldn't work anyway," she says. "I just thought—" She bites her lip. "You're funny and you text a lot and you like to go places. It's nice."

It's very important for me to remember that I'm not the

first person to go through a rough ending. Nadine has a whole history I know nothing about.

"I've really enjoyed hanging out with you," I say, and she puts her mug on the coffee table, scoops up her duffel bag, and heads toward the door.

LATER THAT DAY, I stop by the YMCA to watch my oldest play basketball, and in the middle of a point, while I'm trying to get an action shot, my phone rings in my hands. It's Fiona, the professor who lives an hour away, with the big shiny truck. Why I answer in the midst of the hubbub, I can't explain.

We make plans to go hiking again this coming weekend. It's not easy to hash out the details, with the game noise on my end and what sounds like wind on hers, but eventually we do, and I hang up.

The next time I look at my phone, there's a text from her: *I don't feel like I have your attention,* it reads. *No need to follow through with hiking. Peace out.*

ONCE EVERY COUPLE OF WEEKS, X stops by on his lunch hour to pick up things the boys have forgotten to transfer—our youngest's library book, usually, which I summit his top bunk to retrieve, or our teenager's protein powder. Today, it's our youngest's basketball jersey, but when X shows up, I can't find it.

"You knew I was coming," he says. He glares at my dog, who is growling timidly at him from the sofa, then stomps across my house and into the garage. He returns empty handed. I'm in the mud room, tossing aside winter gloves and tote bags.

"I would appreciate it if you could find things before I arrive," he says.

"I'm sorry, I was in meetings." This is true. Still, I should have taken a minute to dig up the jersey, if only to avoid this exact conversation.

"So where is it?"

"How should I know?"

"Because you're the parent!"

His voice is very loud, mostly yelling if not fully, but I know from experience that if I were to ask him not to yell, he would tell me (very loudly) that he isn't, and then say in fact I am yelling, and then he'd tell me (very loudly) that it's exhausting having to walk on eggshells around me.

"I know I'm the parent," I say weakly.

But I'm done with the part of parenting where I keep track of all my kids' belongings. If something's lost, I help them find it, but my focus these days is on making sure they're maintaining good hygiene, eating vegetables and getting exercise, and arriving places on time. This alone fills a day. X is a more energetic parent than I am, but if he's reciting checklists every time they go out the door, he's only making our collective job harder. *In my opinion.*

I squeeze by him to go into the garage, find the jersey in the car, and return to the house. He doesn't move when I squeeze by him again. Instead, he grabs my butt, one cheek and then the other.

It's not a surprise. He does this a lot. To explain why I've never shut it down would require a book in itself, one about my conflation of love and sex, my history of proving I'm desirable, and my strict adherence to a primary rule of the patriarchy: Never embarrass a man. Not to mention that our children's wellbeing is predicated on us getting along. X is a confrontational and demanding person, but if I could clearly argue a multi-point case against sexual contact between us, it's likely he'd come around. I've thought many times that if I'd trained as an attorney, our entire relationship would be different.

The only time I've truly asserted myself with X was when I told him I wanted a divorce, which means I shocked him, which is fundamentally unkind. The best way to deliver bad news is to prepare the receiver, says my brother, and the best way to receive bad news is to know it's coming.

The last time X and I had sex was the morning I moved out three years ago, as a goodbye. The last time we kissed was right after Y dumped me. "You're a free agent," he said before putting his tongue in my mouth. It had happened before, and twice I'd leaned into it, because making out is fun and I was reveling in the unconventionality of my new life. But after Y, I was a mess. I used my fresh heartbreak, not my gayness, to worm out of it. I'm not sure this situation is possible for outsiders to understand, but I can say that every long marriage is its own brew, and this is ours.

Now, wedged between the dining table and the wall, the jersey between us, I don't know how to respond when he grabs one of my breasts, then the other. I mean, I'm single, he's poly. But the fact is that I don't want to engage sexually with penises, and I don't want to have a sexual relationship with my ex-husband.

Also, the grabbing? Not a turn-on.

So how do I tell him I don't want him to touch me like this? Is there any other way to connect with him? I'm flailing. "I ran into [your ex] the other day," I say.

He and his ex were together for a decade before X and I met. She's also a lesbian—it's pure coincidence, I promise, except that many women of my generation chose to ignore what was fairly easy to ignore. "She said you asked her when you two were going to sleep together?"

She'd told me this offhandedly, like isn't-X-so-funny, but I'd been surprised. To my knowledge, they haven't slept together for decades and she's fifteen years into a monogamous relationship.

"Yeah, so?" says X.

"So you know she's in a relationship, right?"

"Sure," he says, "but so am I."

His hands are no longer on my breasts.

"It feels like the only value women have to you is sexual value," I say. Out loud.

"I don't see the problem," he says. He's kidding, but not.

"So that's true of me, too?"

"You're the mother of my children," he says, sighing.

Rejecting him sexually is rejecting him period; I know this because I know him. I'm sure there's some way for us to relate to each other without sex involved, but I haven't found it and I don't know where to look. Everything having to do with ending a marriage is biased in favor of animosity, and here's X, offering exactly one alternative path.

He gives my right breast a last grope, then says he needs to get back to work. He waves on his way out the door. Usually we hug and tell each other we love each other, but not today.

Endings like mine and X's have a dozen steps, and there's at least one more to go.

Z sent her final text at 10 p.m. on a Wednesday night. After, I forced myself to sleep, and in the morning I called a recently divorced friend and asked her how to file. (I admit that in my freshly broken state, I thought maybe if I took this last step toward singledom, Z might reconsider.) My friend walked me through it, and I filled out the paperwork, and then X and I signed with a notary. The state's mandatory waiting period kicked in when I filed, which was about half the time it took us to hash out and file our settlement agreement, which we did slowly but without much fuss. All that's left now is to schedule the hearing, then that will be that all over again.

MY FOURTH FIRST DATE is Margie, a nurse practitioner and a *hearts-*

over-parts person, which means she's bisexual. She's twice-divorced, once from a man and once from a woman, and petite and blond and very stylish, and when she talks she uses her hands and narrows her eyes in a way I find soothing. We meet at a bar near her house and talk for a couple of hours. I'm heading from here to Lionel's birthday party, where there will be a snake expert and Amanda will be in hostess mode. In my car is a very expensive rock tumbler wrapped in paper printed with turtles.

Margie lives in the house she grew up in. Her parents live a few miles away, in assisted living, and every few days her father comes over without warning to fix things in her house, which I find adorable.

"It's sweet, sure," she says, "but sometimes I'm, like, unprepared for company."

She wears a full face of subtle and expertly applied makeup. When I apply makeup, I immediately sweat off the foundation and smear the eyeliner. Margie and I have stuff in common, actually—we both work a lot and love to kayak and see live music—but there's a fundamental discrepancy in the way we present. Today I'm wearing my cutest jeans and boots and a sweater with a skull and crossbones across the chest, which social media sold to me, but I can't see myself being comfortable dating someone so polished and trim. I'd be constantly sucking in my stomach and worrying about what to wear.

That said, I find it endearing when, in a pause in the conversation, Margie says somewhat timidly, "What's it like for you, having kids? Is that a weird question?"

"It's a great question," I say.

So far, the women I've dated who don't have kids have asked about my kids' ages and names and that's it. They've also made a point of saying they like kids.

"It's like having two things you must do at the same time,

except all day long," I say.

A graduate school professor once told my class of cocky young writers that having children is the surest path to experiencing the full range of human emotions. Twenty years later, I find this insulting. For my generation, staying childless is an act of fortitude and bravery, whether it's intentional or not, which means Margie has accessed at least a few emotions I never will. Not to mention that she has more time and energy with which to make herself who she wants to be.

Maybe it's her birdlike hands or the charming question or my lesbian adolescence, but when Margie offers to pay for our drinks and then invites me to join her for a cooking class next weekend, I accept, saying nothing about my feelings about cooking. We both tap the date into our phones before hugging goodbye, and I drive to Amanda's, wondering again about the logical fallacies of this project of mine. What I'm looking for, ultimately if not today, is that rare, undeniable connection I felt with Z, but to some degree this can be weakly simulated with lively conversation and steady eye contact.

And anyway, what has undeniable connection gotten me other than blacklisted and heartbroken?

THE NIGHT BEFORE THE COOKING CLASS, I'm getting ready for yoga when I receive a text from Margie. It reads:

I wanted to get in touch before tomorrow night to let you know I'm steering toward a relationship with someone. I would love to keep getting to know you if you're up for it, and I don't need to cancel, but I thought you should know in case you'd prefer to do something else.

How can I convey the shot of faith this text gave me?

I write, *I'm so happy to hear that you've found someone. I enjoyed our chat and hope to stay in touch, but if it's all the same I'll take tomorrow night for myself. You are wonderful!*

I send a screen shot of both texts to Amanda. *A master class in how to tell a person you don't love her and never will,* I write.

We don't say master anymore, writes Amanda. *But that's a truly great message. Are you disappointed?*

Only a little. Mostly I'm reassured we're still trying for a civilization here.

It's not a nice thing to say. But the last rejection I received was *Peace out,* and the one before that was Z, and the one before that was Y informing me almost giddily of her imminent getaway with someone else.

How's the weather? I ask Amanda. She and Marcus are back down South, getting the hard sell.

Balmy like my heart, she writes.

THERE COMES A TIME EVERY WINTER WHEN I GIVE UP, usually in the second or third week of February. One day I don't take my morning walk with the dog, and by the end of that week I can't remember how I ever managed to spend time outside at all. I even stop driving us to the dog park, and every other day I come into a room to find a shredded roll of paper towels. It's not my dog's fault, but it's not my fault either—my blood is tropical. Every year, I fall at least once on the ice, too, which hastens my demise. This year, it happens while I'm on the phone with Amanda, and I land so hard on my right butt cheek that weeks later I can still feel it when I do legs-up-the-wall in yoga.

I'm flipping pancakes when Amanda calls to ask if I'm up for a walk across the lake. We do this once a year. It's not an enormous lake, only about four miles across, but the crossing takes hours.

"Can we go Saturday instead?" I say.

"Marcus is working."

"Sunday?"

"Let's go today. Now. Can you go now?"

My children are sitting at the kitchen island, dipping forkfuls of pancake in syrup and bickering. I say to them, "Do you want to cross the lake with me and Aunt Amanda?"

"No, thank you," says my youngest.

"There's nothing I want to do less," says my teenager.

"I'll be there in an hour," I tell Amanda.

I CAN'T EXPLAIN WHY, while I'm waiting outside Amanda's house for her to slip from the grip of her family, I open my least-used social media app and navigate to Z's account, which is public. I barely use this app, and I never followed her on it, but I look at her page every few days. Sometimes the sight of her face makes me maudlin, but sometimes it's just nice to catch a glimpse of this person I liked a lot. I'm predicting today it will be nice, except I can't find the page. It's not there.

By the time Amanda gets to the car, I'm reminding myself to breathe.

She straps in and I hand her my phone. "Take it," I say.

"What's going on?"

"She blocked me. She blocked me."

"Wait, I thought you blocked her?"

I do not have the presence of mind to explain each social media platform right now, nor the difference between disconnecting and blocking. I tell her Z has one open account and sometimes I go there. Privately.

"You do? Does she know that?"

"No," I say, but maybe? "Wait, can you look it up?"

She does. I watch her face as she reads. "*If your account is marked visible,*" she says haltingly, "*then other users can see when you've viewed their profiles.*"

"No way."

"Is your account marked visible?"

"I have no idea!" I take back the phone and comb through

to privacy settings. "Visible," I say shakily.

There's no air in the car.

Amanda gets out and comes around to my side and opens the door. I put my face in my hands. "I'm a crazy person," I say.

"You're not crazy. And you don't know that she blocked you."

I do know it. "No no no no," I say, shaking my head. Amanda tries to pull my hands from my face but I don't let her. "I'm humiliated. I mean, *more* humiliated."

"Take deep breaths, I'll be right back," she says, and dashes into her house.

I'd thought I was getting well, I was over some hump, yet here we are.

She returns with a legal pad and a Sharpie and steps back into the passenger seat.

"Close the door," she says. "Keep breathing."

She turns the legal pad sideways on her lap and writes across it in block letters, then turns the page and does it again.

I'm less crying than baying.

"Breathe," she says again, then goes back to writing. By the time she's done, my breath has mostly returned, but then I glance at my phone and feel woozy. This is humiliation, yes, and also deep regret. If only I were a stronger person, a more disciplined person. If only I were cuter, funnier, calmer, thinner, more independent, less independent, a better communicator, a robot, a superhero.

Amanda tears off one sheet, then another, then another. "Look at me," she says. She holds up one of the signs she's made. "Read it aloud."

I read: *"IT IS COMPLETELY NORMAL AFTER HEARTBREAK TO LOOK AT THE PERSON'S SOCIAL MEDIA OVER AND OVER."*

My own voice is distantly familiar. I can't feel my hands.

She puts the first sign in my lap and holds up the second.

I read aloud. "*I WOULDN'T BAT AN EYE AT SOMEONE ELSE DOING THE SAME THING.*"

This is true. She hands over the second sign and holds up a third.

"*THIS MOMENT IS ABOUT THE WEIRDNESS OF SOCIAL MEDIA, NOT MY WEIRDNESS AS A PERSON.*"

"It can be both," I say, but I'm starting to feel my body again.

Next. "*THE THING I WANT MOST IS FOR Z TO WANT ME, BUT MAYBE I ALSO NEED MORE SIGNS THAT IT IS OVER FOR GOOD.*"

Over for good was exactly my first thought. Had I really been holding out hope?

Next. "*BLOCKING IS CRUEL TO ME, BUT MAYBE NOT TO HER.*"

"That's true," I say. I have no idea what Z considers cruel. But in my clear moments, I know that if she believed something were cruel, she wouldn't do it.

"There's one more," says Amanda.

"You're very good at your job," I say.

She holds up the last sign. I read this one to myself.

THERE IS NOTHING WRONG WITH WANTING TO LOVE AND BE LOVED AND HAVE A HEALTHY RELATIONSHIP.

I exhale.

AMANDA WANTS TO HASH OUT HER MOVING CONUNDRUM with an old-fashioned pros and cons list, so after we've set out across the lake, we drop our hoods so we can hear each other. She's wearing a fleece headband that sends her feathery hair into chaos. The set of her jawline tells me she has a lot on her mind.

"I have something to tell you," she says, talking through her teeth. "He took the job."

I slide a little on a bare patch of ice. "When?"

"I'm not sure, actually. Yesterday or the day before. He told me this morning. He woke me up, actually, which might be the part that annoys me the most."

"He took a job across the country without telling you?"

"I know. I've been that way and back again. I'm sure the neighbors think I'm a loon, the way I yelled."

"This morning?"

"Right before I called you."

We've hit an icy spot and I'm moving fast, almost gliding. Her voice comes through the wind and I keep my eyes on my boots and the hems of my snow pants, which are bright pink. Amanda looks like a lithe ski bunny in her sleek blue snow costume; I look like a Lego person in mine. We're both wearing sunglasses that cover half our faces, and there's a smear of sunscreen on Amanda's chin, which I thumb away for her. It's cold out, but I'm sweating in my many layers.

"It will be fine either way," I tell myself aloud.

"Help me figure this out," she says.

We walk for a while through a high drift, leaving trenches in our wake. "What choice gives you the best chance at happiness?" I say.

"That's the question." She scoops up a gloveful of snow and eats some of it. "Better weather, at least."

"That works both ways."

"You're going to make this difficult?"

"Hurricanes. Storms that might as well be hurricanes. Flooding. Blistering sunburns."

"I give up. We shouldn't move because I might get sunburned."

I hold up my hands. I didn't make the weather. "Money?"

"Much more," she says. "East Coast numbers."

"Cost of living?"

"Same answer."

"Schools?"

"Apples and oranges," she says, but I sense some hesitation.

"Friends?" I say.

She waves a hand. "Next."

"Politics."

"Con."

"Work? I mean your work."

She chews her lip for a while. The ice beneath us is inches thick and dark green, pocked with bubbles and sliced with fissures.

"I need a break," she says.

Amanda's work is like mine in that it waxes and wanes. Heavy weeks, light weeks. Though now that she mentions it, it seems like most weeks have been heavy weeks for her.

"You can always come back," I say. For years, I've made it a policy never to ask what she's thinking in terms of her future with Marcus. A marriage is an inertial mass. It continues unless it's stopped, which takes force.

"We could," she says thinly.

"Does change work?" I ask. "Does it fix things?"

"I think it can. If I'm willing to change."

"What can you change?"

"My expectations."

Your standards, I do not say.

She says, "I'd like a smaller life. Less hustle, more rest. I'd like to make Lionel a hot breakfast every morning."

"You would?"

"It's a way of showing love."

"You already show your love."

"I drive places. I shop for groceries. I don't lose sleep."

"Losing sleep is love? I'm not being skeptical, just trying to understand."

"I don't know. Maybe."

I've thought about this a lot, actually. I know how I show my children love, but I can't say exactly how they best receive it. Their father makes intricate, four-food-group dinners most nights, whereas I roast veggies or pick up burritos. He also makes eggy brunches every weekend, whereas I occasionally make pancakes that don't turn out very well. I take them camping and on trips; he takes them on roller coasters and teaches them chess and poker. I fuss and worry and manage. I make sure their sheets get changed and they have backpacks with zippers that work and shoes that fit. I know the names of their evolving rosters of friends. I ask them about their feelings, and sometimes they even tell me.

"What else?" I say.

"I'd like my home to be quieter. Way less hosting. Fewer neighbors, less drop-in traffic."

I have zero drop-in traffic, but I don't live in Amanda's village. "You can make things different."

"Maybe."

The last mile takes the longest. The wind is high and we head straight into it. Above us, a jet steams noiselessly across the denim sky.

I say, "Last night I dreamed we had dinner with your parents on an enormous mattress, all facing the same direction."

Her father, who invented something having to do with the study of particle physics, died a few years after we met. There were three hundred people at his funeral. Her mother, who taught third grade for thirty-five years, died last year, and there were dozens of people at hers.

"What did we eat?" says Amanda.

"It didn't get that far," I say.

If she grieves her parents, which she must, she keeps it to herself, unlike me. I wore a brave face for years, but now I talk about my mother every chance I get. Your grandmother put citrus down the disposal to make the kitchen smell good, I tell my children. That blanket belonged to your grandmother, I tell them about their favorite. My mother loved pralines-and-cream ice cream, always used very correct cursive handwriting, played the piano and sang often and badly. She went back to school to become a social worker at age forty-five, and her first gig was leading a sexual predator group that met after dark in a strip mall. She was a curious blend of cowardice—in her marriage, in her ambitions for herself—and bravery, in her emotional authenticity. Her emails were like poems, full of new paragraphs and dashes; she died before texting came. When she came into a dim room, she'd say, "How about a little light on the subject?" before turning on the light, and whenever we pulled into the driveway, she'd say, "Home again, home again, jiggety jog!" She wanted to travel but never did. She wanted to own her own home but never did. She fell in love just the once, that I know of. She mourned lost friendships. On the occasion of my brother coming out of the closet, she told me without using the word that she believed she was bisexual. Knowing what I know now, that bisexual can take the shape of being straight for one half of life and gay for the other, as well as many other shapes, I grieve the lives she didn't live. When I left X, my father implored me to think of what my mother would say. I did, and I think she would have said: *Amen!*

I say, "Remember when you talked me down from a panic attack in your driveway?"

"It's been two hours."

"I'm not going to make you do that again."

"I'll do it every day if you need it."

"I know. But I can do this. You don't have to stay for me."

Her glove on the back of my parka makes a shushing

sound. On the far shore, we brush the snow off a bench and sit facing our own tracks. The sun is higher now and I stuff my cap into a pocket. The return trip will be sunnier and the wind will be at our backs. For today, the hard part is over.

AMANDA'S THEORY IS THAT Z got back together with her ex. But Z had described that relationship as full of contempt and unkindness, and who in her right mind would exit my warm, eager heart for that?

When Z asked her questions about our future, I read them as due diligence. I didn't see them for what they were: expressions of fear. Should I have answered differently? Should I have tried playing it cool? Sometimes red flags look very much like green flags, and it's asking a lot of a person to spot the difference.

In the first months after she scorched our paradise, I sent Z three longish emails, all meant to be casual and friendly, asking for nothing but contact. She did not respond. I told Amanda after the first email that I felt like a stalker and she said, "Don't say that. Stalking is a real and scary thing, and you attempting to politely access someone who disappeared overnight is not remotely in the same ballpark."

After the second email, Amanda said, "Please remember that lack of discouragement is not encouragement."

After the third email, Amanda said never to send Z another word. "Listen to me. Listen," she said. "You are not in a movie. You are not in a novel. This is not cute. Picture her rolling her eyes and deleting your heartfelt words as soon as your name hits her inbox. Worse, picture her reading them aloud in a mocking voice to her best friend."

Amanda and I would never do this, and I don't think Z would either. Still.

"Thank you so much," I said to Amanda.

WHEN YOU'RE NECK-DEEP IN MIDWESTERN WINTER and your one living parent calls every morning to check on your state of mind, there's a good chance that it's time to find some sunshine. And when you're from Miami, the simplest way to get sunshine is to fly home.

I've never visited my father without my children, so they're confused when I tell them I bought a plane ticket. "Without *us*?" they say, like I'm testing the laws of physics. At the same time, I buy tickets for them to visit their uncles in California. "Without *you*?" they say.

My father is robust, kooky, and somewhat anti-social, traits he wears more gracefully now than when he was younger. The home he shares with his wife of seventeen years is nothing like the home I grew up in, and their peaceful marriage is nothing like the marriage of my parents. I was raised by an angry, erratic, alcoholic father, and to this day I have a nearly psychic alertness to other people's moods. But age has softened him and he's been sober for years, and though I resent his ability to pretend as if all those years never happened, I will not spend his best years reliving his worst ones.

He and my stepmother spend their days calling across the house to each other. "Sidney!" says my father loudly when she's right next to him. "BILL!" she shouts from the kitchen.

Miamians stay inside in the AC even when the weather's spectacular by any standard of measure, and they only go to the beach on special occasions, if at all. ("Ugh, the *beach*," says my stepmother.) But I want to swim in the ocean, walk on the sand, drive around in the humidity with the wind in my hair, see some art, lounge on their back deck watching lizards dart through the bromeliads.

Before I start my day, I sit in their cramped living room with my father while the TV news plays loudly. I tell him that in my cab ride from the airport, I was stuck in traffic behind a

Jeep with a wheel cover that read *FAMILY FAITH FRIENDS FIREARMS*. We share a laugh.

"Can you believe these bills targeting cross-sexuals?" he says. He often grabs for words and misses, but I don't correct him. "These people are sadists!"

"I could not agree more."

Their back deck is an eclectic oasis: a wide deck painted aquamarine and two dozen colorful pots of lantana and dracaena and stag-horn ferns. My father is a spray paint enthusiast, and each time I visit, a colorful sculpture has been placed in a position of prominence: a yellow egret, an orange alligator, a pink swan, a blue toad. When they met and married, my stepmother lived with six dogs and five cats, all rescues with disabilities: a missing leg, a missing eye, deaf, blind. Those pets died off, and now there is only a stout chihuahua with milky eyes and a habit of rolling on the Turkish rug, groaning in ecstasy.

There's also a tortoise named Humphrey who came with the house when my stepmother bought it. Humphrey lives off carrots and lettuce and broccoli stems my stepmother tosses into the jungly yard, and sometimes he comes onto the deck and stares through the sliding doors like a stowaway. I think he must be very lonely.

My stepmother's arms are covered in bruises of all stages, from sickly yellow to deep purple, casualties of her stumbles. My father installed marine-gauge brass cleats all over the house, and she moves from one to the next like she's playing the calmest game of parkour. They don't feed themselves with meals on regular schedules. They eat bites of chicken salad and key lime pie throughout the day, then go to bed before dinnertime.

Every time I visit, my stepmother pulls out a manila folder and reads me the plan for her funeral. She's written her own eulogy and chosen the music and designated each person's reading. Now, she pulls out a Langston Hughes poem and hands it to me. "You'll read the whole thing," she says. "Tell them it was my favorite when I was a teacher." I scan the page and hand it back. She stands shakily and says, "This is a piece you must read with *emphasis* and *vigor*. My first graders learned it by heart, they knew the hand gestures that go with it."

And then she reads, with gestures: "*Dream-singers, / Story-tellers, / Dancers . . .*"

I cannot envision a future moment when I will stand on a dais at her Episcopalian church and, with gestures or without, read a poem about the profound beauty and meaning of Blackness to a group of wealthy white Floridians. But I'll cross that bridge when I come to it.

When she's finished, she says, "Don't call me Mrs. Daniel when you talk about me." She took my father's last name, which is also my last name. "Call me Sidney."

"Why would I call you Mrs. Daniel?"

"Just *don't*," she says, pointing a bony finger at me maternally. If she dies first, my father will stay in the house until he can't, and if he dies first, she will move in with her daughter. For now, they keep each other alive.

When my father drops me at the airport, he stuffs cash in my pocket and I make a show of rejecting it and he makes a show of insisting, and then we hug for a long time. Every visit might be the last. It would be just like me to forget this fact, so I remind myself constantly.

BACK HOME, BEFORE MY FIFTH FIRST DATE, I connect online with a woman named Jill, whose profile says she's from a small town just east of my city. When I message her, I ask about rivers to paddle in her town, and she writes back that she doesn't actually live in the town she named in her profile. She lives in my city, in fact. *But,* she adds, *I hate this whole county.*

I'm puzzled, but only for a second.

I write, *I think this is your way of telling me that you and I have incompatible politics, in which case I'll thank you for your time and wish you a great day!*

She writes, *lol yea.*

FIVE

MY NEXT DATE IS NOT A FIRST DATE, so I don't count it.

I matched with Dani shortly after I matched with Y, a year before I met Z. Before Dani and I met in person at a dark bar where a thousand tiger-themed figurines and stuffed animals and photographs collected dust on every surface, I let her know that I had recently started dating Y. *Let's have a drink anyway,* she wrote, so we did. We sat at the bar and I drank two soda waters with bitters and lime. She nursed a pilsner but didn't finish it, chatted with the friendly bartender, then tipped a twenty. We never stopped talking. Her work, my work. Her father, recently gone; my mother, long gone. Her dog, my dog. She has a lake cabin up north and a scrum of faithful friends and a weekly winter bowling team. She's very tall and her features are delicate—large brown eyes, short peppery hair, thin arched eyebrows, narrow nose—and altogether the effect is handsome. Her look—crewnecks and baggy jeans and platform boots—deletes her curves. She has very nice breasts, but I suspect she wouldn't take this as a compliment, that maybe she doesn't think about her breasts at all, that maybe they are a nuisance.

At the end of that date, before we parted ways for a year, she said to me, "It's too bad you're coupling up, we could have had some fun," and winked, and my heart did a flip.

It is this flip of the heart, ironically, that makes me cautious of Dani. Less of whether she might break my heart than whether I might end up breaking hers.

We texted from time to time while I was dating Y, mostly to make plans to kayak together, which never worked out. Dani is a serious person, not in demeanor but in values, and she's the kind of lesbian unlikely to be mistaken for a not-lesbian, which is to say an old-school lesbian, what we'd now call a *masc*. Muscles, expensive sunglasses, cocky gait. Someone like Dani has no coming-out story because her gayness was implied, always, and tolerated on the condition that she remained asexual and apolitical. Her parents met a few of her girlfriends over the years, but they never saw her kiss one. Only around her very close friends was she wholly herself.

So it's technically our second date when Dani agrees over text to meet me for dinner at a new Italian bistro on the cool side of town. Again, we never stop talking. She makes me laugh out loud, I make her chuckle. I mention that there's a rodent building a nest under the hood of my car—a mechanic alerted me when I had the oil changed—and she gives a lot of advice and offers to help, which raises a small red flag for me. Dani is a natural caretaker and leader, two terrific traits. But I have a history of falling for strong-willed people and abandoning my own bearings for theirs.

You have to understand: When I left my marriage, I couldn't remember how to do things I'd once known how to do. I didn't recall, in fact, that I was a capable person. I'd let X handle so much of our shared adventures and technology and finances that I had no memory of my own competence. After I left, I re-learned how to start a fire and pitch a tent, keep a budget, fix a toilet, replace a furnace filter, train a dog, landscape and mow a lawn, paint a room, plan a road trip, troubleshoot my technology, all like I was in my twenties instead of my forties. I don't want to forget again, even if it feels good to let another person take the lead.

Still. When we leave the restaurant, I have visions of pressing her up against the brick building, easing my hand under her sweater. But this is the thing: I suspect that if I pressed Dani up against a wall, she'd indulge me for a minute, then turn the tables.

I tell Dani about my lesbian adolescence, my ten-first-dates plan, and even a little about Z. I tell her she's great and I'd like to keep hanging out but I'm not ready to be exclusive. I'm like a shark that will die if it stops swimming, I tell her, except the shark is a middle-aged mother divorced from a man, and the swimming is going on dates with women. The unspoken question is when I'll stop swimming, and for whom.

"You're trouble," Dani says, opening my car door for me.

The way I flirt with Dani is familiar. It's how I flirted all those years of dating men, of chasing their attention. It's easy to slip back in. But when Dani kisses me lightly and walks off to her lowkey luxury car, dangling her keys, I'm turned way on. Her confidence, her maturity. The way she smirks at me like she has my number. Her advice, her supportive nature, even her winky teasing, which charms me as it rings a distant bell. My instincts tell me she likes her girls girly, so that's what I am with her, even though I'm really not that girly anymore, if I ever was.

On the way home, I decide never to sleep with Dani, which seems like something a smart person would decide. I have the feeling that Dani and I could go pretty deep together, in the near vicinity of love if not solidly in its warm center. In my head, there's a nebulous vision of us as a couple, and what I see has sweetness and compatibility, but it also has a slow ebbing of intimacy, a steady rise of resentments, a few good years, a slow painful break. Maybe there was a time in my life when this would have been good enough. But being single has brought me so much joy—and frankly it's been so much *fun*—that I'm not giving it up for a couple of pretty good years. At this point, my swim will stop for the superlative, or it won't stop at all.

A WEEK OR SO AFTER MY DATE WITH DANI, I sleep with Nadine again. This comes as a surprise, given how annoyed she was with me the last time we were together, but we keep in text contact for a few weeks, and then she's back at my house and I'm making us another salad, and before long we've moved to the bedroom, and this time is it much, much better than pretty good.

Y used to lecture me about all the ways lesbian sex is different from straight sex. I understood part of what she was saying, that sex isn't always a straight line to orgasm—it isn't always a straight line in hetero sex either, though it mostly is—but I understand now, after Y and Z and Gretchen and now Nadine, that the fundamental difference is similar to the difference between work and play, or between formal negotiations and idle conversation. Between hiking a path through a forest and flitting through that forest like a native bird. At its best, sex between women is a messy, ecstatic, improvisational fever dream.

I've been asked—I won't say by whom, but her name rhymes with *Bamanda*—whether I miss penises. I do not. Not because they turn me off, but because removing the penis from sex is a bit of sneaky magic. What fills its place is so much more lively and flexible and creative: fingers, tongues, knees, thumbs, toys. Pauses where I lightly tap her clitoris with the tip of my middle finger, pauses where she kisses my thigh while her hair teases my labia, rougher parts where we almost fall off the bed, breathless parts where we might be touching in a way that will lead somewhere or we might be touching in a way that will end in a cozy nap.

If sex with a man is like one of those centrifugal force machines where you send a penny rolling and rolling until eventually it has no choice but to fall down the hole in the center, sex with women is like there's no centrifugal force at all, and after the rolling and rolling the penny starts to dance around the room and out the door and around the block. It's patternless and formless and fully corporeal, and I love it.

And there's a lot of talk, which confused me with Y, but now I get it. The talk is the thing, actually. It's what transpires somewhat naturally with women but not typically with men. At one point, Nadine tells me she likes what I'm doing with my hands, but also there's a spot on the bone under her left labia she'd like me to stroke, and when I do she writhes. At another point, she's touching my breasts and she says, "Do you like it more like this? Or this?" I don't know how to answer. She tries again, like the eye doctor: A or B? B or C? B or D? I think she could make it to Z and start the alphabet all over again.

But it's D. Oh sweet Jesus, it's D.

Later, she asks me what I was doing with my tongue, and I show her, and then she does it to me and I say it's close but not quite right, but after a little tweaking, she's got it.

Am I getting good in bed with women? I believe I might be!

After, naked in bed with a glass of water between us, Nadine tells me a little about her recent relationship, which ended in a way that left her not only sad but confused. No one needs to tell me that all breakups aren't created equal, but I do wonder why so many need to be confusing. When I tell her about Z, it feels as if we've learned something important about each other's tattered hearts.

"Let's talk about what this means," I say to Nadine while we're getting dressed. She did not bring her duffel bag.

"Oh, no ma'am," she says. "I'm here for friends and sex but let's not go overboard."

"So we're seeing other people?"

"I'm not seeing other people, but I'm fine with you doing it."

She high fives me at the door and we make plans to see some comedy next week. Then she calls me when she's home and we get all worked up and end up having video sex, until one of her cats walks in front of the screen and looks me straight in the eye. For a second it seems as if the cat has absorbed her and I'm having video sex with him, and I start laughing uncontrollably and cannot stop.

I'M GOING TO SPILL THE BEANS NOW about the three emails I (unwisely) sent Z in the time after she disappeared.

In the first, which I sent four weeks after her last text, I gave her facts. I told her I'd filed for divorce and that I missed her. I sent strength and peace and wished her all good things. She did not reply.

In the second, subject *It's Been Twelve Weeks*—an amount of time that seemed impossibly long then—I doled out the daily news, including a few lines about my oldest's girlfriend and my nieces and their crushes, and I asked after her funny dog and her friends and family and work. I told her that I needed her to tell me to bug off if she really wanted me to bug off. I sent strength and peace and wished her all good things. She did not reply.

In my third and final email, a week or so before I started my ten dates, I wrote, *It's past time for me to turn this corner. Please tell me you never want to hear from me again. Otherwise I might keep throwing stones at your window, waiting for a light to come on.* I sent strength and peace and wished her all good things. She did not reply.

When humans communicate, there's usually a feedback loop, and when there's not, the silence is terrible. It's not leaving someone that hurts them the most; it's erasing them. Z became my phantom limb, and I became her—what? Her nuisance. Her nag. Toilet paper stuck to the sole of her shoe.

ON THE MORNING OF OUR DIVORCE HEARING, which will happen online, X calls to ask me for a ride home from a town thirty miles away, where later this afternoon he's going to sell his vintage luxury car to some guy who plans to use it for parts.

He's asking for a ride, that's all.

It's true that I'm busy, behind on a couple of deadlines and on the hook to drive my oldest to and from a birthday party, my youngest to and from basketball practice, and myself to and from yoga all in the span of three hours this evening. It's also true that I'm a little sad. I don't mourn the marriage anymore, but it's another change in a never-ending tide of change, and I like change but it's tiring.

I miss my mother very much when I'm in this tidal-change mood, even more than I miss her when I get my hair cut, or find myself browsing for no reason in a department store, or on my birthday or hers. Less than on Mother's Day, which is hands down the worst day of the year.

X asks what I have going on that afternoon, and I tell him. He asks the times—yoga, birthday party, basketball—and computes it all and determines that I do, in fact, have time to drive him.

"If you leave at four you'll be home by five and basketball's not until 5:30," he says.

"None of your ladies can do this?" I say.

Minor is out of town and Major is busy, he tells me.

"I'm sure she's busy, but so am I," I say. "Making money to support our children."

These words feel like crap in my mouth because they are. The truth is that I'm happy to be the one X asks first, the one he bothers, the one he takes for granted. When that goes, what's left?

He goes off. It lasts a while and ends with, "You need something, I tie myself into knots to do it. I ask you for a ride, you don't even think about it. Don't ever ask for my help again!"

"I'm really sorry," I say. "I have no idea why I said that."

He hangs up.

TWENTY MINUTES AFTER I POKE A HOLE in my coparenting partnership, Amanda drops by with a bouquet of wildflowers, which she brought in the basket of her bicycle, then eats noodle takeout standing up at my kitchen counter while I check my watch. Thirteen minutes until the hearing. Twelve minutes. Eleven.

"I remember your wedding," she keeps saying. I wish she wouldn't, but there's something she needs to work out. It's written all over her face, in each magnificent freckle. "You were wearing so much makeup. Why were you wearing so much makeup?"

"I thought I was supposed to. I thought that was what brides did."

I desperately wish I'd become myself much, much earlier.

"Marcus and I had sex that night. I remember thinking that something like forty-five percent of couples don't have sex on their wedding night and wondering if you were going to and then thinking, of course she is, those two are so nuts about each other."

Had we been? The best thing about time is that it fades the hard stuff. But it fades the good stuff, too.

Amanda is staring at me. "I could not admire you more,"

she says, then opens her arms. "Hold me on your divorce day, because it's about me."

"It kind of is," I say. Tonight, Nadine will bring sparkling cider and we'll have energetic, slaphappy sex. The mere fact that this plan exists, that I exist and Nadine exists and this house and my dog and my best friend exist—it's all proof that things are as they should be. I knew this already, but it doesn't hurt to be reminded.

"Nine minutes," says Amanda. "I talked with a lawyer."

"I know. You told me."

She shakes her head. "No," she says, "a local one. I think I might stay."

For one second I feel as if I might get everything I want.

"How does it look?" I ask, meaning the money stuff, the custody stuff.

She smooths down her hair and the collar of her light cardigan. "It's workable. If he goes, we can do a summer schedule, holidays, one weekend a month, that kind of thing. People do it. I'll keep the house, then downsize after Marcus moves."

"Amanda," I say.

She closes her eyes. "I know."

Marcus won't give over his son. And he wants this new job, with the salary they've raised twice during negotiations and the wife on his arm. He won't stay for her, but he won't go nicely without her. Staying won't lead to an amicable divorce. This will be bloodsport.

Seven minutes.

"I'm going to do this alone," I say about the hearing.

She puts the rest of her noodles in my fridge and licks her fingers. "Don't eat that," she says.

"Thank you for coming," I say, like a restaurant hostess. But I'm not here anymore. I'm ahead of time by six minutes.

"Onward," she says, then kisses me on the forehead and

heads out. There's a cowbell on the handlebar of her bike, and she rings it all the way down the street. "Onward! Onward!" she shouts.

I go through the motions of making myself one cup of fresh coffee, and because it's a special occasion, I foam the milk.

Three minutes.

I sit down at the dining table and open my laptop.

Like many things in life, there's nothing to it, after all. The judge is patient and explains every question before he asks it. X's jaw is still hard on the screen, but it softens when the judge asks me to confirm that the marriage is irrevocably broken.

Of course it is, I want to say. It will never break, I want to say. It is in shambles. It is a bunker stocked for generations. If the species can manage to sweat it out, X and I will last forever.

I take a trembly breath. The judge says, "It's not a very nice question, is it? To put it in gentler terms, all this means is that you've decided not to continue to try to repair the marriage in its former state."

"Yes," I say.

When it's his turn, X has no trouble answering.

After the image freezes and the window closes, I shut my laptop and listen to the still house. The hearing lasted sixteen minutes. I am divorced.

X and I had a hard-fought marriage and a hard-fought split. Y and I had a fair first date and, one spring afternoon in my favorite park, came to an inevitable end. Z and I had a sweet, sexy, heady start—the first glimpse of her I got in the flesh, she was coming out of her bungalow, waving cutely— and then bled out on the screens of our phones. We did not give each other a wave or a hug or say Thank you or I'm sorry or Please let me go. Not even Goodbye.

Still, look what she gave me: the nudge I needed to step forward into the rest of my life.

My children are in their classrooms. My dog is napping on

her chair. It is so quiet I can hear the foam breaking in my coffee. I am alone, I am at peace, and I am sad.

IT'S TWO WEEKS before Dani (of the gentle pushing-up-against-the-wall) and I settle on a night to hang out again, but in the meantime we text every day. Spring baseball starts, which, given that I have two kids who play for two teams each, is a full-time load. Dani's a lifelong athlete and asks smart questions about my kids and picks up on truths from my answers. My oldest is a golden boy and likely always will be; school and sports and friends come easily to him in a way they never did with me or X. My youngest, who cracks me up every day, will always struggle with all of it, not because he's less capable but because struggle is in his blood. "He's his mama's kid," Dani says about my youngest, and I have to agree.

She offers to pick up dinner on a night when I work late, and we eat in my dining room with our elbows on the table. We're still talking long after the food is gone. It's been a week, and I'm tired. Somehow, we get on the topic of electric cars. I spend a quarter tank of gas a day when I have my kids, a fact that makes me feel a little panicked. Then we both get on our phones to research makes and models, and I make an appointment to drive an electric vehicle. She'll come with me, she says.

"If you want?" I say, because for a minute I don't understand why she's offered. It has something to do with gender, ironically, and also with the fact that she doesn't know me terribly well. Cars are my father's passion, and in any room, my brother and I are the people you want test driving and negotiating a deal for you, though that's not really how it works anymore. But Dani doesn't know this.

Two days later, we meet in the parking lot of the car dealership. This is where she's bought her last few luxury cars—I'll be shopping from the more modest side of the business—and before we even cross through the sliding doors, a sales guy has sidled up to give her a hug. I wait while they banter. "Not me this time," she tells him, and places her hand on the small of my back. "Her turn."

She has a way of shining light on me. It feels good. Dani and I could have a few great years, I think again, but all of my enthusiastic exploration of life outside the comfort zone would stop. I'm not sure why, but my gut is pretty certain. I want my world to stay open, playful, even a little bit uncomfortable. I want to keep being brave.

I met X just before my mother's cancer returned, and she fought a long time but died three months after walking me down the aisle. There's no one motive for a person to marry, of course, unless you count the patriarchy, but companionship is as powerful a reason as any, isn't it? Plus, I loved him.

Dani's not a see-you-on-the-weekend person. With Dani, I'd gain another driver, another cook, another set of eyes on the homework, a hand to hold on the sidelines, even a second wallet. These are beautiful gifts, and I don't have any doubt that her heart is plenty big to include my children. But.

My sales guy, as it turns out, is a former weather anchor from the news. Dani recognizes him. They chat while I step into this year's version of the car, which is sold out in triplicate. I interrupt them to ask questions about summer mileage versus winter mileage, warranties, local infrastructure. To sell an electric car, you have to sell the whole change in lifestyle, and the weather guy does a good job of it. His father drives this car, he says. And his mother? I ask. She drives the same practical station wagon I do, a car that fits all of our camping gear and the dog, a car for "women in sensible shoes," as I was told when I bought it. Which I realized later was a euphemism and possibly even an insult meaning *lesbian*. My current car suits me, except for all the fuel.

We take out the EV, open the windows despite the chill, change the colors of the dash lights for fun. The weather guy and Dani want me to drive fast, so I indulge them once we're outside of town, but then I relax into the curves and hills of this part of the state, a lush expanse unflattened by the glaciers that knocked around the land before we grabbed it.

It's a good car. It will be finicky—all those bells and whistles—but the warranty is hearty. There will be no negotiating; I'll be lucky to pay list price. But I won't get the weather guy's call for at least nine months if not a year. When we return to the dealership, I write him a deposit check and he puts my name on a waitlist.

I choose the tourmaline blue, a metallic teal the color of the sea and Z's eyes.

FOR APRIL AND MAY, I coast.

Nadine and I see live music and sleep together and laugh a lot, but we don't hold hands in public because we're not committed. We don't sleep together every time we see each other, but when we do it gets better and better. She no longer complains about my bed, and when I spend the night at her place, I discover that she uses not one but two thick mattress toppers, which makes lifting oneself out a pretty serious core exercise. No wonder she finds my bed rigid.

I would be lying if I said I don't wonder whether continuing this ten-date thing is a mistake.

I wonder this with Dani, too. Dani and I meet for meals and check in most days, but we're not committed either. We've kissed a little but so far that's it, despite me wanting badly to drag her by the collar into my bedroom. We do yoga together and lie on the mats after, whispering. She gets my hot tub working and we go in naked and talk until we're pruned. I drive her fancy car into the country with the windows down, blasting the eighties pop station she likes. We take our dogs to my favorite dog park and walk loops until our legs are tired. There's something so warm and comforting, so easy, about being with Dani. Still, I tell her a couple of different times that I don't think we have a future as a couple—this is more my gut's take than my brain's—but she doesn't seem particularly fazed. I'd like to think she's simply enjoying getting to know me, but deep down I suspect she's biding her time. Any day now, I might change my mind.

My kids and I take up pickleball and X plays with us a few times, and then Dani plays with us a few times, and it's Dani, in partnership with my oldest, who figures out the scoring and keeps it all straight. It's also Dani who talks down my youngest when he gets frustrated with his own play. He listens to her exactly like he listens to his coaches, without eye contact but with a tilt of the head that conveys he's getting it. One day after work, she shows up for a game, but I can't leave the house yet because one of my toilets is overflowing and the shutoff valve broke off in my hand.

"Where's the water main?" says Dani as she steps out of her sneakers in my entryway.

We rush downstairs and into the basement storage area, but it's not where I expect it to be. My mind goes blank.

"You don't know?" says Dani.

"Spare bedroom!" I say, and we rush back out of the storage area and into the basement bedroom, which I barely use, and there in the closet is the shutoff, which Dani reaches around me to operate.

As we head back upstairs, Dani says in a chiding tone, "Good thing I was here."

I stop. "I have to tell you something," I say.

She wears an indulgent smirk on her handsome face.

I feel defensive, so I take a breath before saying, "I have this thing where teasing me about being incompetent is a little too reminiscent of the dynamic in my marriage, so I really can't engage with it. This is not your fault, but still."

"I hear you," she says, nodding. "I'll work on it."

"Thank you," I say.

Later that week, there's a warm front and I take off work to kayak with Gwen, and that night when I tell Dani about my day over text, she writes, *Sheesh, do you ever work?*

Then she sends a laughing-so-hard-you're-crying emoji.

I write, *I work quite a bit, yes. Some weeks less than you do, some weeks more. I'm not salaried. My classes are nights and weekends and my editorial work ebbs and flows. Today was light on meetings and deadlines so I took advantage of the beautiful weather.*

I was kidding, she writes. *I know you work.*

Then the next week, when I mention that I've hired someone to install flower beds in my weedy backyard, she asks if I won the lottery. I don't know how to answer.

"I'm teasing," she says again.

Teasing is X's primary way of communicating with me, the oral version of grabbing my butt. It's tricky, because when people are ostensibly kidding, they're under no obligation to take responsibility for their own words, even if what's delivered as a joke lands as a pot shot. I've told X a few facts about the recent uptick in my dating life, and recently he said to me, in lieu of hello and how are you, "Rented any U-Hauls yet?" It's a joke, I know, but how to respond?

"Nope," I answered.

Also, never once in our years together was I able to reassure X of anything, large or small. He was generously reassuring to me, which I leaned on, but when it came to the private island of his worries and fears, he brooked no trespassers.

It's difficult to explain this, but although the way Dani flirts and teases isn't condescending or dismissive, it's in the ballpark. And the way I giggle and play into it is very much on the nose.

If we were together, would I ever get to take care of her?

I do like to be teased, actually. Amanda does it in a way that makes me feel seen and accepted and loved. I want to be teased by someone who knows my flaws and weirdness and limitations and loves me anyway, without subtext or edge, not in a hit-and-run conversational style but in an affectionate bid, a verbal cuddle. It's all anyone wants, isn't it? I want the joking and I want the conversation, but I don't want the former to replace the latter.

A few days later, Dani and I have dinner plans but my youngest's team wins unexpectedly in a single-elimination tournament and has to play at the same time that my oldest is scheduled to play an hour away, which means X, who has the kids this week, needs to be in two places at the same time. He asks me to help and I say yes without hesitating. He does the same for me when this kind of thing happens on my time. I call Dani to reschedule, and when I explain why, she says she understands, no problem. Then she says, "We should talk sometime about how a busy schedule is a trauma response."

"I don't understand," I say.

"There's something you're avoiding. Keeping busy is a tactic."

I don't ask Dani to elaborate because I don't want to. Not because I'm not curious, but because I will not allow other people to tell me who I am.

Dani is otherwise sublime. If I were someone who said things like "the whole package," I would say it about her. And if I were someone without a history of handing over her own self-worth to stronger, more authoritative people, I would be falling ecstatically and unwisely in love with her.

We look at our calendars and choose another date for dinner. Before we get off the phone, she asks if I have afternoon plans this coming Wednesday, then asks if I'll be her ride for a procedure she's having done, an exploratory scope of her throat, which has been closing without warning in an unsettling way. Dani has many close friends, but I'm the only one with a flexible schedule.

I'm eager to do it. Dani is typically the ballast, not the boat. I know this is a big ask even before she says, "I can call a car, it's not a problem," and "You should probably know ahead of time that I'm not the easiest patient."

X, too, was not the easiest patient. Once, he asked me to make chicken soup from scratch, then compared mine unfavorably to his mother's. From then on, I opened a can.

It's been a long time since I've been invited to take care of anyone who is not my child. I tap the appointment into my calendar.

MY BROTHER AND I HAD A SISTER NAMED RUBY, and when Gabe was seven and Ruby was four and I was one, she was killed in a car accident. This was when my father became a drinker. I tell you this because with Ruby suddenly gone, my family blew apart and reorganized in a new way. I became not just the younger sibling but the much-younger sibling. This might be part of the reason why my parents started sending me at a young age to a monthlong, all-girls, Christian summer camp in rural Georgia, where the music director was a woman named Emily Saliers, half of the now-renowned folk duo, the Indigo Girls. I have vivid memories of Emily's gentle voice serenading me to sleep.

So when the Indigo Girls come to town, I go. Nadine's not a fan, but she agrees to be my date and indulges my stories about my homesick, lake-logged camp days. I have long lost count of how many times I've seen the Indigo Girls live. The fact that they're still making music is, in my opinion, a gift to the world.

We have good seats and to reach them we pass every

lesbian in town. It's very hard for me not to touch Nadine when I'm around her, plus it's loud and to hear each other we have to speak directly into each other's ears, so for reasons I can't quite explain, we're entwined for much of the show. Does this make us a couple?

This is the question that springs to life between us later, after an hour of sweaty, ecstatic tumbling in my bed. I search my gut but it's not talking.

"I'm of two minds," says Nadine. We're sitting cross-legged on my bed with the dog splayed out between us, and Nadine's cheeks are flushed in a cute way. "On the one hand it's fun and the sex is good and you're great. On the other hand—"

I'm a little afraid of what she's going to say next.

"—I'm not ready."

I exhale. Nadine and I have talked a few times now about her last heartbreak and mine. There's a little overlap in our stories and a lot of overlap in the damage to our hearts.

She says, "And I don't think you are either."

We're quiet for a minute. I'm surprised to find tears in my eyes. We've been dodging this very conversation, I realize. Nadine and I have a future, but it's not as a couple.

She's ready to start tentatively dating other people, she says, but she doesn't want to sleep with more than one person at a time. So this is it.

"I couldn't do this without you," I say, meaning my healing, my lesbian adolescence, all of it.

"You're welcome," she says, because one of the many things I love about Nadine is that she doesn't shirk a compliment. She knows her worth.

She tells me that at first, she was a little annoyed by all my rah-rah-let's-be-gay stuff, like any lifelong lesbian would be. But she's used to it now, and even kind of likes it.

"So thank *you*," she says.

THE HOSPITAL WHERE DANI'S PROCEDURE WILL HAPPEN is half an hour outside of town, so I pick her up—she insists on going in her own car, but I drive—and after she checks in, we're installed in a small, pleasant room and she changes into a gown. They've given her socks with treads but she refuses to wear them, so I stuff them into my backpack in case she wants them later. While we're waiting for a nurse to start an IV, Dani tells me that last week, when she showed up for her regular appointment to give blood, the nurse had to stick her so many times that both of her arms are still bruised. She's finishing the story as the nurse comes in, and I say, "Whatever happens now, it will be better than last week," and then the nurse asks what I mean, and I tell her what Dani just told me.

"That's not on the agenda today!" the nurse says brightly, her brunette ponytail bobbing. "I've been doing this for twenty years!"

The nurse cleans the back of Dani's hand with a wipe, and I watch Dani's face as the needle goes in. Her lovely eyes widen then shut tight, and when I look back at her hand, blood is running in every direction and the nurse is making panicked motions. Dani looks, too, then starts to try to catch the blood with her free hand. I can't help them, so I watch in fascination as these two homegrown Midwesterners—one panicking, one in obvious physical pain—apologize to each other.

"Oh my!" says the nurse. "That's something!"

"No big deal!" says Dani.

"Can't say that's ever happened!"

"You're fine!" says Dani.

"Let's get you all cleaned up!" says the nurse, grabbing for more wipes.

"Don't worry!" says Dani.

The nurse bustles for a while and bandages Dani's hand without meeting her eyes and, just before hightailing it out of the room, says cheerfully to Dani but really to me, "Let's get someone in here who doesn't know your history, shall we?"

When she's gone, Dani doubles over in pain and I rub her back. "What the hell?" she says when she's able to lie back.

"Oh honey," I say and she shoots me an annoyed glance. *Oh honey* is not her thing.

When she's breathing normally, I can't help but giggle. "So that was my fault?" I say about the nurse's parting jab.

"Yeah, zip it with the next one," she says.

The Midwest isn't always this *Midwestern*, in my experience. But sometimes it is. For my part, I prefer the backbreaking niceness to the way strangers treat each other pretty much everywhere else.

The new nurse is very tall and buxom and sympathetic. I think she has a closeted-dyke vibe, but those are the glasses through which I see the world now, so who knows. She gets an IV going with barely a wince from Dani. The nurse asks a lot of questions from a form, then some off-book questions, including "Where do you live?" and I say, "The west side," which I realize makes it sound like Dani and I live together. But I'd rather be the partner here than the friend, especially if anything else goes wrong. The nurse fusses for a while in a comforting way, then leaves. We like her.

Now we're waiting for the surgeon. Dani is jittery, so I hold her by the shoulder and tell her in a calm voice about one of my students, who's writing a beautiful memoir about her childhood in a commune, and then about another student who's writing a comic novel about an immigrant teen who joins the high school water polo team. She asks questions about them both.

"You have a good job," she says to me.

"I could not agree more," I say.

The surgeon has a Van Dyke beard and kind, lined eyes. Dani thanks him approximately seventeen times, and I ask one question: Could the procedure itself actually solve the problem as well as diagnosing it? The doctor says it might, actually, and Dani thanks him again, and then a helper arrives and they wheel her away.

She's gone about an hour. I work on my laptop and watch the clock. When the helpers return Dani to her bed, she's groggy. The surgeon comes in to give his report—the procedure went very well, and he's optimistic that the problem is fixed—and Dani asks me a few questions—how long she was gone, whether everything went smoothly—and I answer her, then answer again when she asks the same questions again. She lets me hold her hand.

She wants to leave but her blood pressure is too high. The nice nurse is firm about it, but Dani starts to fidget. "I'm ready," she says, starting to stand up, and I say, "OK, sounds good, but let's just wait five more minutes." She lays back and closes her eyes. Then she opens her eyes and asks me the same questions she asked earlier, and I answer as if it's the first time, and then she wants to get up again and I say, "Maybe just five more minutes?" Her blood pressure is still high but it's coming down.

Eventually, she's cleared to leave, and she dresses and then argues respectfully with the nurse about using a wheelchair to leave the hospital. There's no wiggle room. I gather up our things and we go outside and blink in the sunlight and I bring around her car. She's still wobbly, so I ask her to please come camp out on my sofa instead of going home alone.

"All the TV you can binge," I tell her, "and my kids waiting on you hand and foot."

But she's adamant. So I walk her into her condo and get her settled in bed. Before I leave, I kiss her forehead.

"You did good," she says to me.

I MEET MY FIFTH FIRST DATE, Aimee, for a sunrise paddle on the smallest of our city's lakes. She's a travel nurse and shipping out tomorrow for a month in New Mexico. We meet at the launch at dawn—I bring two coffees in travel mugs—and paddle quietly to the middle, linking boats as the sky turns lavender, then apricot. The air is chilly and smells faintly of baked goods.

Aimee is large in every way, tall and strong and meaty, with very short silver hair and lots of gold earrings and one tattoo sleeve, and her voice is silky and deep. She has a shy, lopsided smile that gives me goosebumps. I like the look of her legs, propped in her kayak in shorts, and at some point while we're rolling shoulder-to-shoulder in our boats, I reach for her knee and she shifts to let me, and after the sun is in full view, we paddle back to the beach and load our boats, and then I follow her to her place.

She lives in a one-bedroom cottage in a quiet neighborhood, and her bed is neatly made when we arrive, dappled with sunlight from the window and adorned by one white cat. We get under the covers to warm up, and she tells me she hasn't been with anyone other than her ex-wife in eight years.

"That bodes well for me," I tell her, then I straddle her hips, and the rest is a buzzy, dreamlike blur.

SIX

NOW THAT HE'S IN PRIVATE SCHOOL, Lionel takes a chartered bus, and most days he comes home ready to fight or cry or both. Today, Amanda and I wait for him in the chairs on her front porch, holding mugs of decaf.

There is an anxious flutter in my gut. I'm waiting for her to tell me she's changed her mind again, that she's leaving. I'm open to this news, really I am. This is two-paths-in-a-wood stuff. How could a person not change her mind many times? There's a future she can see, because she's been living it, more or less, for fifteen years. Here or there, it won't make an enormous difference. And there's the behind-closed-doors future, the one she can make for herself. I know what I would choose if I were her, because I did. But I also know that ending a marriage is like unlocking a door behind which a noisy, bull-headed monster huffs. You get back up again, but it takes a while, and when you finally do the world is different at the level of the composition of the air. But right now all she knows is the monster.

She hasn't been sleeping, she tells me in a monotone, rubbing her face. She works all day at the birthing center, then makes dinner, then serves and cleans up, then watches television with Marcus and Lionel, then puts Lionel to bed and goes down to her basement bedroom, then tosses and turns all night. It's difficult to remember what used to fill her time.

"Exercise," I tell her. I'm a big fan of it. Not that I do it all the time, but it's the surest way out of a funk, in my experience. "Me."

When Amanda is feeling low, she stops calling me back. I leave messages reminding her I'm here.

"I'm sorry," she says about going dark.

"It's OK."

Lionel's bus is bright blue with the name of the academy in white letters, and it turns around in the cul-de-sac before stopping to let him off. I haven't seen him in weeks and when he emerges, hands clasped in front of his mouth and nose, I can't believe how fast he's growing. Puberty is wild. Sometimes when my oldest speaks, a sleepy part of my brain thinks his father has somehow come into the room.

"Private school is really a lazy choice," she murmurs as Lionel kicks his way across the lawn. "Set it and forget it."

This is how I've been treating public school, actually. I haven't darkened the door of my children's schools all year.

"Cookies," says Lionel when he reaches us. "Hi, auntie," he says to me.

"Hey, kiddo," I say. "How's my boy?"

"Not your boy." He names my children. "They're your boys."

"You too," I say, and then I have to catch my breath. If Amanda leaves, Lionel goes, too.

In her kitchen, Amanda sets up Lionel with two cookies and his iPad, and we freshen our mugs.

"Does school suck or what?" I say to Lionel before he puts on his headphones.

"Tsk," says Amanda.

"Sucks," says Lionel, rocking on his stool and nodding wholeheartedly. "No friends, no friends."

Throughout elementary and middle school, Lionel had been surrounded by kids who'd known him almost his entire life. They weren't friends with him the way they were friends with each other, but they were nice to him, always gave him high fives and offered him a spot at their lunch tables. Amanda says the new school doesn't have classrooms, it has spaces. Resting space, activity space, learning space, friend space, outdoor space. Lionel reads at a fourth-grade level, which is not nothing, and is a math whiz, though they've told Amanda he probably won't go beyond geometry. He can name the capitals of all fifty states and knows how to use the city bus system and how to bake a cake—skills he learned in the public schools, I'll note. At his new school, he'll make lunch for the ten kids in his grade once a month, and once a month he gets to choose a field trip and the class song, which the teacher will play as the kids stream into the space.

The goal is to trick the kids into thinking they're choosing their own speed and focus. That's my language, not Amanda's. Amanda says it's "child-centered" and that if nothing else, he'll be safe. "You mean like from shooters? Or predators?" I said to her, and she blinked at me. "No, silly, from other kids." I don't understand this logic. Aren't there other kids at his new school? Are private school children inherently safer than public school ones?

Amanda sits on a stool close to Lionel's and rubs his back as he disappears into the iPad. The tinny noise of his TV show comes through his bulbous headphones. I reach over and turn down the volume, and Lionel glances up grumpily, then allows it.

We talk about what we're reading, what we've made for dinner lately. All I make is sheet-pan meals these days, different vegetables each time, either tofu or sausage or garbanzos for protein. My youngest doesn't like any of it and has started to apologize for being a picky eater, which I reassure him he's actually not. I'm just not much of a cook.

Amanda makes beef stews, enchiladas, homemade bread, colorful fruit salads with mint. Lots of garlic, lots of salt.

"I didn't tell you," she says now, "but I had a pregnancy scare."

We are both forty-seven years old. "Adorable!"

"I know!"

"Late period?"

"A week late, and also my nipples were sore and I had all these cravings."

I've been perimenopausal for two years. There are no rules.

"And when it finally came, it was a gusher."

"Yep," I say.

"So there's something I don't understand."

"I probably don't understand it either."

"If I start to feel PMS right before my period is supposed to come, only it ends up being two weeks late, does that mean I have PMS for two weeks? I mean, I feel like I had PMS for two weeks, but I can't tell anymore. I'm so goddamn angry about every single thing anyway."

"I've wondered the same thing."

"Who do I ask?"

"Your doctor?"

"Eh, doctors," says Amanda.

"Your therapist?" I say. Amanda is besotted with her therapist.

"She's younger," says Amanda. "Maybe I'll read a book. Or I'll just let it all be a surprise."

"That's my approach."

Amanda shrugs. Lionel has turned up the volume on his iPad again, and she reaches over to turn it down. He growls at her like a bear cub.

Amanda asks in a dreamy voice about my morning date,

and my head goes a little loopy, remembering. "It was so, so, so amazing," I say. "But I'll never see her again." I tell Amanda that it was slow, then fast, then slow again. Sweaty and talkative, then quiet, then talkative again. We might still be in bed but Aimee had an appointment. After New Mexico, she'll head to North Dakota. We've already swapped texts agreeing this was the sexiest Tuesday morning of our lives.

Amanda listens with her chin in her hand. She blinks away tears.

I cover her hand with mine. "I'm sorry. I walked through fire for this sex life, though."

"I don't think I can walk through fire," she says.

This is her way of telling me she's leaving. Her eyes meet mine and her chin trembles.

"It's OK," I say. "You don't have to."

"I don't even know if I work anymore. Sexually."

I know this fear. "You do."

"Who said one should have as much sex in this life as possible? Mae West? Dorothy Parker? Do you agree?"

"Sort of? But I know there's a robust sex life in your future. And many fallow, sexless times in mine."

She shakes her head. Her bangs have grown out and fall into one green eye. The flesh around her jawline is slacker than this time last year. We are aging well, but we are aging.

"How do you know that?" she says. "I mean the robust part."

"Because your tolerance for less than you deserve will run out."

"When?"

I sip my decaf. "Soonish. Before we're fifty."

"When do we just give up and accept what we're offered?"

"Never?"

"Right. Never?"

"It's OK to coast for a while. Have you told him you were thinking about staying?"

"Nope. What are the chances things will be better there? Ugh, I can't even say it without rolling my eyes."

"It's not zero. Maybe fifteen percent?"

"That seems right. Low but not vanishing."

Both of our phones ding. It's a text from Gwen, a screen shot of a paragraph from an article from *Psychology Today*. Amanda puts on her readers and reads aloud:

"'*The authors compared married mothers to three different categories of unmarried mothers. The findings were clearest for the never-married mothers. Their advantages over married mothers were usually the greatest. They did less housework than the married mothers and spent more time on leisure and sleeping. The divorced mothers also spent less time on housework and more time on leisure and sleeping, but the differences were a bit smaller.'*"

My secret's out! I text to the group.

I would have liked this information twenty years ago, texts Amanda.

Same, texts Gwen. *What's the point of life without leisure and sleep?*

And sex, I think but don't say. Where's that study?

Breakfast Sunday? texts Gwen, and Amanda and I consult our calendars.

Hell yesss, I text.

10a? texts Amanda, and Gwen gives her text a thumbs up.

AFTER I LEFT X, I took a divorce recovery class that met online. There were six women and two men in the cohort, all from hetero marriages. When they told their stories, both men said in so many words that their ex-wives had gone nuts. I had no problem supporting these men—they were both hurting, and they both took a lot of responsibility for the failure of their relationships, as did the women, including myself—but at some point I said, "If every man who said their ex-wife was crazy were right, we'd be walking around in a world full of loons."

I thought so long about leaving my marriage that there was no question I walked out with my sanity intact, despite how hard I grieved.

But not until Y and then Z dumped me did I wonder if those dudes might have been onto something. Didn't I lose at least a few of my marbles when Y told me she hadn't thought I'd *care* that she was dumping me? And when Z followed a text that read *All I can think about is your face* with one that said she was done with me, didn't my brain short out like a fuse?

Wouldn't a person have to be crazy not to go a little crazy?

There's nothing as human and vulnerable and scary and exciting as falling in love. But when it's yanked away, we're supposed to watch it go like sensible robots. And then we're supposed to keep our hearts supple and open them up again, like amnesiacs. We're supposed to draw boundaries but remain open, honor our pain but stay unguarded, break our own cycles but embrace our fallibility. It's a tall order, to put it mildly.

It's hard to know for certain, but I suspect that Z broke my heart not only in the figurative way, but also in the way that means it no longer functions correctly. The gears rusted out and jammed. I couldn't love again if I tried.

MY SIXTH FIRST DATE IS JOYCE, and I like her very much right away. When we're still just texting, I tell her I'm painting my guest room and send a selfie and she says, *You got some in your hair silly.*

Some of the paint is still in my hair when I arrive at her house to pick her up for a visit to the county fair. Her daughter won a prize for a piece of artwork, and though her ex-wife already took their daughter, Joyce wants to see it for herself. The fair is forty-five minutes away. I'm driving because from texting her, I know she drives all week for work. She's a pharmaceutical rep, though that gives the wrong impression. She'd rather be making the medicine than selling it, but she also owns two rental properties plus her house and is aiming toward living full-time from her real estate.

When she steps out of her tidy mid-century ranch, she's wearing shiny blue low-slung pants, a black shirt buttoned to her neck, glasses with mirrored rims, and silver gauges in her ears. She has short, bleached hair and gray-brown eyes and the heavy dark eyebrows of a teenager.

"Hi!" she says brightly, coming in for a hug. "I'm so happy you're here!"

There's no shortage of things to talk about. Her exes, my exes. Her marriage, my marriage. Our children. She wakes up early, like me. She works out using a VR headset and also does jiujitsu. She agrees to go to yoga with me and says, "You know how you're supposed to flow from up dog to down dog without moving your feet? I always have to move my feet."

"I do too," I say truthfully. "We're not alone."

"I don't understand what you do as a job," she says in the car. We talked about it over text but I was vague. She described herself as a lab geek.

"I'm a writer. Only I barely write. I mostly help other people write."

"Can you make money doing that?"

"Some," I say.

Joyce pays our entrance fees and buys a roll of tickets and we study a map to locate the exhibition center. On the way, we stop at a riflery game and she shoots three out of four balloons. It's my turn but I tell her I don't like guns—I don't even let my children have Nerf—and she gives me a chiding look I will come to know well. "I like that you have a lot of opinions about pretty much everything," she says.

"You're a very good shot!" I say.

"My brothers taught me."

Joyce grew up in a big Jewish family on the West Coast. She doesn't go home very often. When I tell her my father lives in Miami and my mother is gone, she says, "I'm sorry. My parents are not allowed to die."

"They won't, I promise," I say.

I don't care for Ferris wheels, so I can't quite explain why I agree to it when Joyce steers us through the rickety entrance gate. We're required to remove our shoes for some reason. Joyce is wearing beaten black Doc Marten boots and socks polka-dotted with her daughter's face. "Mother's Day gift from my ex," she says. I'm wearing sandals and wish badly I had a spare pair of socks. When the tinny metal bar hits our laps, I say, "I didn't want to say anything, but Ferris wheels scare me. Like a lot."

She stares at me with her big eyes. "But you got on?"

I nod. "I didn't want to poop on the party."

"Well, hold on tight."

We start to move, then abruptly stop and swing. A couple loads into the car beneath our feet.

"I mean, I don't think we're going to die or anything," I say.

She takes my hand. "We'll die together," she says.

We shoot up another notch, swinging in the air. I would do anything not to be barefoot right now. When we fall, my feet will turn to mush.

"I had kind of a rough breakup a while back," I say. "It wasn't even a breakup, really, but I took it . . . not well."

"I can tell," she says.

The next time we soar backward into the air, we spend a breath at the top of the wheel. Below us are scurrying bodies and winking lights and above us is a hazy purple sky, no stars yet.

No matter how many first dates you have, the chances of love are still slim to none. That's the trouble with this scheme of mine.

On the way down I can almost understand why people enjoy these rides, and then we're headed back up again.

"Are you going to puke?" says Joyce, cupping her palms and offering them to me.

I shake my head and take deep breaths. "There's so much I want to do before I die."

"Name three things."

We're gliding down and then up again. I break into a sweat.

"More sex with women!" I say.

"Understandable," she says. "What else?"

"I want to be close with my adult children."

"Are you close to them now?"

"Most of the time. Some of the time. It's hard to tell." Once, after spending the day with their cousins, I asked my kids how it was and they both said a few words and scuttled to their rooms. The next day, their aunt called and said my nieces had talked for an hour about how much fun they'd had.

Everyone wants to travel, but I've traveled a lot in my life, and now I want the things that travel interrupts: home, family, friends, peace. So I don't tell Joyce I want to circumnavigate New Zealand, though I do. Someday.

The third is something I admitted to Z, and now it's washed in the residue of her. "I want to make a great relationship," I say. "Sooner or later, I want to find my last-ever partner and show up for her every damn day."

We stare into the darkening sky. Our feet rise on the downslope. My gut rises, too.

"I'll never get married again," she says. "My wedding day

was the happiest day of my life. There's no do-over."

On her dating profile, Joyce notes that she's ENM: ethically non-monogamous. I told her I strongly prefer monogamy, but above all else I'm looking to avoid NEM: Non-Ethical Monogamy. In dark moments, I think this might describe almost all monogamy.

There are half a dozen reasons not to kiss Joyce when, after we've tottered off the Ferris wheel and retrieved our shoes and maneuvered through the crowd to the exhibition center, she pauses to take my hand.

"Friends first," I say.

"Friends first," says Joyce.

But is this one of those times when I think the other person understands me but really she thinks I'm saying something entirely different? I need to work on that. What I'm saying is: I am desperate for love but even more desperate not to repeat the mistake I made with Z, which was falling with no net. If we're friends first, I think, then there's a net, and when I fall, our friendship will catch me.

What I wouldn't give for a monthly coffee meetup with Z, to catch up on her life and catch her up on mine, then go our separate ways. If it sounds unromantic, that's because it is. I wanted to love her, but even more I wanted to know her.

And one thing I already know about this woman is that I want her in my life—and she's hot, frankly, and I wonder what she kisses like—so when she pulls me to her, I go.

OVER THE FOLLOWING WEEKS, Joyce and I see each other regularly. We're taking it slow—this is my request. My heart is beating for her, and that's all I can ask of it. She's a wiz at finding times to see each other. She stops by before work and I make coffee and we sit at my kitchen island talking. On the weekend, we go to her house and sort through two closets of clothes, and I leave with a cropped sweater for myself and seven bags to drop by St. Vinny's. I buy an axe and we split wood together and build neat stacks in our garages, then we're both sore for days. She tells me all about jiujitsu. Sometimes, when she's sparring with a man, she senses something in his eyes and his muscles. He wants to win, of course—so does she—but more than that, he wants not to lose to a woman. His teeth show and his eyes darken, but only for a beat. Then he shakes hands and compliments her skills and that's that.

She buys us tickets to a comedy thing. I buy us tickets to music. She buys tickets to a burlesque brunch. I buy tickets to more music. We go for Indian food and split a mango lassi. One weekday she calls at lunchtime: She's run out of gas downtown and is stuck on a busy street with her hazards on. I grab my gas can and go, and as soon as the gas is in her car, she kisses me quickly on the cheek and whizzes away, like a dream.

But we don't kiss again after the fair. We both want to, but we're doing the friend thing first, and it's so terrific that I wonder if I've been aiming at the wrong target this whole time. Having a friend who comes by for coffee before work? A friend who tells you your new blazer is cute but the color does you no favors? A friend who googles the bites on your ankles to help you figure out if they're from dog fleas? (They aren't. Spiders, Joyce determined.) A friend who sets up mouse traps behind your refrigerator and kisses your dog and brings over unsweetened organic cranberry juice when you have the first inkling of a UTI? It's a dream come true.

But I can't help but notice that Joyce has many more exes than she has friends. I want my proportions to be different. I keep checking the apps, she keeps checking the apps. For me, this is part of taking things slowly, and for her it's part of being ENM.

I also spend some time with Dani, but then she comes down with the flu. I bring her Thai soup and leave it at her door. Joyce goes out with one woman three times, but before they sleep together, they stumble onto the topic of vaccines and the woman explains that vaccines are a ploy to get our information—this is a woman Joyce met through the apps, mind you, which are designed primarily to get our information—and then Joyce asked her who she voted for in the last election, and she said, "The only candidate who wasn't bought and paid for by the establishment." Joyce got the woman's coat and directed her to the door.

"Because he was bought and paid for by Russia," I say when Joyce tells the story again, this time at a dive bar that's hosting a lesbian pop-up.

Nadine is with us, and so is Margie—she's still dating the same person, though when I asked how it's going, she made a so-so gesture with her hand—and I'm sitting on a couch next to Joyce.

"Nonstarter," says Nadine about the anti-vaxxer.

Margie and I agree, but Joyce feels bad about kicking the woman out of her house. "I'm the problem with this country," she says. "We don't even bother anymore."

"You're the *result* of the problem with this country," I say, but I can't really hear anyone and I don't think they can hear me.

"I won't even match with someone who puts 'moderate' on her profile," says Nadine.

"Me neither," says Margie.

"You guys," says Joyce, "*moderate* isn't a dirty word."

"It's code," says Margie.

And then Joyce puts her arm around my shoulders and my hand goes to her knee, and suddenly we are a couple, more or less. We kiss for the second time in the hallway outside of the bar bathroom, then again in the car outside the bar. She takes a selfie of us and puts it online. Caption: *Night out with this beautiful woman.* I resist the impulse to ask her not to tag me.

It's too soon, too early, too fast. All my internal brakes are screeching but for some reason I don't do anything about it.

That night, she sleeps over and it's all great, from the kissing to the sex to the morning coffee. We have half a dozen plans on the calendar. This is happening.

She makes me laugh and she thinks I'm great and I make her laugh and I think she's great, so what else am I looking for?

IN JUNE, X hosts a family dinner for his fiftieth birthday, and the kids and I go early with a platter of fajitas. His sister and her husband and our nieces arrive next, then his parents, and then, separately, Major and Minor and their teenagers. Joyce's kiddo isn't feeling well, so she stays home, though X called me specifically to invite me to bring a plus one. He's a magnanimous, everyone's-welcome person, something I've always admired about him.

Before the meal, we all play Cards Against Humanity in a circle, including the kids. When it's their turn to read cards, my kids swap out the swear words for my sake, and I thank them. On his turn, my youngest draws a card that says something about fellatio and I stop the game to explain it in an age-appropriate way, and he groans theatrically.

My teenage nieces swear a lot, which I find charming— but they also have a habit of making rabid fun of my social media posts, which I do not like at all. I've mostly embraced being old and uncool, but I'd rather not hear about it constantly. When I post a photo of the whole group, my youngest niece makes fun of my caption—*Happy Birthday to X from all the loves of his life*—by repeating it in an exaggerated Valley Girl voice, and her sister cracks up. This is not the first time this has happened.

I open my phone and remove them both from my followers. "I'm sorry," I tell them. "I love you very much, but it hurts my feelings when you make fun of me."

The older rolls her eyes at me and takes a sip of her father's beer.

I wish Joyce were here. She's at ease in groups and likes X, whom she met at my place as she was going and the boys were coming. In the kitchen, X and Major corner me as I'm pulling a seltzer from the fridge. "We need to talk to you about something," says X.

Major is almost his height—way tall—and very pretty in an understated way. She has a sleeve of tattoos on one arm and her long hair is mostly silver. Her three teenagers are funny and sociable and sweet, and she has a way of rolling her eyes at herself and speaking thoughtfully that I find endearing. She doesn't use her sexuality or her intellect to impress X, and he is unprecedentedly smitten with her. If she didn't have another serious partner, I'm pretty sure X wouldn't either.

They want to change our kid schedule, is the gist of it. There's a lot of baffling math, but the bottom line is that since she and her kids are on an every-other-week schedule and her other boyfriend has the same schedule as X and me, she has two weeks a month when she can only see boyfriends with kids around, one week a month when she has access to zero boyfriends, and one week a month when she has to split her free time between two boyfriends.

I realize these kinds of logistics send monogamous, married people casting around for smelling salts, but for us it's pretty normal.

"I'm sorry, I can't," I say. "Joyce and I are on the same kid schedule. If we change, I'd never see her."

This is how X learns I sort of maybe have a girlfriend. "Were you going to tell me?" he says, and I don't reply.

"Hey, that's great," says Major, squeezing my arm. "I can't wait to meet her."

"I like you," I tell her.

NADINE AND I GO TOGETHER to a low-key open mic that happens weekly. She's taking a stand-up class and we're looking for places where she might, one day soon, give it a shot. The open mic happens in the basement of a locals-only downtown bar, the kind of place where people drift in after work and stay until they black out. When Nadine and I descend the steep stairs, we emerge directly into a small, brightly lit room, and a young woman I recognize (from an open mic that Z and I saw on our second date, in fact) looks up at us defensively and says, "We're using this room for an open mic."

"We're here for the open mic!" I say too exuberantly. "My friend's thinking about performing—but not tonight."

"Not tonight!" Nadine makes a panicky motion with her hands.

We sit on a black leather sofa held together with duct tape. Beside me is a college-aged white dude who's chewing a thumbnail and scratching at a notepad. The young woman gets up to emcee. Seven comics, four minutes each, she tells the room in a rushed way. Everyone here knows each other—this is obvious by the way she glances around, skipping over me and Nadine. The young woman is at ease and funny, but the other comics are—this becomes clear when the first one scratches out jokes after he tells them, and then every comic after him does the same thing—workshopping new material.

A very tall trans woman does a bit about the four states where she's considered illegal. Three young guys follow, and each delivers at least one line that cracks me up, though I would not be able to tell them or their sets apart in a dark room. The last comic is a diminutive, white-bearded Latino guy who shouts about how depressed he is. The whole show, which lasts a whirlwind forty-five minutes, is hectic and raw and alive.

Is there anything more full of promise than a first draft?

When we get in the car, Nadine straps in and says, "My

oh my, that was perfect!" and we rehash excitedly all the way home.

SEVEN

JOYCE OR NO, I see no reason to pause my experiment, so I go on my seventh first date with a woman named Chloe, who tells me over drinks about her kids, her parents, her divorce, her childhood, her work, her home, her ex—and asks me zero questions about myself. We're seeing a wildly talented cellist who loops her music using a keyboard she works with one foot, and when the cellist starts to play I lose myself in the show. After, Chloe and I hug goodbye and say we'll be in touch, but we won't be.

Amanda and I squeeze in an early morning walk with the dogs in the middle of the week. The morning is dewy and humid and I'm sweating before we've gone a block. It's been raining a lot. The trees have leafed out in every shade of green and the ground is spongy. Snow has its appeal, but in the spring my city is downright dreamy. Everyone we pass is smiling and sneezing, sneezing and smiling.

"Hey," Amanda says, squeezing my hand, "how's it going with Joyce?"

Joyce. She's now the first person I text in the morning and the last person I text at night. She's gotten into some light trouble at work for being late because once we start talking it feels like there's no natural place to stop, so we don't. All I've ever wanted is a relationship where the conversation never ends.

"She's one of the most fun people I've ever known," I say.

"How often are you seeing each other?" says Amanda.

Two or three times a week, is the answer.

"Do you miss her when you don't see her?"

"I do! I have all these things I want to tell her, so I text her like twenty times a day."

"Like me," says Amanda.

"Yes, in fact."

"And?"

"And is that maybe not how this is supposed to go?"

"I wouldn't worry," she says. "It all seems really great."

"And the sex!" I say.

"Is it the kind where time doesn't exist?"

"Yes. No time at all. And also we laugh so much."

"I'm happy for you," she says, bumping my hip. "And so jealous I could puke."

THERE'S NOTHING SPECIFIC THAT I DON'T LIKE about Joyce. She's thoughtful and smart and funny, and completely open. In bed one night, she says, "I want to tell you I'm falling in love with you and you don't have to say it back," and I say, "I want to say it back but I'm not ready," and she says, "That's OK."

There's a pressure building. It off-gases between us. I kiss her as often as she kisses me, I'm every bit as hungry for her in bed as she is for me—still, there's an imbalance. She won't let it go unchecked forever. We were friends first, and I have no rules about my children meeting my friends, and neither does Joyce, so we've already met each other's children. If we hadn't been friends first, I doubt either of us would have made introductions for several more months.

That said, a very specific feeling comes over me when

Joyce tells me that her ex-wife told her that their daughter, who is ten, mentioned my name twice at dinner the other night.

We're working on different painting projects on the same wall. She's on my extension ladder, using a two-inch brush to painstakingly cover the dark living room molding in white, and I'm below her, priming my mantle to take a few coats of yellow lacquer. She has the more finicky task—I'm no good with precision.

"Wait, say that again?" I say.

"Relax, it's not a marriage proposal."

"I know. I'm just—she's what?"

"She's happy we're together. She thinks you're good for me."

My only thought is: *Oh no.*

"I need to move slow," I say. "Slower. I'm sorry I haven't said this before. I don't always know my own mind."

This is true. I always know what I'm supposed to be thinking and feeling, but I don't always know the real stuff.

With Z, there was no discrepancy.

I'm a little afraid of falling in love with Joyce, but I'm more afraid of not falling in love with her. She's not perfect—she chastises me regularly for things I'm too old to be chastised for, like not taking daily vitamins or not keeping enough toilet paper under the sink or spending too much money on tickets to see music—but still, she is a gift. What does it mean for my future if I can't open my heart to her?

She adjusts on the ladder to look down at me. "Is this because of Z?" she says, not particularly nicely.

She knows the outline of the story: I met Z, I fell for Z, Z dumped me in a text, Z no longer acknowledges my existence. To an outsider, the whole story is defined by the way it ended. But I don't see it that way. For me, the end is a hideous, scaly tail affixed to a shimmering sea maiden. It makes no sense, pasting something ugly onto something beautiful. Part of the reason to end things more cooperatively is so the tail isn't all that lasts.

What does Z remember, if she thinks of me at all? My petulance, when I asked over text to please talk face-to-face? My earnest emails, reporting the minutiae of my life and begging her to tell me there's nothing between us?

We both grew scaly tails.

"Let's define some terms," says Joyce, her face close to the molding. She's doing a bang-up job, one inch at a time. "What is slow?"

I no longer have any sense of what slow means for me. With Z, I would have posted photos online and made vacation plans by now. With Joyce, I'm reluctant to put down a fully refundable deposit on a weekend rental.

"I'm going to tell you my brother's rules," I say.

"I want to know your rules," says Joyce.

"He's smarter about this stuff than I am," I say. "And I think I agree with him."

"Gay men aren't like us," she says.

"I think his rules come from being a therapist, actually."

"OK, tell me," Joyce says, looking down at me over the rims of her glasses. I'm trying her patience.

"He says to wait six months before becoming exclusive or using the word *girlfriend*," I say.

"Too late."

"And nine months before saying *I love you*."

"Too late, more or less."

"And no moving in for eighteen months," I say. "Because that's how long it takes for people to remove their masks."

Z called this early-relationship masking the Date Suit. We all have one. My Date Suit is funnier than I am, much sexier, and has fewer opinions. Z's Date Suit replies to texts and emails, haha.

"Shit," Joyce says, and uses a damp cloth to thumb away a spot. "No one said anything about moving in."

"I know. I'm just telling you his rules."

"I'm glad those have worked for him," she says.

"Going slow means building trust before acting like the trust already exists."

"But it does exist."

"It exists provisionally, because there's nothing that's undermined it."

"You're assuming something will?"

"Not at all. All trust is provisional. The only thing that makes it permanent is time."

"But trust can always be broken."

"True," I say.

"So you're just talking about playing defense," she says.

"I don't follow."

"You want to deny a certain depth of feeling until enough time has passed that you think you're safe. But you're never safe."

This feels both true and not true. And it's dawning on me that we're having a debate about—what? Pace? My needs? The fact that I'm not head-over-heels in love with her? Or the fact that I don't trust her nearly as much as I like her. This is instinctual, and there's no amount of conversation that will make it otherwise.

"It's true that I have my defenses up," I say.

"Like Fort Knox level."

"I don't think either of us knows what Fort Knox is, but OK."

Joyce steps backward down the ladder and moves it two feet, then climbs back up. "Fort Knox is where our country keeps its gold. Most of it, anyway. Named for the first Secretary of War."

She knows stuff. It's something I like about her. When we

started hanging out, she told me all about North Korea. Did you know that all North Koreans have a *songbun*, which is a score that measures your social value? Did you know that North Korean adults have to choose from fifteen state-approved haircuts, except that unmarried women must keep their hair short?

"I need to go slow because I need to build trust between us."

Joyce is quiet. "OK," she says finally. "But for the record, I do think you're falling for me."

For the record, I think this is a possibility, too. And if it's true, or almost true and getting truer, then what's the point of pretending otherwise? Because my brother says to? Decades ago, before either of us was married, Gabe said something offhandedly about how we both have rosacea, so we shouldn't do anything harsh to our skin, like chemical peels. I had no plans to get a chemical peel, but the next time I was at the dermatologist, I asked if I should be doing something about my rosacea, and the doctor looked at me over his eyeglasses. "Who said you have rosacea?" he said.

"My brother," I said.

"Is your brother a dermatologist?"

"He's a relationship therapist."

"You don't have rosacea," said the doctor.

To Joyce, I say, "After we've spent more time building trust, we'll be able to move forward without feeling anxious about it."

"I don't feel anxious," says Joyce, but she's got the paint brush handle between her teeth and her words come out muffled. She reaches toward her back pocket for the damp rag and the whole ladder sways toward me and I rush to press my body against it. When the ladder's steady again, she says, "Did you think you were going to have to catch me in your arms?"

"I thought you were going to spill paint all over my floor,"

I say.

"I wasn't worried," she says. "*I trust you.*"

"You don't understand," I say. "I can't trust anybody this fast." Not again.

"And there it is," she says.

"There what is?"

"There's Z. It all comes back to Z."

Does it? I don't think so. But because of Z, I know that people can be opposing things at the same time. Z was both warm and ice-cold, trustworthy and unworthy of trust, open to me and entirely closed. I'd lost love before, but I'd never experienced romantic dissonance.

Once, Amanda said to me, "Z gave and withheld in exactly the right proportions for maximum torment. Not on purpose, but still."

Am I doing the same thing to Joyce? What's healthy and what's Fort Knox?

At this point, I've known Joyce almost as long as I knew Z. If I'd met her first, would she have absorbed all the love I had on offer? Or would I have wanted this slower pace anyway, instinctively, because different people have different chemistry?

Something else my brother says is this: It's a miracle love ever works out.

ONE WEEKEND MORNING, Joyce hands me an unwrapped plain cardboard box the size of a man's wallet. Inside are two diamond studs with gold collars.

"Classic?" she says.

This is the word I've used to describe the kind of jewelry I like. Pearls, studs, gold hoops.

We slept at her house and I'm still in my pajamas. The light coming in through her picture window is weak and uninviting, but we have plans for the day: shopping, groceries, a portrait exhibit downtown.

The earrings have the kind of backs that screw on with a tiny release lever. It takes me several minutes to get them into my ears, which is how I know, even before Joyce hands me a dark red clamshell box with the famous jeweler's name embossed on the top, that this is no casual gift. The first box was a decoy. These cost her a couple of mortgage payments. The bait and switch doesn't sit right with me.

The earrings are beautiful, but I can't wear a couple of mortgage payments in my ears. Before today, the most expensive jewelry I owned was a pair of cruelty-free diamond studs X gave me for our tenth anniversary. Once, recently, I lost one in the hot tub and had to drain the whole thing to find it. I know how much those cost because the transaction showed up on our joint credit card.

When you don't know what to do, do nothing, says Oprah. How, in this situation, do I do nothing?

"This is too much," I say, admiring them in her hall mirror.

"When I find the right gift, I buy it," says Joyce, gently pinching one of my earlobes. "They look amazing on you."

There is suddenly, on this slow gray morning, a lot going on: conflicting gift boxes, exorbitant jewelry, a new girlfriend smiling back at me in the mirror. The cute fleece I bought Joyce for her birthday, on sale no less, seems like the present of a friend, not a girlfriend, and suddenly I'm pretty sure I know which one she is.

"I'm uneasy," I say to Joyce.

"Why? They're just earrings."

Joyce is saving to buy another rental, and twice in the last couple of weeks she's offered to cook instead of going out, to spend less money.

"I feel uncomfortable."

"You're doing that thing where you name your feelings," says Joyce.

"Because I don't know what my feelings mean," I say.

"Just wear them today. See how they feel." She pulls my hair away from my ears in a way I find possessive. "Try to enjoy them, babe."

I wear them. To the outdoor mall where we buy candles and soaps for my nieces and potted plants for Joyce's coworkers. To the art gallery, where I thumb one earlobe compulsively as we step from portrait to portrait, holding hands. To the sushi place, where we sit at the bar and eat from one large plate. Twice, Joyce brushes away my hair to admire the earrings. She looks pleased and I feel . . . branded.

Joyce watches me eat. "You don't have to keep them," she says. She doesn't seem gloomy or hurt, just disappointed.

"I'm not ready to be in a fine-jewelry place," I say.

"Just sleep on it," she says.

So I do. And in the morning, when we wake up together at my house, I wait for Joyce to blink open her eyes, and then I say, "I can't keep them. I'm sorry."

She stretches cutely and gives me a humoring smile. She's wearing a tank top and her breasts swell resplendently from the arm holes. My dog nuzzles her hand and Joyce rubs her obediently. It is lovely to wake up in the morning with this woman in my bed, her warm skin and disheveled hair, the promise of her company. Why can't I cross the distance between us? Why does Joyce's generous gift feel like an interruption of intimacy instead of a hastener of it?

"It's no big deal," says Joyce. "Maybe I'll keep them until you're ready."

"Please return them."

It's one of those moments where you don't know what to do with your hands. I kiss Joyce and step out of bed and start to get dressed, only I'm not sure what I'm dressing for.

"I'll be back," I say.

I stand in front of the coffee maker, then carry two mugs back to bed. When I'm settled in, I say, "Remember when we talked about going slow?"

"I know. I'm sorry. I didn't think it was a big deal."

"It's OK." But I feel like I'm trying to see through a fog. "But can I ask you—why did you buy them for me?"

Joyce sips her coffee and shrugs. I see her vulnerability. I don't know what I did to earn it, but I won't pretend it's not there. I put an arm around her and kiss her hairline.

"I wanted to show you how much I care about you," she says. "I wanted to demonstrate my commitment."

And there it is. I can talk all day about going slow but the fact is that Joyce's heart was never going to be bridled, and why should it be? If it were me and Z in bed drinking coffee, wouldn't I be grinning at her and thinking idly about a distant day when I might get down on one knee?

Once, after Z and I talked on video before bed, I woke up in the middle of the night, thought of something she'd said, and started laughing, all alone in the dark. The dog startled and left the room. In the morning, I texted Z: *I think I have a crush!* She texted back, *What a coincidence! I have one too!*

Joyce says, "I keep thinking you're going to tell me this isn't working for you."

"It's not working for me," I say. It comes out without forethought, but I know it's right. "I don't want to lose you from my life, but I can't do this."

She nods. "It's OK. You tried."

"I'm so sorry," I say. "It's not you."

"Oh, I know it's not me," she says, and then we both start to cry.

EVERY SPRING, X puts his motorcycle into heavy rotation. It's a joy for him, a welcoming of a new season, a return home. He wears leathers that weigh as much as a toddler, and never rides without a helmet. He put each of our kids on the back for a ride around the block last summer, and our oldest hopped off and said, "That is not for me!" But the youngest was in thrall.

So it's not a question of doubting X's level of caution when, in response to a text asking what I'd think about him letting our youngest ride on the back of his bike from time to time, I write back, *No, absolutely not.*

Three days later, X requests a video chat, and when we get on, he says he'd like to have a reasonable discussion about taking our youngest places on the motorcycle. "Nowhere busy, never the highway, all back roads," he says up front. "He really, really wants to."

"He's eleven," I say.

"At what age will you be OK with it?" says X.

"He can make the choice when he's an adult," I say. "Eighteen."

"OK, Nana," he says, referring to his mother.

"I'm flattered to be compared to your mother," I say sincerely. "Thank you. And she would agree with me, I think."

This is dangerous territory. I'm grateful to remain a part of X's family, but I'd never ask them to side with me over him, not even about this.

"Saying not until he's eighteen is absolutist. That's not even an attempt to compromise."

This is true. I don't want to compromise. I want this to go away.

"Can we talk about it again when he's fifteen?" This is our oldest's age. By then, our youngest will at least weigh over one hundred pounds. His helmet will actually fit.

"You're ignoring the upside," says X. "I went out with this super sexy woman the other day—I'm seeing her again tonight, she's so hot—and she told me all about her happy memories of riding on the back of her dad's bike when she was a little girl."

Half a dozen snarky responses flit through my brain. *If she thinks so, I'm in! But only because she's hot!* I say nothing.

He says, "I'm saying you're ignoring the cost of keeping him off the bike."

"I think he's forming other happy memories," I say. "And we live in a city." But this is barely true. There are plenty of roads where there are no big intersections, very little traffic. "Also, he's our risk-loving one already. What message are we sending?"

"We're sending the message that risk needs to be tempered with caution and experience," X says.

This is an excellent point. I'm about to say as much, but X is sliding downhill, gathering speed, and it's my first response—*absolutely not*—fueling him. No one likes to be told no.

I'm about to say something about sleeping on it, maybe talking with our youngest together, maybe agreeing on a number of rides and the length of each, to keep my anxiety in check and our child's expectations low, to send a clear message that this is a pretty big deal—but X says, "I mean, give me some credit for even caring about your opinion."

I zip up.

He says, "I'm completely within my rights to take him anywhere I want to without your permission. I could take him on the interstate tomorrow, and there's nothing you can do about it. You can't even go to court over this."

Court? Like the court of *law*?

"Thank you?" I say.

A few weeks before our divorce date, he let me know that he'd added a line to his side of our financial disclosure statement, some account I hadn't known about. "You'd never know about it if I weren't telling you, so give me credit for doing the right thing," he said at the time.

But you do have to tell me, I thought. That's what *financial disclosure* means.

Now, I have that same feeling of being squeezed into a corner, collecting my rights to my chest like squawking fledglings. My compromises, low-hanging fruit to start with, feel like rotten droppings now. Are we talking about our child's safety or are we talking about dominance?

I change the subject, then call Amanda as soon as I'm off.

She's between clients. "Sorry," she says. "I owe you a call. Shitstorm here, but what else is new."

"Must rant," I say.

When I get to the part where he deserves credit for caring about my opinion, she starts laughing and doesn't stop for a long time. I listen happily.

When her laughter ebbs, she says, "Yesterday I brought up how Marcus took the new job without talking to me about it. I was saying I'd like some things in our marriage to change, silly me. And he said, and I quote, 'Tell me why you think my work decisions have anything to do with you.'"

Now I start laughing and can't stop. "Are they absurd, or are we?"

"I'm biased," says Amanda. She goes quiet. "I'm worried about us. You and me, I mean."

"I'm not," I say, though this is not strictly true. "Till death do us part."

"What on earth am I doing?" she says.

"You're going with the flow," I say.

"I'm scared," she says. "I miss you already."

I'm nodding at the phone but I can't speak. A small part of me is letting her go. I don't know if this is self-preservation or defensiveness or what, but I know I have to fight it with all I have.

THE FOLLOWING WEEK, Chris Pureka returns to my favorite venue, this time as the headliner with a trans singer whose core following has been with him since before he transitioned. When Nadine and I arrive, there are very few open seats. We end up in the back row, unhappily, and I go to the bar to get us drinks.

The bartender and I gab a bit—and do I sense a ghost in the shadows as I turn away from the bar? Or am I imposing this retrospectively? Nadine and I sit quietly for a minute, and I make a joke about something and she makes a joke about something, and then, minutes before the show starts, I glance up over a bramble of dark heads, and there's Z.

She's standing at the front of room, facing me, talking to someone in the front row.

My first, fleeting thought is: Hi! How are you? It's so great to see you! You look terrific!

I grin at her without thinking.

In the next second, my body goes cold. I can't look away from her—she is such a welcome sight—but once I do, I can't bear to look back. My vision narrows and heat fills my chest, my gut, my useless limbs, my slack jaw.

This is the physical experience of shame.

I talk to myself in my head: *You are not garbage. You are not garbage.*

Then I try to catch her eye.

All she needs to do is look slightly over her friend's head to spot me. I wave in her direction in a quiet way, then in a less-quiet way. There's something in the way she's standing, in the fixed expression on her lovely face: I can't know this for certain, but I suspect she has spotted me and has decided to pretend she hasn't.

"I'll be right back," I say to Nadine, and she puts out her hand to hold my drink. I negotiate four pair of knees to reach the aisle, then walk out of the bar into the night.

Amanda answers right away. "What happened?"

"Z is here."

"You don't have to stay. Make up an excuse."

"I'm not garbage," I say. "I'm not garbage?"

"You are not!"

"I waved but she didn't see."

"Can you do that? Just say hi? That's exactly what you should do."

"I tried. I'm trying. What a relief it would be."

"Has the music started?"

"Any minute."

"Go home," says Amanda. "It's not worth it."

"But this is *my* show."

Z isn't a Chris Pureka fan, not by a long shot. There are many events where I might worry about running into her, but this is not one of them.

"I've been looking forward to this," I say.

"But can you enjoy yourself?"

I don't have an answer. From outside, the venue buzzes with human noise. The opener will start any minute. Maybe it's Amanda's soothing breath on the line, maybe it's my own deep breaths, maybe it's Nadine, waiting for me—but the hot shame is ebbing. I can feel my limbs again. The venue is laced with white lights and each gives off a fuzzy halo in the darkness. The world is so glorious sometimes, so full of music. I feel so much gratitude when I'm not feeling like refuse.

"It was bound to happen," I say glumly, which I now realize is precisely what I've been waiting for all this time. So often when I'm in public, I keep half an eye out for two people: the woman who elbowed me in the nose in the lake on my last birthday, and of course Z.

This is one of the reasons I can't understand Z's insistence on zero contact: It was inevitable that we would run into each other. But it never crossed my mind until now that a person can ghost another person IRL. But—my goddess, if someone could answer this, please—*why*? Isn't a friendly hello infinitely easier?

"Just say hi," says Amanda. "No big deal."

"Right. I will. Just hi, right? Nothing about being in love with her? Haha."

There's a pause. "I've never heard you use that word before."

"I haven't. I'm not allowed."

There's a shift in the hum coming from inside. The opening act.

I say to Amanda, "If you'd told me I wouldn't be over this in eight months, I would have told you that's nuts. This is not a reasonable refractory period."

"It takes what it takes," she says, quoting my brother. "I always think of church when I hear that word, by the way."

"Like refectory? I do that with *conservancy* and *conservatory*."

"Oh! I know you have to go, but I just listened to an interview with the Dalai Lama, and I have to say I was not impressed! What's all the fuss about?"

"I'm not sure, but I think maybe don't admit that to people? Other people, I mean."

"Send updates, please. You're very much not garbage."

WHEN I RETURN TO NADINE, she asks in my ear if I'm OK, and I nod and take back my drink. She's looking at me and I squeeze her knee. I'm so grateful she's here.

The opener's name includes his chosen name and his deadname, which I find curious and touching. I find him totally sweet, actually, and I'm a fan by the end of the set, but when he talks to the crowd I can't follow what he's saying. It's like he's above the water and I'm deep under it, blowing bubbles.

Z is no longer standing in front of the stage, so I scan the crowd and find her across the aisle and a few rows up from me. In the second that I spot her—her welcome profile, her eyeglasses reflecting the stage light, her expression open and light—I also spot the pretty, spunky-looking woman sitting comfortably at her side.

Amanda was right.

I take a few more deep breaths, but the music is good and Nadine's warm arm is resting alongside mine, and now I know that what happened between me and Z was, for her, a cul-de-sac back to familiar love. Maybe even a bid for her ex's attention.

What a fool I am.

But it doesn't hurt to know she's back with her ex. It hurts less, in fact. The hot shame is gone now, and what I feel, watching their two profiles, is a feeling of grace. *Go with goddess*, I think to them.

IF MY GOAL IS TO INITIATE some normalizing, casual interaction, then the set break is the time to make it happen. The lights come up and everyone heads toward the bar, including Nadine, but then my old neighbor Lyn comes over to say hello. We stand in the aisle chatting for a while, and I almost forget that I'm in the midst of an emotional emergency. When Nadine comes back, I introduce her to Lyn, and we're still chatting when the lights dim again.

As Chris Pureka steps into the spotlight, Z and her girlfriend walk up the aisle and take two empty seats in the front row. As they turn to sit down, I put on a smile and wave again, broadly.

Nothing.

They're in a direct line between me and the stage. I can't watch Chris Pureka without also watching Z. Her girlfriend is truly lovely, not just in appearance but in bearing. She has a wise, game, intelligent face. Anything Z conveyed that was unflattering is merely breakup byproduct under the reunion bridge.

After the third song, Z wipes under one eye. Maybe she has an itch, or maybe this music does the same thing to her heart that it does to mine.

It's a testament to the artist that I'm able to relax into the show. They pull me into the palm of their music and hold me there. I want it to never end even as I wish desperately for this whole night to be in the past.

After the lights are up, I run into another friend and introduce him to Nadine, and we all chat in a normal way. I lose track of Z and her girlfriend and don't look for them. I tried to say hi and I failed. Maybe she didn't see me, or maybe she deliberately decided not to recognize me. Or maybe she no longer recalls that I exist.

There are so many things I like about Nadine, and one of them is that she doesn't ask me to explain my strange, quiet behavior. I don't make excuses. I don't say I'm tired or have a headache, I don't say nothing's wrong when she asks. I tell her I need a little time, and I'll be in touch in the morning. Then I take myself home and get into bed and sleep for twelve hours straight.

TWO DAYS AFTER THE SHOW, I send Z a text despite Amanda's warning not to. I convince myself that all things being equal (are all things ever equal?), the right move is to send a friendly note. The worst-case scenario if I send it is also the most likely scenario—she won't respond—so it seems there's little to lose except my own sense of who I am. I write:

I glimpsed you at the Chris Pureka show—weren't they great? That was a pretty energetic crowd! I'm glad you have love and comfort by your side, and I wish you all good things.

"BALONEY," Amanda says when I report back. We're walking a loop at the dog park. "You're not *glad* she's back with her girlfriend."

"Yes, I am."

She gives me a look. "Why?"

"Because it's what she wants. If it weren't, she wouldn't be doing it."

"Hrmph."

"Maybe *glad* is strong," I say. "But it's a relief, and if I'm annoyed by anything, it's that she's had this information that would have made me feel so much better, and she chose not to share it."

Amanda gives me her disagreement frown, which deepens the lines in her neck. I mimic her, deepening my own. There's this certain feeling I have when having a logical discussion about something emotional, like my brain and heart are both itching to cross a threshold, but they can't pass at the same time—the threshold's not big enough. They're not jockeying for space, though, they're deferring to each other. Like, After you! No, I insist! Please, I'll wait. No, I have nowhere to be, I promise. You're divine! No, *you're* divine!

"I feel like she hoarded the info," I say. "Like, 'I see you're bleeding out, but these are my last two Band-Aids.'"

"You're saying it makes you feel better to know she got back with her ex."

"Definitely."

"I don't think it's reasonable to assume she would guess that. I wouldn't."

"That surprises me. It seems obvious. And I'm not sure why you're always defending her."

"I'm not defending her. I'm disappointed in her, frankly,

and if it were me I would've given you a friendly wave, because what does that cost. But that's not her gig, apparently."

"Hmm," I say.

"I think it's reasonable that she might feel uncomfortable not only about running into you, but running into you with her girlfriend. And I don't think it would occur to her that getting back with her ex would make you feel less hurt."

"I contain multitudes!" I say to Amanda.

"You do."

"Here's a fact," I say. "I now know that she's back with her ex, and it makes me feel a lot better."

She shrugs. "How much better, would you say?"

"It's hard to calculate, because being snubbed—"

"She did not *snub* you."

"Jesus, Amanda!—because being snubbed set me back a good bit—"

"That wasn't *snubbing*. You didn't say hello, did you?"

"I actively tried to catch her eye in a cordial and un-private way."

"Maybe she didn't see you?"

"Maybe I'm invisible!"

"Snubbing's a strong word."

"*Ignored*," I say.

"Go on."

"So being ignored set me back maybe, oh, thirty percent. A good bit. I'm telling you that when I saw her my body stopped working properly. I would never have thought I wasn't worth the price of one friendly hello. So maybe I was fifty percent healed before the show and now"—my breath catches—"maybe twenty percent?"

"I'm sorry, honey. I'll always say hello to you. Hello!"

"Hello! But knowing she's back with her ex also makes me feel maybe twenty percent better."

"So back to forty percent?"

"I'm toggling between thirty and fifty, but I'm moving forward."

"Setbacks happen." She gives me a side hug. "I have a headache for no reason."

"Aw, I'm sorry." I rub her back.

I'm telling Amanda the truth. I know the difference between established relationships and potential ones, and I know what it is to seek stability over possibility. I know I offered Z peace and safety and comfort, but I also know to accept it, she would have needed to trust me. And for reasons I can only guess, I didn't earn her trust in the time she gave me to do so.

Which, to put it mildly, I regret very much.

THIS TIME, Z DOES RESPOND. Hark!

The message lands while Amanda and I are walking, but I don't check my phone until I'm home. Her name on my screen sets off a carbonated feeling in my brain. I sit down. The world beyond the screen dims. She writes:

I'm sorry I haven't responded to your messages. I tried but I didn't know how. Your language is so, so intense. I just cannot handle your intensity.

My entire life, I've been told I'm too intense, too much, too too too.

My words are intense because my feelings are.

She asks no questions, so why do I write back? Because I am an idiot. Heartbroken, heartsore, and heart-stuck.

I know re intensity, I write. *I'm sorry. I really cared about you and I can't understand why radio silence is the only option here. I acknowledge that it's your right—really—but I wish I could understand it.*

Why do I use the past tense? Maybe it will soften my intensity.

But that tense choice is my only untruth, not just in this message but in all of them. Can she say the same?

There are plenty of people who can accuse me rightly of avoiding intimacy and vulnerability—Y and Joyce, to name two—but Z is not one of them.

She does not respond.

Z AND HER EX BROKE UP roughly six months before Z and I met. They were both on the apps; I swiped right on both of them, not knowing they belonged to each other. Before Z and I had even shared a meal, I'd told her I was progressing gingerly because of my breakup with Y, and she expressed some concern that I wasn't ready, and I met her concern with respect and reassurance.

In what world would I have turned around and said, "By the by, are you over *your* ex?"

A world in which people don't tell you what they don't want you to know, is the answer. Our world.

But bear with me. They're together—maybe they'll move in, get married—but right now, if someone casually asked Z how long they'd been dating, would she say four years except for that one span when they dated other people? Or would she simply say four years and leave it at that?

She'd say four years and leave it at that.

You see where I'm going with this. In a very real way, Z has arranged reality so that she and I never happened. She never went online, we never met. And if we never met, then why would she wave hello across a crowded room? Why would she greet a stranger?

THE DAY AFTER Z'S TEXT, I'm sitting in my car in the high school parking lot, waiting for my oldest, and I am suddenly sick of my persistent impulse to return to the texts Z and I exchanged, to prove to myself that there was something between us. The astonishing, contradictory fact is (this is my brain speaking, while my heart cedes right-of-way) that our chemistry and connection and all the warm and *intense* feelings we both expressed—it all amounts to nothing.

Not a goddamn thing.

I'm having an overdue epiphany right here in the high school parking lot while staring dully at the school's Pride flag, like the overthinking middle-aged changeling I am. And as the backpacked students spill down a grassy knoll toward our battalion of idling cars, I understand that what Z and I shared *does not matter.* It's so much smoke long since blown away. It's not even history, because like blown smoke we matter exactly as much as if we never existed.

We were—*we were, we were, we were*—and also we were not.

Erasing what happened between us is not a two-turning-keys situation. She turned hers, as was her right to do. Poof!

Something that is nothing requires no record of itself.

I disconnected on social media because it was painful to see her there. Deleting our thousands of words to each other is different, but both moves are about forcing myself toward acceptance: Not only is she permanently gone from my life, but the words we exchanged mean nothing. They weren't lies, but they weren't the truth by a mile. We didn't break up, me and Z. We un-met.

I've never been moved to make theoretical art. I write primarily to understand my strange self and secondarily so my children will know me, and when I am gone—early, I predict, like my mother—I will have existed. What I wouldn't give to have whole books composed of my mother's words.

Now, heart beating hard, I open my phone and search and swipe, then do the same in the trash folder. The words Z and

I gave each other, the lion's share of which were kind and funny and warm and charming and loving and fun as any I've ever exchanged with anyone, are gone.

My kid opens the passenger door and asks for a banana. There's one on the seat because I brought it for him—but maybe he thinks it's there because it looks nice?—so I hand it over and ask about his day ("Good!"). As we maneuver past a line of buses, I shiver a little, but I do not cry.

ONCE, Z TEXTED ME after I'd gotten into bed and turned off the light. We hadn't seen each other for two days. *Send me a picture of your face*, she wrote.

I sent her one. It was very dark. *I miss your face*, I wrote.

I miss yours! she wrote. *That's why I asked you to send a picture!*

But did that happen, really? I think I remember, but I can't prove it.

FOR A WEEK, Amanda sends check-in texts every morning, and around the same time my father texts updates on his latest weight loss plan. For every five pounds, he tells me, he's going to reward himself with a vanilla milkshake from Burger King. He also tells me he's been reading some modern philosophy and has come to believe that he is a Secular Buddhist.

I'm so happy you've found yourself! I write to him.

Amanda calls one morning while I'm still in bed. "Wait," she says.

I wait. My phone dings. She's sent a short video of a deer peering into someone's kitchen through a sliding glass door.

Amanda says, "For like five minutes, I thought this animal was a donkey."

The deer really, really looks like a donkey. It's the angle—

he's all ears.

"A donkey would be funnier," I say.

"Yeah, deers are duds."

"Also this," she says.

My phone dings again. It's a link to a *New York Times* piece headlined "The Hidden Truth of Menopause." I click on the link. Below the headline is a line indicating how long the piece will take to read.

"Twenty-eight minutes?" I say to Amanda.

"I know!"

"Why does that make me a little angry?"

"Because any menopause expert should know we don't have that time, and if we do, we're using it to enhance our souls or rest our bodies."

"And *that's* the hidden truth about menopause," I say.

"You take this one. Give me the highlights," she says.

We hang up. I read half of the article, then send her a text. *I put in a good ten minutes and learned nothing noteworthy*, I write.

She gives that message a thumbs up.

Here's my personal truth about menopause: It's kind of exciting. OK, not purely exciting, but a little. My body is evolving for the first time in decades, having a second puberty. It looks more or less the same—maybe there's a newish fullness to my jawline and a slackness to my upper arms—but inside I feel evolution, not in the way of decay but in the way of rebellion. All bets are off. What was old is new again. It's a pain, for sure, and though I can abide the hot flashes I know for some they're intolerable. If I miss a week of yoga I have trouble not falling over while putting on socks. Sometimes I feel angry for no reason, so I keep my mouth closed and my brain occupied. Before I quit drinking, wine had started to give me a headache. Now, sometimes I get headaches for no reason. I only need one cup of coffee a day, but I have trouble focusing on a book. My hips ache in bed. I open my web browser to search for something and can't remember what. Last year, I made plans to visit my brother, but when I tried to check in for the flight, I was startled to realize that I'd never bought the tickets; I'd only reserved them. I didn't even know you could reserve plane tickets, yet somehow I did!

Whether any or all of this is menopause, I have no idea.

WHEN X NEXT BRINGS THE BOYS for their week with me, my youngest comes in barefoot, carrying a pair of sneakers. My oldest makes three trips from the car: two loaded dumbbells, a weight bench, an enormous tub of protein powder, two Nike boxes, a bulging backpack full of what must be bricks, and his favorite hairbrush. Everyone hugs me, including X, who's chipper. "Let's get this show on the road," he says. "I have plans."

Last week, when we had dinner with the kids at his house, X told me he and Major had had their biggest fight ever. It was about nothing, he said. They'd both been drinking. When I offer him a drink now—I keep a bottle of bourbon for him— he says he drank too much last night and doesn't need one now. He had the kids last night, so I ask what he did and he says nothing, just hung out with Major and the kids at home, playing games. I do not say, "You drank so much while hanging out at home with the kids that you're abstaining twenty-four hours later?" I say nothing.

And I don't say anything when, after I ask the boys to start a fire in the wood fireplace—it's unseasonably cold—he says, "You know, Major just had a gas insert installed!"

Or, after my youngest asks if we can order sushi for dinner tomorrow, X says, "Major and her kids are having sushi tonight. Right now!"

Or, when I report to the kids that the hot tub is on the fritz again but the internet gave me some ways to troubleshoot, he says, "Boys, we really need to get in Major's hot tub again!"

There's no use in pointing out that X doesn't care for hot tubs, gas fireplaces, or sushi. Didn't care for these things, I should say. He used to be monogamous and is now polyamorous: People change. Though is he, actually, polyamorous? Because I haven't heard Minor's name in months, and I barely heard it then.

What do you get when you cross a polyamorist with a fixator? The father of my children!

I have no problem normalizing his polyamory for my kids, but I'm not crazy about normalizing fixation. I'm no stranger to romantic obsession, of course—you're holding proof of this in your precious hands—but around my kids, I keep my mouth shut about it.

YOU MIGHT ASSUME THAT AFTER MY SISTER'S DEATH, my parents would have brought a little perspective to life's inevitable knocks, but this was not the case. When my brother came out of the closet during his junior year of college, my parents jumped together into a well of existential angst. They denied facts. They told no one. They refused to talk to Gabe about his love life. They drank.

I'm not sure what changed—though I wish I could ask my mother this exact question, among one hundred others—but after about four years, my mother joined a Parents and Friends of Lesbians and Gays chapter that met at the Jewish Community Center, and within a few months, she was not only out loud and proud, but also declared herself a closeted Jew. She started advising me to make more Jewish friends—"They have better values," she told me repeatedly—and talked about converting. She was interviewed by the local TV news for a segment called "How to Cope if Your Child is Gay," which I possess on VHS tape.

My father eventually got on board, at least with Gabe's sexuality. One summer about five years after Gabe told them, they loaded up their car and drove from Miami to San Francisco, where Gabe had recently moved, and on the way they stopped at the home of every friend and relative in driving distance to share their news. Gabe and I called it their Coming Out tour.

I'm thinking about all of this on the day after the last day of the school year, in the waiting room of a hair salon. I'm full of a giddy eagerness for each new day, as if I've just recovered from a bed-ridden illness. In the upper Midwest, summer is brief but intense and full of play in water and on land. I've already started to tan from daily laps in the community pool. My children will soon start to complain that they're bored. All three of us have haircut appointments with the same stylist. My oldest takes the first and my youngest takes the second. After my oldest is done, he and I wait together on a firm leather loveseat, staring at our phones.

Mine rings in my hand. It's my brother. "I have a question for you," he says.

"OK," I say, "but if it's about Christmas the answer is I don't know."

"It's not. I was just thinking about something. Do you think you didn't come out for so long because I came out first?"

This is a question I've asked myself. What's done is done, is my feeling. Our parents came around; I have no one to blame but myself. "It never occurred to me that I could choose a less conventional life," I tell Gabe. "Not just a gay life but all of it—the marriage, the kids, the house, whatever. Kids aside, I didn't realize that wasn't my best future. If there are other reasons, they're minor in comparison."

"But still," he says.

Sometimes when my brother and I are in the same place,

I am overcome with shyness. I cope by being well-mannered but closed to him, as if we are co-survivors of the same war instead of lifelong trustees of each other. I do this because I fear vulnerability in general, and also because vulnerability with Gabe is the most vulnerable of all the vulnerable. To be vulnerable with him, I need to feel very strong.

I feel strong now. "I love you," I tell him. "I know how hard those years were on you. I thought you were incredibly brave. I made my own choices."

"I was just thinking it would have been hard not being the straight one."

"It would have been. But I wasn't longing."

"I think you're brave, too," he says, and then Elton starts barking and Gabe says he has to go.

My oldest runs his long fingers through his newly trimmed hair. A stylist—not ours—comes into the waiting room with a freshly coiffed older Asian woman on her arm, and a middle-aged man hops up to hand the woman a walker. "Ready for lunch, Mom?" says the man.

Mom nods and nudges her walker toward the door. If her life had not ended, my mother would turn eighty-one years old today.

"Don't forget to bring your earrings next time, Hyun," says the stylist, which I interpret as an offer to put in the woman's earrings for her. This gives me a feeling of profound peace. The world is full of people helping other people. It's full of angry men with guns and unquenchable wildfires, too, but the good stuff is every bit as irrepressible.

I hope that one day I will be a very old woman, and a person I trust will help me with my earrings.

I nudge my oldest's knee and gesture discreetly at the grown son escorting his mother out the door. "That's going to be you and me someday," I say.

"If you're lucky," he says, and concedes a sly, sweet smile.

I HAVE ZERO DATES LINED UP, but it still feels as if I'm romantically entwined when, in one kid-free weekend, I go kayaking with Dani and then to Joyce's house to help put together her kiddo's new loft bed, and Nadine and I go out for breakfast and then spend an irresponsibly long time shopping for house plants. I'm hanging on to these terrific women, looking to turn each of these low-potential romances into high-potential friendships, something that I'm starting to regard as much, much more precious than any romance.

That said, I have the sense that Dani is waiting me out, and though I'm still given to thoughts of pushing her gently up against walls, I'm also still mostly certain that we don't have a rosy future as a couple. And Joyce has said a couple of times that she isn't sure she can keep doing the friend thing at all, given that she's still hurting from the earring-breakup, but I've been steamrolling her into staying my friend, which I should have known would·not end well.

Nadine, though. I'm starting to think she'll be my friend for years and years, like Amanda. Sometimes I call her before I put myself to bed, and she's watching *The Shining* for the seventy-ninth time while also working on a painting, and I tell her something funny my kids did and she tells me something funny her coworkers did. I've introduced her to Joyce, too, and they swap stories about being gay in the nineties, about Dykes on Bikes and Guinevere Turner movies.

Nadine has other plans the night Joyce and I go together to Dyke Dive, a monthly dance party DJed by a very talented Indigenous woman whom half the crowd wants to sleep with. Dyke Dive moves around each month, and this month it's at my favorite small music venue, the place where Z and I saw comedy on our second date, and where I failed to successfully say hello.

I'm waiting my turn at the bar while Joyce dances. The main bartender here is an affable, gray-bearded bear of a man who is right now being overly apologetic (*in my opinion*) toward a twenty-something masc who's giving him hell for failing to keep their credit card on file. After I put in my order and the bartender goes off to grab my NA beer, I glance down the bar and recognize my most recent online match, a tall, sinewy Puerto Rican woman with a bookish air and curly black bangs and pink cat-eye glasses, whose name is Esther.

I feel nothing.

Esther is waiting to order, so without thinking, I say her name until she looks my way and recognizes me, and then when the bartender returns, I ask him to put her drink on my tab, then sidle through the bodies between us. By the time I get to her, she has a can of beer in her hand and she's thanking me in lieu of hello.

I'm trying to come up with something to say, but then Joyce appears next to us, blond hair catching the flashing lights. Esther's face tightens with the understanding that she's now standing between two women who want to talk to her.

"It's OK," I say to her, putting my arm around Joyce. "We're good friends."

Esther says, "I'm not sure online dating is for me, I might go off the apps."

"I've mostly met friends there," I say. Then say I need some air, and as I back away I hear Joyce say to her, "So I was hoping I'd run into you tonight . . ."

There's an old-fashioned water cooler in the corner, and I fill a cup and drink it down and fill it again. I search myself for feelings about leaving Esther and Joyce to their conversation and I come up empty.

Then Joyce is back, sparking with something heated and sharp. "I should have guessed you'd matched with her, too," she says.

We're in thorny territory. "I'm not interested, no biggie."

"I don't need your permission to talk to someone, but

thanks. You bought her a drink?"

"It wasn't some big gesture."

"Then why'd you do it?"

Because it seemed like a cool thing to do, is the answer. "The timing worked out. I didn't mean to step on your toes."

"Didn't you?"

She's wearing a slight smile, so I'm wearing one, too, but I can't read her. Does she want to talk or pounce? "What's happening right now?" I say.

She looks me in the eye. This is a woman with grit, which I respect. She says, "The fact is that I'm only trying to meet people to get over you, but I can't get over you when you're around all the time. And I want you to meet someone so you'll have someone else to drag places with you."

"Ouch," I say. "That's not how I work."

"That's how everyone works."

"I don't agree."

Her smile disappears. "That's because you don't understand how hearts work."

"I am not going to engage with you right here and now," I say.

"Why?"

"Because I feel a lot of aggression coming from you and I don't know how to handle it."

"Aggression? There's no aggression coming from me. None!"

But she's practically yelling, and I'm starting to panic. I don't know how hearts work? I am all heart. My heart might be a lumbering, ragged thing, but it's enormous. Leviathan. Pumping hard.

Joyce steps out a side door onto the deck and for some reason—loyalty? foolishness?—I follow her. The music hushes.

"I told you weeks ago I couldn't be your friend," she says, "and you wouldn't accept it."

"You're right, I'm sorry," I say.

She steps away, then turns back, and her eyes are clear and determined, a shade short of cruel. "I'm sorry I said that to you," she says. "But I can't be your friend, and you need to accept that and stop pushing me. I'm going to get a ride home, and then I'm going to disconnect from you on social media, and I'm asking you please not to contact me. I don't want anything to do with you."

I'm stunned. I can't speak. And I can't say any of the things I want to say—please don't, for one—because she's asking me not to, and I can't pretend to make things right anymore because she's telling me very clearly that it won't work.

"I'll miss you," I finally say, and she walks back into the bar, loosening noisy revelry into the quiet night. I walk to my car alone.

LATER THAT WEEK, Dani and I go out for drag bingo, then finally sleep together. Before it happens, I say, "Can we do this and still not be a couple and still be friends?" And she says, "Let's see how it goes," and then her mouth is on mine and her fingers are competently working the buttons of my shirt.

Sex with Dani is different from anything I've ever experienced. Like a new door to a new room, one where I'm treated like a goddess. At one point between rounds, I'm lying on my stomach and she tells me there's a place along every woman's spine that begs to be touched. I think this sounds like a line, but it turns out she's right.

In the morning, when she invites me to spend my next kid-free weekend at her cabin, I hedge. There is so much I want to share with Dani—sex is only part of it, though I don't deny it's a big part—but I know better than anyone not to overpromise. Love is not the sum of its parts.

"I'm still dating other people," I say.

She crosses her arms. "Why?"

"Because I'm a lesbian adolescent."

"You're a what?"

"A lesbian adolescent. I'm trying things and gaining experiences. This is my journey." I sound like a heavily hashtagged social media video, and not one I'd choose to watch.

"You'd rather go on a date with a stranger than spend the weekend with me?" she says.

"I want both."

"Do you have feelings for me?"

"Yes. And also I don't think we have long-term potential."

"Skipping to the end still, after this?" She backs toward the door, putting on her sunglasses. "I think it's best if you don't call me," she says, and walks out.

EIGHT

I FRAY. I intend every day to go to yoga but end up skipping, my house is a mess, I nap every afternoon, my children survive on screen time and cereal and pasta. I gain weight and grow three pimples on my chin. There's a sound in my ears like a tiny bug's flutter. I've had my period twice in five weeks, once heavy and once very heavy. What this means, I don't know and I don't care.

I'm jumpy all the time. My children call for me and I yelp. My phone dings and I startle. My dog spends every minute at my side, offering her soft ears to my fingers. Nadine stops by with milk after I mention there's none in the house. It cheers me, seeing her, but when she's gone I fall back into my funk. I ache physically and take ibuprofen a couple of times a day. I do the laundry but don't fold it, and soon my children and I are swiping through the baskets for clean underwear. I institute movie nights and order pizza. It's all I can handle.

The days are long, and I go to bed with the sun in the sky. I wake in the middle of the night with a feeling of dread. I let the air conditioner run freely. I can't read. I don't visit social media. I do my paid work in a joyless, head-down grind. I create nothing. I take my youngest to a birthday party at an indoor trampoline park and spend two hours in a broken massage chair with dead headphones in my ears and a book closed in my lap. Two days later, my youngest complains of a sore throat. When it doesn't get better, I take him to the doctor and he tests positive for strep.

Maybe I have strep, too, though the timing is off. I go to the doctor and she agrees it's likely, but I test negative. She prescribes antibiotics anyway, but Nadine says not to take them if I'm negative, so I don't. Nadine thinks it might be mono, but I don't have another medical appointment in me. Gwen reminds me about her psychic but I say no, so she recommends her energy healer instead. I make an appointment online. Amanda is busy selling the birthing center and closing her practice, so I don't go into it when she checks in. Fine, I tell her, everything's fine. But she knows better. She orders large containers of egg drop and hot-and-sour and wonton soup to be delivered to my house, and over the course of a week I make my way through them gratefully.

In my head, I have long conversations with my mother.

And one morning I have a fresh thought: Maybe I can stop trying so hard to give Z up. Maybe this is just what life is now.

This reassures me. Gabe is right: It's all just grief. Living with grief I can do. I've been doing it for years.

REIKI IS PRONOUNCED *RAY-KEY*. I'm not sure how I pronounce it, but the energy healer, whose name is MaryAnn, corrects me as I sit down in a kilim armchair in her office, which is one block from the cottage where X and I lived during our childless years. I parked in front of the old house for nostalgia's sake and thought about a morning when X and I were lying in bed and for some reason I sang him a Patty Griffin song, and when I was done, he said, "That was so beautiful," and I had the clear thought that it is a lucky, lucky thing to find someone in whose arms you can rest. We had something special once upon a time. What do I gain by forgetting this?

MaryAnn wants to know what brought me here today. She's wearing a mustard-colored tunic and expensive boots and her ropy blond hair falls past her shoulders. It feels like a long time since I've talked about Z, so I'm surprised when I start crying. Our first video chat, our first date, our first kiss in my car, our second date, the first time we had sex, the second time we had sex, the questions we covered on a floating dock in a swimming pond, the excitement of deciding to start something together, her abrupt cancellation. My stupid emails. Seeing her at the Chris Pureka show. Her one text. Deleting us.

"I'm perseverating," I say, quoting my brother. "I am so tired."

"I don't understand," she says with a head tilt, as if I've skipped part of the story. "She won't talk to you? I thought that behavior was for young people."

I nod. We're on the clock here, and this is not cheap. "How does this work? Are we already doing it?"

She tells me to take off my shoes and lie down on a padded table. She places a pillow under my knees and a heavy blanket over my body, all the way up to my neck. I close my eyes. Her voice is like warm iron and she smells like fresh earth. I am desperate to be soothed.

She says softly, "Can you name the feelings that came up as you told me your story?"

"Yes."

"What are they?"

"Shame. Regret. Confusion."

"Can you tell me your wish for yourself right now?"

I swallow a sob. "If she's forgotten, I want to forget too," I say.

I don't want this, actually—why don't I want this?—but I want to want it, which is close enough.

"Can you tell me where the grief lives in your body?" she says.

Can I? I scan myself. In my gut is a hot nest of worms, and in my chest is a clammy, pumping fist. Am I allowed to have two places?

"Here." I touch my breastbone. "And here." I touch my stomach. But don't I also feel grief in my knees and my shoulders? Does anyone point to their eyelids, their lower lip, the arch of one foot?

She warns me before the soft plank of her hand meets my body. It rests there, and my buzzing mind contracts until all I hear is her breathing and my own, and all I feel is the weight of her hand.

"When you're ready," she says, "I want you to gather those feelings of shame and regret and confusion right here in your torso. Call them all together."

The worms wriggle. The fist clenches.

"Now in your mind's eye, form a sphere made of light around your body, three feet in every direction. Imagine yourself standing in the center of this sphere. It pulses with light and warmth and energy. It's yours, you can reach out and touch it, you can rest inside it."

I exhale.

"This is the sphere of your power. Fill it with peace and strength."

This reminds me of something, but I don't remember what.

"Now, and this is the hardest part, I want you to summon—I'm sorry, what is her name?"

I manage to whisper Z's first name.

"I want you to summon Z to the outside of your sphere. Right up to the edge of it."

She's right, this is not easy. I haven't allowed myself to conjure Z's face since I last saw it in life. Her exquisite face.

How I relished the minutes I spent looking at it.

"Look her straight in the eye, and tell her your wish," says MaryAnn.

My voice breaks, but I do it.

"Now I want you to create a cord that stretches from your torso to Z's feet. It's straight and wide enough to fit all the shame and regret. It's unbreakable and never clogs."

"To her feet?" I say.

"To her feet. Because in a minute, once the cord is in place, I'm going to ask you to gather your bundle of shame and regret and confusion and push it into the cord and let it slide all the way to her. Not yet but get ready."

Soft footsteps pass outside the door. MaryAnn's hand pulses on my chest. The worms writhe and the fist tightens, and I gather them together. The bundle knocks uneasily against my solar plexus. It's in me but it's not of me. The cord is smooth and open and the bundle fits with room to spare, but I don't let go of it yet. The sphere is all light. And Z is there, a human in a body, her own sphere and her own bundle and her own cord stretching only she knows where.

"I'm not ready," I whisper.

"Shh," she says, "take your time."

I feel a slaking in my heart. Inside myself, I take a step back, away from Z and the cord. The bundle starts to slide.

"Directly to her feet," says MaryAnn, and then the bundle is gone.

"What will she do with it?" I say. I've left sense behind, but then again I haven't made much sense to myself for a long time.

"You're giving it back because it belongs to her."

Where was Z, in the physical world, sometime between 1:15 and 1:30 that Thursday, an afternoon when the air smelled faintly of an algae bloom? Was she at her desk or walking her dog or texting her girlfriend or having a snack?

Did she feel a tickle in her thumbnail, a spasm in her funny bone? Did my face fly into her brain and out again, like a winged ghost?

The bundle emerges from the far end of the cord, but that's as far as I push it. I gently nudge Z back, away from the bundle and from me. I don't want to keep it anymore—progress!—but my bundle of pain isn't Z's. She didn't mean to make it and she doesn't deserve to carry it.

"Your sphere is getting brighter," says MaryAnn. "It's full of your self-worth and strength and hope and love. It's a force field and cannot be pierced or diminished. And it belongs entirely to you."

MaryAnn's hand leaves my body. I miss it. I open my eyes.

"So that's reiki," I say.

"*Ray-key,*" she says.

AFTER, IN THE LOBBY, I LOOK IN A MIRROR at my own face, and I see the chin zits and eyebags and extra pounds—and something else. Peace.

I walk a block to the co-op grocery and wander the aisles for a long time, touching the smooth boxes of teas and inhaling the briny air of the olive bar. I choose good bread. I choose rich cheese. I scoop three kinds of olives into a large container. I feel like a placid, satisfied zombie, and want never to come alive again.

WE'RE PACKING UP HER HOUSE TOGETHER when Amanda tells me she applied to work part-time at the school where Lionel will be a student. It's a Catholic school with desks and grades, and costs three times as much as Lionel's woo-woo school here. There is one classroom where the special needs students from every grade are sequestered, and Lionel will wear navy chinos and a white polo shirt every day. This school is all the rage in her new city, recommended by every executive's wife—and a couple of lady-executives themselves—and, according to Amanda, the only other viable option is a different Catholic school with no special-needs classroom at all.

"Which school did the husbands recommend?" I ask, and she blinks at me indulgently.

Amanda's packing style is to wrap items inside other items: Lionel's seashell collection inside his socks and underwear, candlesticks inside sweaters, the Taylor Swift bobblehead I gave her inside two placemats. If she has her way, no packing material will infiltrate the entire move. There are as many soft things in her home as hard things, she told me, and now we're testing that theory.

We label boxes and leave them where we fill them. The movers will handle it from here.

Somehow, while absorbing Amanda's news, I lightly cut my finger on a butter knife, and Amanda says, "Let me get some lemon juice for that," then goes back to wrapping things in other things.

"I don't understand," I finally say.

"Don't judge," she says.

I stop wrapping. "OK, I won't, but what?"

"I'll be a teaching assistant, basically."

I let it sink in, but not for as long as I should. "At a wealthy Southern Catholic school? Why?"

"I said don't judge!"

It had never crossed my mind that she might not rebuild her midwifery practice, if not open another center.

"Why?" I say.

She holds up a framed photo of herself and Lionel and Marcus wearing matching chambray shirts and white jeans, sighs onto the glass, then wipes it with her sleeve and swaddles it in a tablecloth.

"Just to get settled," she says to me, and in her voice I hear resolve. This move, this marriage, this family—it will work because she will make it work. She's the captain of this ship. I've been outside the bubble long enough to no longer remember why I wanted in, but I'll be damned if I'll make Amanda follow me.

Except.

I put down a pair of rooster-shaped salt-and-pepper shakers she bought during her Country French phase. "Just help me understand," I say.

"I'm going to take some time off, more or less."

"By working part-time at a middle school?"

"—is the kind of thing you will not say because you're not judging."

We pack quietly for a while. A silver trivet with the date of their wedding engraved on it—why? A bamboo salad bowl the size of a dog bed, and a pair of tongs with mother-of-pearl handles. I'm not going near the photos on the wall, but I start on the artwork, taping each piece into blankets and suturing them with painter's tape, then leaning them against the back of the sofa, like quiet guests.

While I work, I count my breaths to keep myself from speaking. An hour later, the walls are bare and so are all the surfaces. If not for the boxes stacked here and there, the house looks like something from a magazine. Sterile, unloved, very pretty.

Amanda goes to the kitchen and pulls down one of the mugs we left unpacked for these final days, then fills it with white wine from the fridge. It's 11 a.m.

"Is it good money?" I say.

"Do you know anything about private school?"

This is as close as Amanda usually gets to snapping at me. All these years, we've been so gentle with each other. We've always known what this friendship was worth.

"So that's a no. Is it . . . good benefits?"

She glares at me over the top of her mug. "It's reduced tuition. By a third."

"You can get mad at me. It's OK," I say.

"I am mad at you. I'm fucking livid."

"Just explain it like I'm a kindergartener. I'm grasping at straws here."

"Marcus thinks—"

I put down the packing tape. Not quietly.

"—it will help Lionel acclimate. And for community," she says.

Does this make sense? Through a certain lens of priorities. Marcus's priorities. Or priorities that prioritize Marcus. Which, in Amanda's world, is the same as prioritizing the family. The Family. A tiny, self-perpetuating cult.

I have the feeling that I'm missing something, because have I really spent an hour idly wondering about this job bid while she seethes at me? But then I remember that she's moving and really, really sad.

"Tell me," I say.

"You know I love you and I'm rooting for you, but do you know what it's like to have a best friend who's been grieving for what, ten months? Over a person she knew for ten minutes?"

"No. What's it like?"

"It's tiresome."

"So moving is a relief?"

"Maybe." Her face falls. "No, moving sucks. I'm sorry. I don't know what I want. I can't picture the future."

"It's OK."

But it is and it isn't. My lifelong experience with other people's anger, to say nothing of my own, has long since taught my brain how to shut down and leave my empty body behind to absorb the blows. Before I learned this, I lashed back, which was much worse. Now the ugliest my anger gets is a snotty retort I immediately regret, and even those are rare.

"I can't even imagine your life sometimes," she says, but the bite has gone out of her voice. "You're going to teach a class on the road, really?"

This is a twist. In ten days, Amanda and I will stuff her husband's car full of valuables and, together with our two dogs and all of Lionel's reptiles—Amanda promised they will remain inside their containers—drive thirteen hours to her new home, to open up the house and gather supplies. We'll have three nights before Marcus and Lionel arrive via airplane, and I'll drive home with my dog in a rental car.

I keep my voice neutral. "What are you talking about?"

"That's what you said. We're stopping halfway so you can teach a class."

This is from a conversation we had a week ago, when I told her I'd booked us a hotel room between her former home and her new one. I was letting her know the logistics were taken care of. And yes, I teach a monthly evening class, and I plan to host it from our hotel room. I reminded Amanda to bring headphones so she can tune me out. I'll wear headphones, too. What's the problem?

"We're stopping to sleep," I say.

"After six and a half hours? We'll barely be out of the Midwest."

Is it my imagination, or does she say *Midwest* with a shade of disgust? Enjoy those hurricanes! I want to say. How much did you pay for your sixth-acre of sinking marsh? Live it up while you're still above sea level!

I say, "You don't want to stop until we've cleared the Midwest? What is that, Kentucky? That's fine, we'll just leave earlier."

She's visibly gritting her teeth. "I don't want to stop, period. If we're going, let's go."

"That's fine. I mean, personally I enjoy sleep, but I'll cancel the hotel. I'll still need to stop somewhere to teach."

"Why?"

"Because, I don't know, on the road there's dropped service and all that."

She buries her hands in her hair. "I thought you might cancel one class. I can get myself there faster without you."

"Jesus!"

I put down a vase the size of a bassoon. I cannot cancel class. I can reschedule, with some lead time, but I can't just cancel. My income depends on me showing up. She should understand this.

"I didn't realize getting there fast was the point," I say. "I'd rather not cancel."

My husk-body is straining toward the door. I've been at Amanda's house every morning this week, not writing and not prepping for class, skipping yoga and rescheduling meetings.

"Do you want to go without me?" I say.

"I want to be alone," she says.

No one has to ask me twice.

"I'll call you later to apologize," she says as I open the front door.

"Good!" I say, and as I close the door behind me, I hear her say, "I love you!" and I say, "I know!"

SUMMER HAS CRACKED OPEN and baseball is in full swing. The day after my argument with Amanda, I can't focus on work, so I put my kayak on my car and go out on the water, fighting hot, gusty wind. I stick mostly to the creeks and inlets, and when I paddle onto one of our lakes, the waves push me around and I spend a while watching kite surfers launch into the air, suspend breathlessly, and crash down again. Weather treats us more gently here in the middle, but that doesn't mean it has no teeth.

That weekend, the kids and I pack up and drive a few hours so my oldest can play in a baseball tournament with his travel team. X will ride his motorcycle down to watch one game, then go back home and take care of my dog, and my youngest and I will stay overnight in a hotel with the rest of the kids and parents. As soon as we arrive at the field, my oldest jumps out of the car to get himself eye-blacked by his friends, and this is more or less the last time I see him up close for two days.

The sun is very strong and the wind dies and I sweat in my camp chair. I send my youngest to concessions three times for snacks and drinks. X joins us on the sidelines during the second inning. At one point I yell, "You've got this!" to a kid who's swung twice without making contact. The coaches ask us to "make noise" and "get loud." This is part of my job as a sports parent. But immediately, X turns his back to the game to say not-quietly to me, "If I were that kid, I'd be so annoyed with the random lady cheering on the sidelines. I'd be like, 'Shut up, lady.'"

"Hmm," I say.

The next time I cheer, he says it again using different words.

I stop cheering.

After our kid's team wins, we go together to a chain restaurant for lunch. I pull out Bananagrams while we wait for our food, and we're halfway through a game when it arrives. The server is a young Black man with long, thick eyelashes and a Pride flag pin on his lapel. As he places our meals on the table, I notice that every dish is served in heavy single-use plastic. I say, "We just throw this all away after?" to the server, and he shakes his head like he's with me and says, "I know, definitely not my choice," and we share a grimace.

When the server leaves, X shakes his head at me and says,

"Jesus, it's not his fault, for fuck's sake," as if I've just given the kid a piece of my mind.

I stammer something, I don't know what.

We finish Bananagrams and play again. I win, then X wins.

What do our children think about these exchanges? Will they speak to people they love this way? Will their mentally healthy Gen-Z partners know how to shut it down?

It might seem like a poor choice to not say something like, "Please don't speak to me that way," or "My behavior does not reflect on you." But speaking up is a firestarter, and I don't want to start a fire. Not now and not the next time or the next. I quit the low-ranking job I held so long in this workplace, so why is my old boss still telling me what to do?

Z AND I NEVER SPENT THE NIGHT TOGETHER, though we planned to, because X gave the boys the stomach flu and they gave it to me. Z went on with her life, and at some point during those hazy days, I whined over video chat that the only thing I wanted to eat was a brownie, and an hour later my doorbell rang and I opened it to find a bag of brownies on the welcome mat and a delivery person driving away. At another point, I whined on video chat about feeling anxious about us. We were barely ankle deep before this heavy pause, which felt like tricky timing. She chuckled and told me not to worry, she was good at waiting. The next day, I texted her: *Hey girl*, and a photo of myself holding a thermometer—my fever was gone—and she gave the photo an exclamation point.

I can't remember—was it that afternoon or the next when she showed up at my door? We'd shed half our clothes before we made it to the bedroom. The fun part was so far from over.

ONLY A DAY HAD PASSED between me leaving Amanda's house

and her calling to apologize and asking me to come back, and we ended up laughing together on Lionel's top bunk while prying solar system stickers from his bedroom ceiling.

So it's not because we're in a fight that I'm dreading her going-away party a week later. On the morning of the party, I take an hour of hot yoga, but I fall out of the balance poses and end up in child's pose through the final vinyasas. When I get out, I turn off my phone and take myself on a three-hour paddle down a local river. After, I sit on a bench overlooking the water and drink kombucha.

I stay at the party for only an hour, long enough to eat two tacos and watch Amanda's good friend from her village give a funny and warm goodbye speech, which she ends tearfully, touching the corners of her own eyes. (I like this friend very much, though once she came to my house with Amanda, and as she stepped into my foyer said to me, "I can already tell that this is the nicest house on the street!" I had no idea how to respond.)

I wave goodbye to Amanda across a sea of heads, and the look she gives me is wise and contained, like she's been swallowed by an invisible viper and is being imperceptibly squeezed to death. When Marcus's gaze swings my way, I narrow my eyes at him.

I PARK IN HER DRIVEWAY just after sunrise the next morning. We situate the dogs in the backseat of Marcus's SUV and the reptiles in the trunk, then stuff the car with suitcases and boxes and valuables wrapped in beach towels. Amanda is wearing sweatpants and unlaced sneakers and the bags under her eyes are blacker than I've seen them in years. Neither Marcus nor Lionel comes outside to say goodbye, and I don't go inside. I realize that engaging in a cold war with Marcus will only make Amanda's life more difficult and our friendship less steady, but

I can't help myself. While Amanda is packing the car, I sneak around the side of their house to Lionel's bedroom window. He's on his bed with his iPad. I rap on the window and wave wildly so he won't be alarmed, and he waves back for a while before getting up to face me through the glass. He says loudly, "You're driving to the new house!"

"Yep!" I say. "I wanted to say goodbye."

"Goodbye!" he says. "Have a safe trip! Drive safely! Be safe!"

"Goodbye, my love!"

Then I duck out of sight like I'm magic.

We stop for gas right outside the welcome sign to her village, and Amanda asks me for chili-cheese Fritos and Hot Tamales. A road trip never feels like a road trip until I've been on the highway for an hour. Now, we're just running errands. I hand Amanda my phone to choose a podcast while I go inside. I get the snacks she requested, plus two bananas and a bag of baby carrots. When I come back out, my phone is in her lap and she's gazing out the window—at a walk-in hair-cutting place where neither of us has ever been, a sandwich chain, a local coffee shop where once she had a nosebleed all over the table while I rushed around grabbing napkins. The grocery co-op, the grocery megalith, the budget grocery. The credit union where once she withdrew so much cash to pay under the table for her kitchen renovation that we spread it out on her bed and took photos of each other rolling around in it, then took off our tops and held hundreds against our nipples and took selfies and sent them to our husbands. (X joked, "I'm on my way!" and Marcus didn't reply.)

That was another life.

My phone in her hand is muted but we can tell it's ringing because Gwen's face is on the screen. I lean over to swipe to answer but leave the phone in Amanda's hands. Gwen's voice fills the car. She asks Amanda questions—How do you feel?

Do you have a pillow for car napping? Are you taking I-39 to avoid Chicago? Is it too late to pick me up?—and Amanda answers in a monotone, like she's decamped her body.

At a stoplight, I take the phone. "I think our friend is disassociating," I say to Gwen.

Amanda says, "I am the opposite of disassociating. Everywhere I look, associations."

The bagel place where we used to meet on Sunday mornings. The Dairy Queen where we took the kids no fewer than a dozen times. The bike path she took to work. The hospital where Lionel was diagnosed when he was two, where they operated on his heart when he was four.

The restaurant where Z and I once shared a bowl of butterscotch pudding while touching feet under the table.

Amanda hands me her phone and tells me to turn it off. I pull a fleece blanket and a small pillow from the backseat and pass them to her, and in a minute only her hair is visible. "Good night," she says. We drive south.

AMANDA DOESN'T STIR until the car starts to buck. We're in southern Indiana, we've gone through an entire tank of gas, and there's nothing around but a farmhouse across a field. How I managed to ignore this car's many warnings, I have no idea. I pull onto the shoulder and tell Amanda to wait, then walk up the highway and squeeze around a fence post and head to the farmhouse. I knock on the door and ask the woman who answers for a ride to the nearest gas station. She waits for me to purchase and fill a red fuel container, then drives me back to her house, and when I offer her cash for her time, she waves me off and trudges back inside. I cross the field again, squeeze around the fence post again.

Amanda rouses when the car starts, and then we're off. At the next exit, I gas up the car while Amanda runs the dogs around an empty field.

At some point in the last hour or so of the day, I glance over to find her sitting straight up, blinking at the windshield.

"You're awake," I say quietly. "Eat a banana. Drink water."

She does.

"Did you dream?"

She nods. "Of the beach."

Was I there? I do not say.

She says, "You were there. I was shouting at you."

"Why? Was I drowning?"

"No, I was. And you were just standing there, watching."

The sun is setting behind us. Humidity presses against the car.

"Do you want me to tell you not to do this? I will."

She shakes her head and her thin blond locks catch shafts of sunlight, like an angel's. "Too late," she says.

I RESCHEDULED MY CLASS, of course. We stop at a hotel before midnight and sleep in the next morning, and Amanda offers thinly to drive while yawning, but I'm wide awake as we cross another state line and stop to fill the tank. I put Amanda's new address into my phone, devour a burger and fries from a drive-thru, and crack the windows.

Miles of highway pass beneath us and the sun is so bright I'm wearing my darkest sunglasses and a baseball hat pulled over my eyebrows. We play a game: I sing a song lyric I like, and then she sings one, and then it's my turn again.

I start. "*I wonder if she's changed at all, if her hair is still red.*"

"*You kept me like a secret, but I kept you like an oath,*" sings Amanda.

I sing, "*If this is love, I want my money back.*"

"*But you don't really care for music, do you?*" she sings.

A long time passes. When I speak, Amanda's knee jerks like she was dozing.

"*I guess I should've closed my eyes when you drove me to the place where your horses run free,*" I sing.

"*Y'all haters corny with that illuminati mess,*" she sings.

She falls asleep again, this time in a broken-neck pose. I want to prop up her head, but I leave her alone.

When she's upright again, rubbing her neck, I sing, "*Can I handle the seasons of my life?*"

"*She doesn't want to leave, she's just wondering if there's life out there,*" she sings in a twang, and we're both giggling as we cross the border into her new state.

AMANDA'S NEW HOME is a shambling Victorian on a small, bustling island, across a dead end from an inlet beach. I pull into a narrow grass drive and park under a green-and-white striped carport.

"Come see," says Amanda.

We step into the humid early evening. Fireflies blink in the crannies of bright green ferns. She passes a side door—the house is heavily weathered and somewhat short of grand, which I like—and across a brambly back slab, over a spit of scraggly grass, toward a wobbly pier. The house backs onto a marsh and is bound by water on three sides. The heavy air smells like earth.

I follow her to the far end of the dock. An egret takes flight from a wood piling, the top of which is soft under my palm. The waning sunlight has a sepia cast. We take off our shoes and put our feet in the water, which is not much cooler than the air. Beyond the marsh is the bay, and beyond the bay is the ocean.

"OK, this is not bad," I say to Amanda.

"It was my choice," she says. "I put my foot down."

"I can tell."

"I'll be out here every sunset," she says.

"You will," I choke out.

"I've made a decision."

I brace myself, I don't know why.

"I'm going to have an affair," she says.

Toads growl around us. "You could have done that at home."

She shakes her head. "No. I can reinvent here. No one knows me."

"You're diving straight into his world," I say. She's already visited the homes of three of his colleagues. She joined a pickleball league organized by the Board Chair's wife.

"I'm not going to do that. I already told him. I'm not going to parties, I'm not hosting dinners."

"You're working at a middle school."

"There's nothing wrong with that. I'll still have my own money. Anyway, get on board. I'm going to have an affair. Affairs, maybe. For sex and love."

There are alligators in these waters, plump on herons and watersnakes. They're too lazy and well-fed to aim for us, but they're here.

"I'm asking you to consider whether this is a realistic plan. Are you just asking for a different kind of . . . unease? Who's going to pack his bags and keep his schedule?"

"He can pack his own bags."

"You're choosing an affair here over a divorce at home."

"Yes." She scoots on the dock until she's facing me. "I have something to tell you."

"OK?"

"It won't be easy to hear. It's about Z."

My gut skitters.

"What I want to tell you is that it's not love," she says to me. "You don't love her."

I exhale. This is old news, actually. According to my brother, what I feel for Z is something called *limerence*, which has nothing in common with love except for the inconvenient fact that it feels exactly the same. Love is based on time spent together, loads of it. There's no love without time. My grief is about lost potential, though this makes it sound like an investment scheme when in fact what I lost was minutes of laughter, deep kisses and light ones, loose and lively conversations, shared glances and buckets of popcorn and inside jokes. I never pressed my forehead to hers and felt her breath on my face. I never reminded her about an appointment or asked if she'd heard from her sibling or sought her opinion about whether I should color my hair or leave the gray alone. I'm not in love with her, no, because the stairs I was climbing toward love crumbled. I landed in the wreckage and I'm still there.

Amanda says, "If you let her go, you'll find someone better. I know you will."

"I know." But I don't know.

"Let her go. It's time. Promise me."

I can't lie, but I can promise to keep trying. "And you? Who do you love? Do you love your husband?"

She faces her new watery queendom, teeming with life. "I love Lionel," she says.

THAT NIGHT, we inflate air mattresses on the screened upstairs porch. The moving van will arrive tomorrow mid-day. We'll spend three days putting things in drawers and on shelves and folding boxes and buying cleaning supplies and filling the pantry and painting Lionel's room a soothing dark gray. We'll choose expensive patio furniture and put it on Amanda's credit card. We'll check out the nearest library—a dud, all business books and no armchairs—and find a place to get manicures.

She'll turn on her phone for a few minutes every morning over soft-boiled eggs, and for a few minutes every evening over hearty salads on the dock. Once, we will watch a mother alligator slide by with her many babies of all sizes, and twice we will watch an egret dry its wings on a piling. We'll let the dogs run on the beach and prune the bougainvillea that spills over the sunroom. I'll press some of its papery pink petals between the pages of my book and put more in baggies to take home for my children, and for my mother, though I can't say how or why.

At night, still sleeping on the porch even though the beds are all set up, we'll talk about her future paramour. He will be stuck, too. They will lie to their spouses to snatch hours together. They will invent a whole new world for each other. They will never resent each other's home lives or ask for more. The sex will be, it goes without saying, hot and tender, but sometimes they won't even have sex. Sometimes they'll just lie in each other's arms and talk and laugh. He will understand in a way Marcus never has that she is made of magic, and he will adore her.

"What will you tell Marcus when he asks if you're cheating?" I ask Amanda.

She takes a big bite and wipes salad dressing from her lip. "He won't," she says. "But if he does, I'll ask him to tell me what makes him think my sex life has anything to do with him."

AN HOUR BEFORE THE AIRPLANE carrying Marcus and Lionel lands, I hug Amanda and settle my dog in the backseat of the rental car. I set my course to a small, pet-friendly beach with a sandy boardwalk and dunes stippled with tall grasses, and I swim in the Atlantic until I'm brined. Then I shake the sand from my hair and put the sea to my back.

MY ADOPTED HOME STATE is simultaneously landlocked and hemmed on two sides by lakes so massive they have their own weather, their own smatterings of shipwrecks. The Third Coast, t-shirts proclaim. I hesitate to spread word about the pristine analog enchantment of these shores, their old-growth forests and rustic spits of civilization. Nothing to see here, coasters! Keep your yacht-salted bays, your vacation compounds, your underfed sea-beasts. You've locked in the best Earth has to offer, really! We're awash in milquetoast envy—no need to check on us!

Thirty-five thousand islands spill across the five Great Lakes, and when I learn this fact from my youngest—I'd like to think he learned it in school, but in my heart I know he learned it from the internet—I know we need to go.

There was almost no travel in my marriage. Too far and too expensive, X always said. A year after we split up, I saved up to take my children to Alaska, where I'd never been. The next year we went to Costa Rica and swam in waterfalls and hiked through the cloud forest. Then we fell in love with road trips, and I drove us to Maine, the Carolinas, Southern Utah. This year both kids are locked into sports all summer, but I carve five nights from the calendar and book a rental cabin perched on a cliff overlooking the sea-lake to our north.

On our way out of town, I voice-text X to tell him we're stopping by his house to pick up my youngest's shoes. "And to pee," I say to my phone.

"And poop!" says my oldest loudly.

"And fart!" says my youngest.

"And spit!" I say.

"And sweat!" says my oldest.

"And sneeze!" says my youngest, then the message sends.

As we drive, the temperature drops and the woods thicken. We're as far north as you can go without bordering Canada. I live along the 43rd parallel, but these islands are just north of the 46th. These facts meant one thing when I landed in the Midwest twenty-odd years ago—it took me the better part of a decade to learn how to dress for winter—and something different now, as wildfires decimate Maui and hungry, warm-water sharks roam the coast of Maine.

My dog explores the woods while we unpack, then returns carrying a deer leg in her jaw. My children play rock-paper-scissors for the second bedroom and the younger wins and the older takes the living room sofa. In the morning, we drive to a state park and spend hours jumping from a cliff, swimming through gentle swells back to shore, skinning our knees on boulders. I jump first, to make sure that the lake floor is deeper than it appears, and because I want them to remember me this way: arms open mid-air.

I splash around in the water while they jump again and again. They beg me to judge each of their jumps according to specific merits, on a scale of one to ten. I tell them in addition to splash volume and leg positioning, I'm also judging on panache. There are the usual jumps—pencil, cannonball, can opener—and then each kid does a specific dance on the way down—the floss, the moonwalk, the running man—and then there is a Guess What Animal I Am round. First, the oldest is an elephant and the youngest is a chimp, and about three jumps later the youngest hits the water face-first while impersonating a shark, and comes up crying.

"It was just like hitting a mattress," he tells me, gulping water. "Soft and hard at the same time." He climbs back up the cliff, wiping his face with the inside of his elbow, long hair swinging.

The waves are high and crash over my head, and the water is cold but I warm to it. I grow pruny. My dog settles on the cliff edge above me and crosses her paws. My youngest wins the competition, but only by a hair.

After, damp and bone-chilled, we go into town and eat

pizza and then get ice cream. My youngest asks for a cup but is handed a cone, so he asks for a spare cup and is given one. Then, as we're crossing the street to shop for souvenirs, he's carrying the cup in one hand and the cone in the other, and he trips a little, sending a scoop from his cone into the air. He tries to catch it with the cone and then with the cup but misses both times, and the second the ice cream hits the pavement, he scoops it up and puts it back on his cone and keeps walking like nothing happened. I double over, laughing so hard I can't speak or see through my tears, and my children come to my side and wait for me to calm down, and then we go buy a Christmas ornament, a 3D magnet with blue water and a little ferry boat floating inside, and—my youngest's choice—a red rubber pig that snorts when you squeeze its flanks, which I almost throw out the window on the ride back to the cabin, after asking him repeatedly to stop making its noise.

"Why did you buy it if you didn't want him to use it?" says my oldest, and I tell him I have no idea.

At night, we eat microwave popcorn with M&Ms mixed in while watching campy horror films. During the scary bits, I watch my children instead of the television. Even when the killer jumps out of a pantry wielding a knife, the muscles of their beautiful faces remain still.

In bed alone, I read a novel about a woman whose wife is slowly evolving into a sea creature. When we get home, there will be school supply shopping and sports practices and the days will shorten and our tans will fade, another summer downshifting and falling behind. But we have four days left— hiking waterfalls, browsing bookstores, kayaking together into mossy sea caves, bickering over the snorting pig—and I will clamp joyful arms around every hour.

MY EIGHTH FIRST DATE is Lucinda. She reaches out through the apps, but it's not the first time we've exchanged messages. I'd forgotten, but months ago, shortly after we swiped right on each other and before we met in person, Lucinda sent a note saying she'd met someone, and I wrote back to wish her well.

The relationship you so generously wished me well in ended badly, she writes this time. *I'm putting myself back out there. Are you still available, by any chance?*

As a matter of fact! I write.

The morning of our date, I text Lucinda, *Good morning! Happy Friday! We have a date tonight.*

She texts, *Good morning! I am looking forward to it!*

I text, *Are you a person who would enjoy seeing a 6-second clip of video wherein two teenage girls make an appeal to their missing sister … and then it gets really funny? (The premise, I'll admit, is not funny.)*

I ask this while lying in bed with my dog, psyching myself up to do yard work. Normally I'd text the video to Amanda, but we're not back there yet.

Love all of this. Please send, writes Lucinda.

I send it. After asking their sister to please come home, one sister says, "Oh, and Steffie P. from bio is pregnant, like she's pretending she's not but—"

And then the other sister says, "—But she's been wearing these big sweaters and—"

The interviewer cuts them off.

Lucinda sends seven laughing-to-tears emojis, and I write, *I love teenagers. If this video is fake, that's information I don't need.*

IT RAINS SO HARD AND SO LONG the day before our date that cars stall out in the streets and are abandoned at odd angles, like pieces on a game board. When I arrive to pick her up, Lucinda's front yard brims with standing water, so I text her to let her know I've arrived, then stand in the high ground in the middle of her street, alert for cars. I've washed my hair and put in my big gold hoops and an underwire bra and a sleeveless dress. A couple shuffles by. Minutes pass.

Then there she is at the door, and as she starts down her front steps, she gives a hearty hello and then slips a little on the slick sidewalk. Soon enough, we're both in my car and I'm pulling away from her house.

Right away, it's a yes. Her bearing—she's very tall and wears her height like a good suit—and her straight dark jeans and boots and the salted brown hair that curves inward at her shoulders. I like her voice, which is smooth and deep, and her prominent chin, and the way she nods while I'm talking. We chat on the way to the bar about something or another, and just as we're pulling up, she says, "I've been told I'm a bad driver."

I check my rearview and put the car in reverse to parallel park. There's a line of cars backing up but this will all be over soon. As I reverse into the space, I say, "People don't usually admit they're a bad driver or have a bad sense of humor. Is this a good time to tell you I'm not funny?"

She laughs. I like it.

About my smooth parking, she says, "You did that under several levels of pressure, and I'm impressed."

"It's only because I'm on cocaine," I say, I have no idea why. I've never even done cocaine.

"Yeah, you're not funny at all," she says.

The bar is in an old house. Next door is a pretty good pizza place that delivers to the bar, so that's our goal, dinner and drinks. Inside, we wander a little before choosing a round table on the main floor. It's dim and loud. The trans woman tending the bar is unflappable and sexy, and the only reason I can speak normally to her is that I'm feeling so solidly positive, ten minutes in, about Lucinda.

I am on my eighth first date, and my wild heart is beating.

WE TALK ABOUT allergies (her child's) and body image (my oldest's) and medical micro-dosing (her field), and our marriages. I tell her about losing Joyce and Dani, and she tells me about a similar experience. She asks if it's painful and I admit that it is.

"My friend hasn't come back yet," she says. "But I hope yours do."

She orders the pizza. It comes tepid and burned on the edges and uncooked in the middle and neither of us complains. She eats and drinks more slowly than I do—most people do—and there are only a couple of times when I don't know what to do with my hands.

There are a few pauses. We let them stand.

"I like your dress," she says.

"I like your face," I say.

"I like yours, too," she says.

When she goes to the bathroom, I text Amanda: *IT'S A YES*.

She sends back three crossed-fingers emojis.

TWO HOURS PASS. The date is simultaneously perfect and also lightly laced with something I can't put my finger on. Something unsaid. A reluctance on her part, which triggers a reluctance in me. It could be that I just don't do it for her, but I don't think she's shedding disappointment or disinterest, exactly. She's full of compliments and wisecracks. The pizza gets cold. A guy clearing tables asks twice if we'd like a box, but we say we're still working on it. She's not standoffish, but she's not flirtatious, which makes it easier for me to be not-flirtatious, which means I'm fulfilling my self-assigned mantra for this date: *I am brave and honest first, charming a distant second.*

She's into music and plays guitar in a couple of local bands. I invite her to see music with me tomorrow night, and she thanks me and specifies that she has plans. She does not say that otherwise she would love to.

Can I see myself spending more time with this woman? I most definitely can.

There's a pause. I say calmly, like some supernatural version of myself, "I would like a second date. If there is going to be one—no assumptions—is there anything we want to cover before the first date is over?"

Right away, she's nodding. "You're a very straightforward person," she says.

This is something I've been told many times. Since Z, I'm much more interested in whether other people are straightforward.

"I'm heartbroken," she says.

I sit back, then lean forward.

"I thought I was ready," she says.

"How long has it been?" I say.

She thinks. "A little over a month."

A month, a minute, a Mississippi second. "That's a very short amount of time," I say. I feel for her. Stepping into the supportive friend role is not my first choice, but now there's no choice at all. "What percentage of your feelings are angry ones?"

"I think that's the next stage."

They had one big fight, she says, that's all.

So it's not over, I do not say.

We talk a while about anger. It's not an emotion she allows herself, she says. This is a red flag, because conflict avoidance tends to get conflict un-avoidant people in trouble.

"My next relationship will be a calm one," I say.

"I've been so—so—so happy all week, looking forward to meeting you. I thought I was good to go—then today I started crying and couldn't stop. Can't stop."

She's crying now. I don't mind.

"I've been there," I say. "Do you want to go, or would you rather sit a bit?"

"Pretty soon," she says, nodding.

She apologizes a few times—about the tears, about jumping the gun—and I tell her not to. I'm not uncomfortable, I tell her. It's the truth.

"I can tell. You're very warm."

"Thank you."

We small-talk on the ride back to her place, and when we get there, I pull into her driveway. I don't cut the engine. She starts to get out of the car, then pauses with her hand on the door handle. She says, "I should say, heartbreak aside, I don't see us in a romance, but I'd like to be friends."

I take this to mean she's not attracted to me physically. It's a bit of a shiv to the ego, but it's also just another bend in the road.

"That's OK," I say. "Friends is great."

"Cool," she says.

"Be good to yourself," I say. "I'd give you a little advice, but really there's only time."

And Amanda, Gwen, ray-key, tarot, sex with strangers. Sheeting storms of tears, empty acres of loneliness, windy gusts of confusion. But here I am, more or less whole, and the biggest shock to me isn't that I like talking to Lucinda almost as much as I liked talking to Z—it's that I'm speaking like a person on the far side of heartbreak. This is staggering. Have I made it?

When I get home I text her: *Thank you for being vulnerable with me. Sleep well.*

And I text Amanda: *I won't go into it via text, but suffice to say I'm very very very disappointed.*

Except I'm talking to my phone instead of using my thumbs, and it comes out *fairy fairy fairy disappoint.* I let it stand.

YEARS AGO, I read an interview with a famous writer in which he claimed he had a strong Pollyanna streak but wasn't interested in scrubbing himself clean of it.

I also have a strong Pollyanna streak and am sticking with it.

On our first date, Gretchen (of the bloody sheets) told me she'd read that a crush is nothing more than a temporary suspension of the brain's hunt for attachment. A glitch, more or less.

Maybe this is true, maybe not. But a crush is also a reminder from the universe that the heart works and potential exists. What a beautiful thing, just to like someone a whole lot.

A COUPLE OF WEEKS LATER, while I'm getting ready for yoga, my phone dings. It's a group text from one of my cousins to me and Gabe: Our ill aunt fell out of bed and needs surgery to relieve compression in her spine. There's another surgery after this one, and by the time I get myself on a plane and to the hospital, my aunt's lost all movement in her hands and can no longer sit or stand. She's breathing on her own, though, which everyone is treating like a very big deal.

This is aging: One day you're complaining that your niece gave away your favorite skirt, and the next day you're lucky your lungs work.

My cousins are my aunt's local caregivers, so I relieve them to sit by my aunt's side for six days. I take meetings while nurses bustle in and out. I hold her hand and show her videos of my dog and children. I move her hands for her and remind her where she is when she gets scared. There are yellowing bruises all over her shoulders and upper chest. "They pinched her," says the nurse when he sees me looking. "They do that when they want her to come back."

She's moved from critical care to not-quite-critical care.

She can't swallow without coughing and twice an hour I clear phlegm from her mouth using a suction tool, and it collects in a cup like radioactive waste. The first two days, she's awake and wants to talk, so we do. She talks about her dog, Scotty, who lives with friends now. She misses him terribly. She talks about losing her home, moving away from her city and friends. She talks about never having had children, then realizing it was too late, then grieving.

At some point, she says, "I had planned to spend the spring traveling." Her traveling days have been behind her for some time. One of the last flights she took was to see me, before I had my kids.

"Where were you going to go?"

"To see you," she says, like it should be obvious.

The sky outside is pale and hazy. The nurse brings in assistants to help change my aunt, including a compact Latino dude with trim facial hair who does a few squats before taking hold of the padding beneath my aunt's slack body. "Here we go!" he says, and the muscles of his back flex under his tight t-shirt, which reads DO YOU EVEN LIFT, BRO?

On our third day together, my aunt is grumpy and sleepy. The employees at her assisted living facility have been trying to kill her, she says. Well, not kill her—she walks it back—but they want her to fall, for sure.

"Why do they want you to fall?" I ask.

"Who knows!" she says, rolling her eyes.

She presses the bedside button and they don't come, she tells me. She screams for help and they tell her to be quiet and get back in bed. The rent at this place is ten times my monthly mortgage, which may or may not mean anything.

Before I leave to sleep at the hotel next to the hospital, she invites me very politely to sleep in the chair next to her bed instead. We both look at the chair, where I've been sitting for eight hours, and then back at each other.

"Maybe not," she says.

The fourth day she's not grumpy, but she's sad. I walk a circle around her unit, looking for ice chips. Every patient I pass is open-mouthed and tubed. Every patient's body is arranged in a way they did not choose for themselves, as is my aunt's.

She naps for three minutes every ten minutes or so. This restlessness reminds me of my mother's last days, when she was never fully awake or fully asleep. The body fights stillness when stillness is its only option. This makes complete sense to me.

The day before my mother gave in, she sat up in bed—this alone was medically astonishing—reached for my arm, pulled herself to her feet, and led me toward the front door. "I'm going home," she said over her shoulder. I had no idea what we were going to do when we reached the door, but she didn't make it that far. She sat down on a bench in the foyer. "What are we doing?" she said to me. It was the first time I'd heard her voice in a week.

"We can do anything you want," I said. But then the nurse arrived and put her back in the hospital bed, and that night, while I was sleeping, she crossed her hands over her waist, nodded goodbye to the night nurse, and died.

On my fifth day at the hospital, my aunt fades in and out all day long. One of her feet moves in circles under a sheet, as if demanding attention. At some point, she wakes from a two-minute nap and says, "I was dreaming."

"Your feet were dancing," I say.

"It wasn't that kind of dream," she says. "Everyone was wearing swimsuits."

Her face is my mother's face, if I don't look too carefully.

She tells me her teeth are moving in her mouth. I ask her to open up and peer in, using my phone for a flashlight. Besides one that has browned since the last time I visited, they are all intact.

"Oh, good," she says, and closes her eyes.

When she opens them again, she asks me where we are and I tell her.

"At the last place, there was all this stuff buzzing through the air," she says. "Like dandelion spores with tiny engines."

"There's nothing like that here," I say, "which I find disappointing."

"Don't be disappointed. Those thingamajigs were nasty."

She asks me to be her puppeteer: "Grab my arm and pull me to the left," she says, and when I do, she tells me to pull to the other left. Her left leg spasms several times an hour, and when it happens, she closes her eyes and purses her lips, and I rub her swollen calf. The spasms make her pee, and frothy yellow liquid rushes through a tube like it's on a wild ride. When I pull my hand away from her calf, there are fingertip-shaped dents in her skin.

She winces in her sleep and wakes up and looks at me. "I pooped, I'm sorry."

"Oh? I can't tell," I lie.

I call the nurse and she comes in to say she'll be back with help, then she comes back again ten minutes later and says the same thing. My aunt falls back to sleep, grimaces, then wakes to say that she likes this nurse but she liked yesterday's better, then falls back to sleep again.

Before I get in a cab to the airport, I read to her, and at some point, she stops me and says, "I don't know any of those people you're talking about."

"They're made up."

"Like so-ci-e-ty," she says with difficulty. Her eyes open and find me. "I love you."

MY NINTH FIRST DATE, Naomi, texts a lot before we meet, and though it's been a while since I found that part enticing, I'm intrigued by her photos of her dog in a bowtie and of herself in a kayak wearing a tank top, by her messages asking me what beverage I make to start my day and offering facts she learned from a podcast about paprika. The night before our date, we video-chat while I eat a salad and she eats leftover meatloaf. I like the way she moves around while she talks, unselfconsciously spotlighting the underside of her chin, then her hairline, then one ear. I like the way she focuses on some distant point while she's talking, then returns to check my face. I like the way her thin, scissory fingers move near her jawline. I list the ingredients of my salad in order of how much I enjoy them, cheese first and broccoli last. I give her a tour of my living room and kitchen without moving from the couch, and for a while we talk about my goldfish, who I adopted from my sister-in-law, who had adopted it from a friend. I tell Naomi, shamefully, about the time I bought two tropical fish and six ghost shrimp and the goldfish, whose name is Lucy, ate all of them in the course of one day. I feed and talk to my goldfish every morning, and sometimes I explain to her that she's really not supposed to have survived as long as she has. I have twice googled how to painlessly euthanize a goldfish, but Lucy lives on.

Naomi tells me that once she stayed in a hotel where you could request a companion goldfish for your bedside, and even though they had been clear about not allowing guests to buy the goldfish, she got attached and tried to convince them to let her take it home.

The morning of our date, I send Naomi a close-up of my face, with one finger pointing to a pimple blossoming from my bottom lip.

#thisisapimplenotacoldsore, I write.

#itchosealovelyplacetogrow, she writes back.

If I had to name each contour of my nervousness before Naomi and I meet, the list would go something like this: What if she's attracted to my brain but not my body, what if the whole thing is more awkward and embarrassing because expectations are high, what if we don't connect, and what if we do?

Because there's truly nothing terrible about being on a date where there's no there there, except that after several of these, one starts wondering if she's abused her meeting-new-people muscles and they've given up. Over the course of one summer when I was twenty-five years old, I ate so many mangoes that I gave myself an allergy—the science is sound.

We've planned an ambitious evening. My brother would not approve; first dates are supposed to be short, little more than a meeting to plan a slightly longer meeting. When I pull into her driveway, she comes bounding out with her long-legged, floppy-eared hound, giving me a thumbs up when I ask through the open window if I can park there.

We hug. It's going to be OK.

Naomi is very, very pretty, wearing joggers and a thin hoodie. There's nothing wrong with makeup and tidy outfits and coiffed hair, of course, but when a woman is very put-together I'm reminded that I'm a bit of a slob. Though I made a modicum of effort tonight—I spritzed my curls and put on my cutest sneakers—I'm happiest in jeans and tank tops and maybe the occasional V-necked tunic. A couple of the women I've dated have worn the kind of makeup that my mother wore, foundation and blush and eyeshadow and eyeliner and mascara, form-fitting Moto jackets and shiny boots and a tasteful ring or two on each hand. I have no problem with this in theory, but in practice I end up feeling like a thundering amorphous blob beside them. I feel beside them the way I feel beside men, in other words.

Naomi wears oversized tortoise-shell glasses, and her wide smile boasts two gold caps, one on either side of her upper jaw. We set off on foot toward a beer garden on the nearest lake. I use a waist leash to keep my hands free, which means my dog roams ahead of me. Naomi's dog is trained to sit at every curb, so my wayward dog and I are halfway across the street before I realize I need to wait. At the beer garden, I take both dogs while Naomi gets our drinks, and then we find a table near the water. It's windy and her curly silver hair blows around her face, occasionally weaving behind her hip eyeglasses, and she gently frees the locks with gel-manicured fingers. I stop one of her hands mid-air and peer at her nail color.

"Terracotta," she says, letting her hand rest in mine. "Matte. I wanted them to look like little pots."

"And they do!"

There's not a high wattage of electricity sparking between us, but there is something. Gameness, maybe. Grace.

Her phone vibrates and she picks it up and squints at it. "Oh, no," she says.

A work crisis. I tell her to go handle it, I'll hang with the dogs.

My city is usually lushly green in spring and summer, but it's been dry and a gritty wind blows. The wind will die with the sun, but until then it will set us all on edge, like the slightest-ever headache.

The dogs settle down separately, eyeing each other. Naomi is under the awning of the bar, the phone against one ear and her palm against the other. She's gone long enough for me to finish my can of fake beer. When she comes back, apologizing, I shrug and tell her we have plenty of time. "Do what you need to do," I say.

This is a tough one. Taking a work call during a first date could be a turnoff, but I want to see this stuff up front. If you're a person who checks the messages on her watch while I'm talking to you, I'd rather know now.

But it's not disengagement she's showing me, not poor manners. I can tell by the way she flashes those gold teeth and eyes the locks of my hair that fall across my neck. It's comfort. And why wouldn't I want her to feel comfort with me?

She tells me about her work—big job, many moving parts, days full of meetings and interviews with media—and I tell her about mine. We talk about where we've been, where we want to go. Who we've loved, in brief.

My mantra for this date, which I gave myself because Amanda hasn't been in touch, is: *My vision is clearest when I view life through a lens of hope and gratitude.*

But if I'm honest, I don't feel hopeful. I'm day-old bread, crustier every hour. Still, when we walk back to her house, the wind at our backs, my dog stops at the curb with her dog, and they wag their tails against our feet.

We leave the dogs at her place and go to dinner. The restaurant is wallpapered in a nouveau-art pattern, the lights are low, and the waiter is very talkative. With our drinks he tells us how the restaurant started, and with our first round of plates he tells us about their plans to expand, and when he leaves us to our cooked dates and cauliflower and shashitoes, Naomi says, "I could listen to him talk all day. Wait, scratch that, I thought he'd never leave."

For reasons I cannot explain, this makes me laugh almost silently until tears run down my face. She watches me with a pleased expression, and when I finally wipe my tears, she says, "I could watch you laugh all day. You're missing a tooth!" We talk about our teeth over a skillet cookie topped with avocado ice cream. Then somehow we wander onto the topic of the difference between soil and loam and silt, but we can't come to any conclusions and neither of us picks up a phone. I pay the check, but before I sign the bill, I say, "Let's rank everything we ate from least favorite to most."

She holds up a finger and says, "First, I'll say everything was tasty and the company even tastier, but my least favorite was the cookie—too rich—followed by the cauliflower . . ."

Our rankings are exactly opposite with the exception of the cookie, which is also my least favorite. I agree that the company is tastiest. I'm just starting to get the full picture of her: She's an oddball, for one thing, prone to witty retorts and casual puns and made-up songs and obscure references to commercials from our childhood. At one point she raps the entire bridge to a song from our teen years, one I'd never have remembered otherwise. Her humor is the egoless and generous kind, where you feel welcome to join in and nothing is too silly or weird. I already know that she's not like anyone I've ever met.

When I drop her off, I'm not sure if we'll kiss goodbye, but she makes it happen. She's several inches taller than I am, so I tilt my chin upward, and at the end of the kiss she nibbles my upper lip.

We make another date for the following weekend. In the interim, she drops a wrapped package at my door. Inside is a tri-fold foam display board, like a school science project except half the size. It's layered in green and brown craft paper, with pictures and words in her artsy handwriting, titled SOILS &

SUBSTRATES. Each type is illustrated and labeled, and on the third panel are drawings of three states: the one we live in, the one she's from, and the one I'm from. Beneath each state is information about that state's official soil. Florida's is Myakka fine sand, and it's found primarily in palmetto forests.

I take a photo of the project and send it to Amanda, who responds, *Marry her!*

To Naomi, I write, *Your science project is so impressive, thank you! P.S. My best friend says I should marry you.*

She writes back, *Today I installed deck lights and programmed them to a scene called "dreamy dusk" to woo you, but if we're getting married I guess they're unnecessary?*

Let's woo each other anyway, I write.

SEX WITH NAOMI IS SOMETHING ENTIRELY NEW all over again. It's calm, for one thing. Energetic but deeply hypnotic. When I come out of my stupor I can't recall exactly what happened, though I remember how it felt. She's a mover; she twists and bends and rolls and flips and I am right there every time, an extension of her. Her bed is dressed in luxurious navy linens that all end up on the floor, and when she tidies up after, she puts all the pillows back in their places, including an accent pillow in the middle. Her bedroom is painted a warm rosy white and one of her closets is paneled in cedar and filled floor to ceiling with dozens of pairs of boots.

In the morning, I sit in an Adirondack chair in Naomi's lush, colorful backyard while she gets dressed. She comes out in full workday getup, fitted jumpsuit and high-heeled sandals, carrying a tray of yogurt and granola. We eat and talk and swat at a persistent yellowjacket. She tells me about her two small tattoos, one on the underside of each wrist, and then segues into a story about seeing Haley's comet from her family's backyard when she was eight years old.

As I listen, I start to feel the blood drain from my face and the tips of my fingers go cold.

It's as if my body senses a predator, though the only person here is a kind, funny, goofy, wonderful woman. But here's a fact: In a few minutes, I will drive myself home, and by the time I get there, Naomi might have already sent a message telling me it's over.

Z's goodbye note had the tone of a surgeon talking to a patient who might sue: cool, professional, uninvolved. Either she felt she couldn't say she was sorry, or she wasn't.

What feels to me like a promising start with Naomi could feel to her like a terrible mistake.

My brain knows that it's unlikely Naomi will send such a message—she's shown nothing but enthusiasm, right down to the way she stoops to kiss my dog goodbye—but my heart braces anyway. I'm going through the motions. It's time to leave.

Last night, at some point during our long tussle, I said, "Where's your emotional wall?" and she said, "What emotional wall? I like you. I trust you." But I've heard this before.

A COUPLE OF WEEKS BEFORE SCHOOL STARTS, my brother and his husband call my kids and beg them to convince me to drive us to Taos, where they're spending a month for my brother-in-law's work. It's a twenty-two-hour drive to New Mexico, but for some reason I agree. I rent a minivan so each human gets a row to litter with snacks and electronics and stinky feet. I cover the dog's seat in towels, which she immediately nudges out from under herself. On the drive, I listen to ten episodes of a lesbian podcast and my children dive inside their screens. After twelve hours, we stop at a hotel and they put on their swimsuits. My youngest begs me to join them at the pool, but

I'm already in my pajamas in the big, clean bed. My body's given out.

When we arrive the following evening, Gabe is making a video and his husband is on a conference call. After they're finished, we all go for a walk through low hills covered in sagebrush. The dogs walk shoulder-to-shoulder—they know each other from previous trips—and the children run ahead, run back, run ahead again. I hold my brother around the waist as we walk, until his dog steps on a cactus and comes limping our way.

The adobe ranch is decorated exactly how you think it would be: lots of stamped metal and paintings of Indigenous people in hats, bunches of dried chiles hanging over the back deck, split wood beams, Spanish tile in the bathrooms. In the distance are the Sangre de Cristo mountains, which for most of our visit are capped by dense, moody clouds. I spend a lot of time watching the sunlight morph over the range. My youngest collects rocks for tumbling and my oldest practices driving with his uncles in their electric car. We all make dinner together and play round after round of Bananagrams. We watch *Close Encounters of the Third Kind* and spend hours inside a wacky interactive art installation I find impossible to describe. We visit the Taos Pueblo during a rainstorm and go whitewater rafting on the Rio Grande. I buy everyone crystals.

At night, I share a bed with my youngest. His watch, a hand-me-down from his brother, flashes in my face when he moves, so I ask him to please take it off. He doesn't respond so I ask again, and again he doesn't respond so I ask again, and then he says calmly, "Please stop saying that, Mama," and rolls away. He doesn't remember in the morning.

My dog loves running in the low hills behind the house, and each evening I pull cactus splinters from her paws, though she doesn't seem to mind them. A field mouse with cartoonish ears lives in a woodpile behind the hot tub, and the dogs sniff at the pile until it scurries across the terracotta patio.

Naomi and I text throughout the day. She sends me a photo of an apple she's about to eat, then one of her dog on her sofa, then one of herself in front of a green screen at a TV station, right before she's interviewed about the non-profit she runs. I watch the interview itself online and try to find distinctions between her television persona and her real-life persona. I can't find any! I'm a little flummoxed by her. She asks if I've read or seen *Dune*—I have not, but now I'm imagining us watching it entwined on her big orange sofa, the dogs draped over our legs.

She writes, *I ask because they have the ability to travel by folding space and I was going to offer to fold space for you so your trip would be shorter.*

It feels strange, being missed.

But I don't want to go home, not yet. Outside of these short trips we snatch from our schedules, Gabe and I live separate lives, which is fine but also profoundly sad.

If I had to do it again, I write to Amanda on our last night, *I'd settle down near my brother. Why didn't I do that?*

What else would you do differently? she writes. *Would you marry X again?*

Yes, he loved me through a time in my life when I had trouble loving myself, I write.

Would you swipe right on Y?

Yes, I'm grateful to her for many reasons.

Would you swipe right on Z?

How can I say no? How can I not?

If I could give myself back the energy I've spent on Z, I would do it in a heartbeat. But I wouldn't give away one minute of the time I spent with her. Not one.

Yes, I write, and leave it at that.

Once, not so long ago, I was brave. I remember.

SIX WEEKS PASS. I'm still braced to be unceremoniously dumped, but it doesn't happen.

Naomi spends the night once during my child-free week, then twice during my next child-free week, then three times. My youngest's baseball coach is the lead singer in a local band, and I invite Naomi to join me and my children at a patio show he's playing, where people trip over our dogs and I spend one hundred dollars on lemonade and nachos. The whole set-up is a miscalculation on my part—it's loud and crowded and hot. But my youngest exchanges many kisses with Naomi's dog while my dog looks on lazily, licking her own freckled snout. After glancing up to meet Naomi, my teenager tends to his screen except for the minutes he spends scarfing the nachos and asking for more. We play one round of Bananagrams and Naomi almost wins, but then my youngest comes from behind, and gets so excited that he leaps up and knocks the table and the tiles go everywhere. We all scramble to collect them, except for the teenager, who strokes his hair into place and takes a selfie while I kneel to reach the tiles under his chair.

Naomi is lovely in a sundress, lugging a large bag of dog-water and contingency plans, and I am my usual scattered, seat-of-the-pants self, and my oldest is robotic and my youngest is a ball of glee and no one can hear each other and there's no shade and we're all sweating, and it doesn't matter. After the music, my children and I say goodbye to Naomi at her car and get into ours, and my dog climbs onto my youngest's lap to put her head out of the window, and we drive home through the humid evening.

Naomi and I spend half an hour on video chat every night. I send her a photo of myself in my camp chair at the ballpark, holding up a warm cookie I bought from concessions. She sends me a photo of herself in her kayak, her dog's ear against her cheek. I send her a link to a lesbian artist and we both buy framed pictures of women kissing each other; mine are mermaids, hers are fifties-era office ladies in pencil skirts. When my children go to X's, I bike to her place with my dog in a trailer, and we sit on her back deck drinking kombucha on ice.

She lost her father four years ago. She doesn't speak to her mother. We talk about her memories of her father and how they differ from the memories of each of her three sisters. "I used to think they were wrong," she says, "but now I think all of us are right."

"No two people have the same parents," I say, though I think Gabe and I come close.

Her father was Turkish and Muslim and superstitious, she tells me. He was handsome and knew it. Once a year he went to New York City to buy new clothes, and when he died she and her sisters couldn't bear to give them away, so each has a few of his fine garments in the back of a closet. He believed pulling dogs' tails gives them diarrhea, and killing a spider would make it rain. He could make a sheep sneeze by tickling it behind the ear. He caught flies between his palms and delivered them outside. He asked his children to keep his ashes on the highest shelf in one of their houses, so he would be far from underground, and he demanded his ashes not be divided so as not to dilute his spirit. He believed it was bad luck to keep unworn shoes any way other than side-by-side, as if they might walk away by themselves.

Naomi can name every plant in her own yard as well as mine. I find a woman online who's selling native perennials and Naomi pours over the list, choosing for me and for herself, and then we drive out to the woman's farmstead together, holding hands.

She clears out a drawer for me in her second bathroom. She clears out a drawer for me in her bedroom dresser. It's not even close to my brother's eighteen-month waiting period, but I not only move in a toothbrush, but also pajamas. I look at my own messy drawers, but I clear out nothing.

Another month passes. One night when I'm alone without my children, organizing my junk drawer and doing laundry, I find myself wondering why I'm not with Naomi instead.

What are you up to? I text.

I'm eating a sweet potato, she texts back. *And missing you.*

We show up an hour early for a talk by a trans actor who wrote a memoir, then share a sandwich in the long line. When we're about thirty people from the front, a guy comes around and tells us the venue is full. Naomi and I disperse with the crowd, holding hands, and on the way back to our bikes, we run into three people I've dated and three people she's dated. One of the women she dated is coiffed and dashing in a cowl-neck tunic and leather boots, and she looks me up and down, smirking.

One morning, after a night spent partly entwined and partly taking turns telling our dogs to get off the bed, there's a ruckus in the backyard, where Naomi has let the dogs out. She comes back to report that our dogs fought. "I felt exactly like I was prying apart two teenage girls pulling each other's hair," she says.

My dog lost. There's a bloody puncture wound above her eyebrow and another beneath her chin. The next day, Naomi talks to a dog trainer and comes up with a plan. The foresight, the commitment, the can-do attitude! When I'm next at her house, she carries into the backyard a piece of flat wood, which she will use to separate the dogs if they start up again. They don't; they ignore each other. After Naomi eats her breakfast of yogurt and granola, she lets her dog lick the container, and then she lets my dog lick the container. Her hair falls into her face as she coos to them. Her joggers hug her hips. She's what my mother would have called, in complimentary terms, *womanly*. My mother would approve.

We meet Nadine for a drink. It goes well, I think, but then

Nadine calls me later. "Are you and Naomi still dating?" she asks.

I don't understand the question. "Yes?" I say. "That's why I wanted you two to meet?"

"You're not . . . a *couple*," she says.

I think she's saying we're not *couple-y*. I've been intentionally ignoring the question of what happens to my experiment if my ninth date becomes a relationship that lasts—well, forever. So what's the right word for me and Naomi at this point, three months in? Shouldn't the word for people who are still getting to know each other be different from the word for yearslong partnerships?

"OK," I say, and change the subject.

In bed, I hone my skills on Naomi, and she's sexy and vigorous. I tell her what I like to get going, and she does it expertly. Where's the friction, the texture, the shaky sea legs? Where's the bump on which we'll snag? I keep looking, but I can't find it. When it's just the two of us, I feel a lightness and ease I typically feel only when I'm alone. When we're apart, life goes on as normal except for a quiet feeling of patient connection, like an invisible outstretched hand. There's been no pushing toward declarations of love or exclusivity, and yet both feel inevitable, in time. Maybe we're not a *couple* yet, though I'm not sure what Nadine is looking for other than more use of the word *we* and public displays of affection, which aren't really my style—but we're flowing in that direction, and what's the rush? I've never felt so accepted at the level of *pace*.

Still. I said I would go on ten first dates, not nine. My profile is still active but I have no impulse to check the apps. If there's any doubt in my mind about going deeper with Naomi, it takes the form of a hazy question mark that hovers over the memory of the woman from the Goddess Plunge last year. Who is she, where is she, was there something there or did I imagine it? If there was something, how would it compare to this untroubled, halcyon thing with Naomi? It's unlikely that any relationship could be more fun or peaceful or sexy or full of potential, but it's also not hard to imagine that a loop that opened that day might never close.

There's Z, too, of course. The hazy question mark of her has faded a lot, but it's not gone.

One afternoon, I watch Naomi bend to attach a leash to her dog and feel the last of my ramparts eroding. It's not an easy feeling, but it's not difficult by a mile.

NAOMI BOOKS US A WEEKEND at a rustic, lesbian-owned resort and we take a ferry across a Great Lake to get there. The swells are so high that the ferry's galley stays closed and the crew goes around handing out ginger ales and vomit bags. My stomach is calm, but we choose seats up front, close to the bathrooms, and are treated to a show of passengers holding their guts and clinging to the handrails, their sights set on the bathroom doors, like climbers scrabbling toward a peak.

Naomi opens a bag of potato chips and wedges them between us. "The best seats in the house," she says as a green-skinned teenager limps out of the bathroom toward her tattooed boyfriend.

We brave the rocky stairs up to the sun deck and lean into the wind, hair whipping. The boat pitches and we sway like drunks. Back home, wildfires are soaking the air in a silver haze, but in the middle of the lake, the sky is blue and clear. I've missed it.

Back in our seats, Naomi tells me the story of the SS Edmund Fitzgerald, then sings me the song by Gordon Lightfoot. It's illegal to dive the wreck, she tells me. There are twenty-nine bodies still down there, preserved by the cold minerals. I start thinking about waves crashing over that ship, or ours, and I start to feel a little nervous. There's no sight of land in any direction.

When a crew member offers me a white bag, I say to her, "Is this normal?"

I'm thinking she'll say, "Yep! Nothing to fear!" but instead she says, "Not at all! I've never seen waves this high!"

Naomi chuckles for a long time.

The sound of retching comes from the starboard side of the cabin, then the port stern, then directly behind us.

"I wonder what all these people had for breakfast," says Naomi.

"I wonder how the dogs are doing," I say. They're downstairs with the cars, side-by-side in wire kennels.

"Will we find them covered in each other's puke?" says Naomi.

"Maybe they're pretending to surf, yukking it up," I say.

I clap when the ship docks, but I'm the only one. While we descend to the car and dogs, I tell her that on a police report the word for vomit is *emesis*, and she says, "I knew that but I don't know how!"

The dogs are clean and waggy-tailed, and we drive off the ship into the sunshine.

WE SPEND A DAY picking strawberries and biking trails, then another driving the scenic highways, stopping to sample cheese and dried cherries and artisanal fudge. She buys me a mug, I buy her a locally made anklet. She teaches me about Petoskey stone and seasonal poverty in the Upper Peninsula, where she was born and raised. She likes welcome centers, so we stop at three of them. At one, she buys a tour guide and reads aloud from it, adding her own commentary: "John Greene was a logger in 1829 who [raped the land and] taught settlers how to harvest corn [which was information he stole from the native people, to whom he and his family spread disease]."

In a boutique, I hold up a neon yellow leather evening gown that costs $1,998. "This would look good on you," I say.

"This would look good on you," she says in a gay-themed gift store, holding up a tank top that reads, *I PREFER cooking but sometimes EATING OUT with my GIRLS is fun.*

"Too subtle," I say, so she pulls out a men's t-shirt with a picture of two male silhouettes having sex on a boat that reads, *I SUPPORT OFFSHORE DRILLING.*

"Better," I say, and pull out one that says *WATERSKIING MAKES ME WET*, which she buys for one of her sisters, who was on a college waterskiing team.

I make peanut-butter-and-jelly sandwiches and we eat them on the road between towns. We stop to take a photo of every post office we pass. Each is tiny and just short of quaint. We take a selfie in front of the area's famous dunes but we don't climb them. We keep driving. The oaks and maples that reach over the road come in seven shades of green, by our count. Sage, emerald, juniper, pine, lime, olive, and grass. We name as many of the fifty-four nations that make up Africa as we can. I get twenty-one, she gets forty-two, including Côte d'Ivoire. "How could I forget Senegal?" she asks me sincerely. I ask her to name all the wild cats and she names the obvious ones, plus ocelot, civet, and lynx. "What am I forgetting?" she says, and I say, "I cashed out at mountain lion."

I buy a watercolor kit, she buys a deck of sapphic tarot cards. I buy my children local chocolates, she buys postcards and writes them out in the lamplight of the cabin. In the evenings, she makes elaborate mocktails. She packed a psychedelic mushroom candy bar, but I've never done mushrooms and chicken out. We have sex every night and every morning, and all day I find myself touching her: her knee in the car, her silver curls in a store, her bare upper arm with my lips. We talk about words we mispronounce accidentally—

detritus and *athlete* for her, *mauve* and *potable* for me—and words we get wrong on purpose.

"I'm spectacle there's a gas station between here and the cabin," she says in the car.

"I'm not peculiarly worried," I say.

"But are you defiantly certain we shouldn't turn back?"

"To be pacific, we have enough to get home."

"But how much do we have atlantically?"

"I feel pre-science that it will all be fine," I say.

"You've blinded me with pre-science!" she says.

We nap in the muggy second bedroom with the dogs at our feet. There's a bookshelf full of lesbian romance books and she reads the racy parts aloud in a stage voice. She weaves leather cord over rocks we find on the beach, gusseting them prettily, then writes our names and the date on the biggest one, to leave behind. She tells me about the baby goat she and her sisters raised when they were children. His name was Squirt, and he was so friendly that the farmers who took him appointed him stud of the following generations, to spread his good cheer.

"He earned his name," I say, and she snickers as if no one has ever said that before.

At night, I lie on the couch reading, and she brings me squares of chocolate.

Is this the caretaking I want and need? Is it the care I can take? What else could I possibly want?

I want to tell her I'm falling in love with her, but I'm afraid it will be like when I tell someone I'm about to orgasm, and saying it aloud vanquishes any possibility of it happening.

I HEAR THE ELECTRIC SHIVER IN AMANDA'S VOICE before she tells me she's met someone. On her end of the line is the repetitive sound of a knife hitting a cutting board. I wonder if this means she's back on full-time cooking duty, but I don't say anything. Even I chop vegetables from time to time.

"It's nothing like what I thought it would be," says Amanda in a dreamy voice. "I don't know how to put words to it."

"Tell me."

"I can't." She's covering her mouth with one hand, I can tell. "I feel so ashamed all the time and also completely free and happy."

"Don't do the guilt thing," I say. "Waste of energy."

"I can't help it."

"I know." We're programmed. But who would deny Amanda some spot of complicated happiness? How is finding joy inside her marriage even possible? And who among us lives willingly without joy? Isn't that the greater sin?

"Is Marcus sleeping in your bed?"

"No," she says, sighing. "Thank heavens."

In addition to what's new in her voice, there's something missing—resentment. Anger. Maybe cheating is one way to forgive your husband for being your husband. Maybe one man earns the other some slack.

"You know I want details," I say, "but I'll wait until you're ready."

"One detail," she says.

I wait.

"He's very . . . generous."

She's covering her mouth again.

"Can I assume that you're saying he's generous in bed?"

"Yes."

"And can I assume that we're talking about oral sex?"

"Yes. It's—I had no idea."

"And when you say *generous*, are you saying he spends a lot of energy on it, or are you saying he does it, period?"

"Both!"

"That's wonderful! I'm so happy for you!"

"I'd forgotten how good it can be, all of it. It's been so long."

This silences me for a beat. "I wonder if forgetting is a way of protecting ourselves."

"Yes! I feel awake."

This is the heart of it, isn't it? At any given moment, we are awake in our lives or we are not.

I say, "I feel like talking on the phone should feel the same because we did that before, but it doesn't. I don't know how to say everything I want to say."

She's chopping again. "Like what?"

"I want everything good for you. Does he tell you you're beautiful and sexy?"

"He told me this morning! Twice."

"Did you believe him?"

"I did. I do."

"Are you scared of blowing up your marriage?"

"I'm not scared at all. I feel very brave. And a little sad."

Her voice wavers, but only a touch.

"Why sad?" I say.

"I want to tell someone I'm sorry. I am sorry, I really am. But this is all I have."

There are so many paths available to us if we're willing to take them. And lest we forget what we're reminded of constantly, time is passing very fast.

"I'm so happy for you," I say.

"I'm sorry," she says softly.

"Is that for me or the universe?"

"For you. I'm sorry I had to leave."

From now on, our friendship will be gagged by distance. Updates will lag and whole events will go unshared. Part of me would rather give her up than live with this, but I won't.

"Here's your mantra," I say. "*I'm doing what I have to do.*"

"I'm doing what I have to do," she says.

AT A CRAFT FAIR, I sit in a quiet room with a tarot reader and watch her lavender fingernails turn over my cards while Naomi waits for me outside. The wisdom sounds smart and relevant as the reader's telling me what the cards say—what I've left behind, what I carry, what the future holds—but leaves my mind as soon as I've stood up from her table. This is what happens almost every time I have a tarot reading, so I'm disappointed but not surprised.

I read a book about the Enneagram. There are nine types, and I'm a four, which is the most complex type (these are the expert's words, not mine). Fours are passionate and introspective. They tend to keep their own counsel. They believe they are inherently broken. They get swept away by their own daydreams. They spend a lot of time and energy trying to figure out why they are the way they are. They want to be seen and heard and ultimately known and understood, all of which takes time most people are unwilling to give.

Fours are afraid of their own ability to be alone.

Fours tend to obsess, especially when betrayed.

Fours won't let go of their pain until they've learned from it.

ONCE, after we had gotten into our separate beds six miles apart, Z sent me a photo of herself as a child, maybe ten years old. In the photo, she has excellent posture and one hand in her front pocket.

Is it wrong that I'm kind of attracted to the way you're standing in this photo? I wrote.

No. I think I'm attracted to the way I'm standing! she wrote.

Were you always sexual? I mean, were you like a sexy child? I think you were.

There was no message for a minute, then this:

I can't type because I'm laughing so hard at that question, but I think the answer is yes.

TEN

IT FEELS AS IF all the away baseball tournaments fall on my kid weekends and all the home ones fall on X's, but I don't look too closely at the calendar. And I like the away games, mostly. The Field of Dreams—or the Field of Middle-Age White Men's Dreams, as I take to calling it after three different baseball dads tell me they cried the first time they visited—is only a ninety-minute drive, and the team stays in a hotel with an arcade and pool in the atrium. My oldest goes off to be with his friends and on the group chat some of the parents are organizing a trip to the local casino, but I'm in bed before they settle on a designated driver. I don't know how other families cope with their schedules, but I cope by taking these minutes to myself, canceling the roar outside the room with headphones, and pulling a book close enough to read with my aging eyes.

There's a knock at the door. My oldest has forgotten his key. He retrieves it, then is off again.

Then my phone rings. It's X on the screen, looking grim. Our youngest has vomited several times, he reports. I dropped him off this morning, bright-eyed and grateful to not spend a weekend watching baseball, and now he is leaning in a rubbery way against his father's shoulder. "Poor baby," I say to his sweet face, and he nods very slowly, like a cartoon sloth.

THE HOTEL RECREATION AREA CLOSES AT 11 P.M., and the noise dies, and my body relaxes. I put away my book after my oldest is back in the room, and then there's only the soft light of his small screen. (He used to read before bed. I ache to think of his boredom-free childhood.) I sleep well and am ready to spend another day in the sunshine, but my phone rings again when I'm brushing my teeth. It's X. "How's our boy?" I say when I answer.

"Better," he says, "but I'm calling about Annie."

Annie is my dog. X is talking very fast. "She's OK, don't freak out. But she ate something and started vomiting and wouldn't stop, so I brought her to the emergency vet. We're here now. They're pumping her stomach."

"I'm coming," I say.

Another family agrees to take care of my oldest and sends me off with their well wishes. He wants to come, too, but I convince him to stay and play. "Daddy says she's going to be fine," I reassure him. I don't say that I'm afraid X might be underreacting even as I'm afraid I'm overreacting.

X sends me his location and I aim for it. I'm driving twenty miles over the speed limit past stubbled cornfields and silver silos. Annie is three and a half years old. She's been with me since she was one, though her age is the rescue's best guess. She was picked up pregnant on the street in Texas and gave birth to five healthy puppies shortly after being installed in a foster home. The local rescue said she was a cattle-dog mix, but the Texas paperwork claimed she was a boxer mix. Both of these breeds worried me; I didn't want a high-energy dog. But the foster reassured me that she was very mellow, which turned out to be true. Other than following me everywhere I go, Annie doesn't need much beyond love and food and the peanut-butter spoon from my morning smoothie. She loves being in the car and the kayak and tolerates the trailer behind my bike. She sleeps exactly where another person would sleep in my bed, with her head on a pillow, and when it's cold she finds my flank and burrows in. She bares her teeth at other dogs sometimes, but when I *tsk* her she looks up at me guiltily. Be nice, I tell her, and she wags her tail. She wags her tail all the time, for no reason and for every reason.

When she sits for a treat, I think she looks like an alien wearing a dog suit, an imposter, her eyes sliding sideways as if asking, Are they buying it? Am I giving earthdog?

Annie is the kind of dog who goes missing only to be located in my body's blind spot, her snout grazing the backs of my knees. She's the kind who sniffs my mouth after I eat but never licks me. She's the kind who's already in the backseat of the car when I'm still looking for her in the house.

You're the best dog in the whole world, the kids and I tell her constantly. The sweetest, the most loving, the most adorable. We're the luckiest. When she wants attention, she rolls over and punches one paw into the air and my kids pretend she's knocked them out. When I want to act like I'm the kind of dog owner who has her dog's respect, I tell her to get down off the sofa, and she immediately does, then gets right up on the other sofa. Then I tell her to get down from that one, and she does, and gets right up on the first one.

I try not to fawn over my dog, but the fact is that she is one of the great loves of my midlife.

AT THE CLINIC, the receptionist points me into a room down a wood-paneled hallway, where I find X sitting on the linoleum floor in cargo shorts. Annie is curled in his lap, small as a puppy. He looks up as I come in—there's someone else in the room, a flash of white coat—and then I'm on the floor with them. When I put my hands on her soft freckled ears—everyone comments on how soft she is—she half-opens one hazel eye, and this is when I lose it.

"Don't move her," says X quietly, so I wedge myself into them like the other side of a dome, so she's nestled between the two of us.

"What's going on?" I say in a whisper. I can smell X's breath and skin, I can smell Annie's.

"They pumped her stomach. We're just waiting to see how she responds."

A form shadows us and speaks. A female voice. This isn't Annie's regular vet, who is a white woman with a diamond the size of a bird's beak on her ring finger and who, I've been told by several people, is outspokenly MAGA. I've been meaning to find a new vet for years.

This vet is also white, though all I see of her at first are her sensible clogs and veiny ankles. Her voice is rumbly and nasal but very calming. She says, "Annie is a lucky girl, she got here fast. It's all about timing with these things."

"What things?" I say.

The vet says, "We think she ate either moth balls or—"

"Snail bait," says X shakily.

X is in a yearslong war with the slugs who find their way into his house. Last time I was there, I found one by the downstairs toilet. It's been months since he last put out snail bait, he says—he didn't think it would still be there.

"But Annie doesn't eat things," I say nonsensically. Her ear twitches. Her chin and cheek rest on X's thigh.

But it's true: She eats her food and the carrots or peanut-butter spoons I give her and occasionally licks up a piece of salmon skin I drop on the floor. She's not a scavenger.

"She eats peanut butter," says X. "It's peanut-butter-flavored. It even looks like peanut butter."

"She may not have ingested much and she got here fast,"

says the vet. "Her bloodwork is good, but I think we should keep her for observation, at least for a few hours. Just a precaution. Most dogs in these cases come through just fine."

This is when I look up into the vet's face, which is very pretty with her downturned pink mouth and laugh lines and watery green eyes. She is slightly pigeon-toed, something I've noticed subconsciously. Her face is very familiar, but it's not until she's left the room and X has gone home and Annie is nestled in my lap, snoring softly, that I realize how I know her.

IF ANNIE PEES, she can go home. If not, she has to stay overnight to receive fluids. After an hour or so, a tech comes in to invite us into the backyard of the clinic, where there's a small, fenced lawn. Annie gets to her feet just fine, but she won't leave my side, so I step slowly around the perimeter of the yard until she finally squats.

"Hooray!" says the tech. "Let's get you two on your way."

There's no sign of the vet in reception, but I'm alert to the periphery of my vision while I pay the bill and try to concentrate on the receptionist's instructions about fluids and rest.

Just before we turn to leave, the vet rushes into the waiting room in her quiet clogs. "Wait up!" she says.

She runs her hands through her hair quickly—it's shorter than I remember, with more layers around her face—and slips out of her white coat and hangs it on a hook filled with leashes, then sweeps by me to hold open the door. Annie and I step outside. At my car, I load in Annie first, then the woman opens the driver's door for me in a way that tells me what's coming next.

"You've healed," she says, lifting a hand to my cheek. She doesn't touch me, but I feel almost as if she has. Then she puts her hands in her pants pockets and leans against the car door.

"I've wondered about you."

"Same," I say. "How's your right hook?"

"Would you believe I took up boxing after that? I'm pretty good!"

"Really?"

She nods slowly. "No."

I laugh, then cover my mouth with my hand.

"I'm Nova Weston," she says, putting out her hand. "Can I have your number?"

X CALLS AFTER WE'RE HOME and we video chat while I lay on the couch with Annie, rubbing her belly and plying her with sips of bone broth from a bowl. "Don't worry," I say, because he looks guilty. "Dogs eat stuff. She's fine."

"What if I'd left the house? What if I'd waited to take her in?"

"That didn't happen."

"Ugh, I can't even think about it."

I can't either. But what's the point of this?

"You're so annoyed with me all the time, this would have been the last straw," he says.

"I am not." But of course I am. I've been half-annoyed with him for months. It's no way to live.

"I feel like I'm always saying the wrong thing with you," he says.

"I'm sorry," I say.

"Just try to give me the benefit of the doubt, you know?"

It's easy to forget how much you like and love a person when you're fighting for your independence from him. But X has always come through for me when it matters, and this game we're playing together is a long one, and when it comes down to it, quibbles aside, there's no one else I'd rather have on my team. Co-parenting is a heavy grind for a lot of people, I know, but for us it's been a pretty good fit. And it could be better.

"I'm going to work on it," I say.

THAT NIGHT, NAOMI ARRIVES with her dog and a backpack full of distractions—supplies for making felted rocks, an erotic coloring book, fancy black licorice. She sits with Annie while I shower. After, we all settle in my bed and the dogs fall asleep. We talk quietly about things that have nothing to do with pet emergencies: how to prep your hair before swimming laps; her high school history teacher, who refused to believe it when she told him that Jimmy Carter was once a peanut farmer; her mother's horses, who her mother loved caring for more than she loved caring for her children; creative pursuits we no longer pursue. Pottery for me, woodworking for her.

She names all the joinery methods she can recall, then demonstrates each using her hand and my hand. The butt joint, with our two pointer fingers pressed together. The dovetail joint, with our fingers zippered. The rabbet joint, with her palm folded over my fingertips.

It's always a bummer when the weather starts to turn. When I say this, Naomi speaks softly so she won't wake Annie. "Yes," she says, "but soon it will be cold and the sun will go down early and it will snow. And we will come in from the snow and stomp-stomp our boots and throw our snowy jackets over a chair, and the dogs will shake-shake themselves dry, and in the evenings we'll make sugary teas and eat warm, tasty, lemony soups, and when we go out to shovel, we'll wear big, cozy mittens. And all winter long, we'll leave our mittens in places all over town, and sometimes I'll borrow your mittens or you'll borrow mine, and we'll go together to buy new mittens and leave those places, too. The dogs will wear sweaters and—"

"I have to talk to you about something," I say.

SOMETHING VERY COOL ABOUT NAOMI is that she doesn't freak out. Her hand remains in my lap, her shoulder pressed against mine.

"Hmm," she says after a few quiet seconds. "You're saying . . ."

I'm supposed to finish this sentence. But can I turn the squirrelly rationale in my brain into a statement, and one I'm not ashamed to make?

Also, something is happening in my gut. It's remarkably similar to the writhing nest I brought to reiki. Fear of making the wrong choice, of losing this thing we've got going. This thing that feels almost like an incarnation of exactly what I've been hoping to find.

"I want to check off this box," I say tentatively. "I want to put my tenth first date behind me."

"What if I had been tenth?"

I think about this. All I would have to do is massage some numbers, actually. I could decide Dani counts, even if she wasn't a first date. Wouldn't I rather feel I'd cheated a little at my own game than like a person who can't appreciate what she has? Like a person who will hurt the woman I'm falling in love with?

Naomi is no fool. "You could check a box with anyone," she says.

"That's true."

"You like her."

"I don't know her." I'd liked all of the women I'd dated, at first. "The chances that one dinner changes anything for anyone are slim to none."

"So far, they're one in nine," says Naomi.

What remarkably good odds! I should be taking this win and running with it. If Naomi had been my second or third date, would there have been a fourth? It feels easier to abandon a project early on than now, so close to the end. But I'm the one making the rules here, so aren't I the one who gets to break them?

Only in a romcom does attraction + meet-cute + a couple of laughs in a clinic parking lot = love.

"They're one in a thousand, at least," I say.

She sighs heavily, but she's still here. "Are we talking about one date? Four dates? Sex? Meeting the kids?"

"One date."

"This is like a game show," she says. "She and I will sit on stools facing you and you'll tell us each how great we are, blah blah blah, and then you'll *pick*."

Her voice cracks a little.

"Pick me," she says.

Once, years ago, I accidentally kicked a full can of white paint down the stairs in my two-story rental house, and I feel now exactly as I'd felt as that can went tumbling end over end toward disaster, ruining not only the wood floor and my chances of recovering my deposit, but also my weekend. At the very least here, I've ruined our weekend, and at the most, I've lost the kind of potential that comes along—well, not often.

"Wait," I say. "I don't want to do this. I'm an idiot." Inarguably.

"What are you hoping to hear from me? I'm not promising to say it. I probably won't."

It's been four and a half months, me and Naomi. We've gone away together, and she's met my kids but never slept over when they're home. We have not told each other we love each other, but it's coming. Soon. What we have is real. I can feel its reality in the contours of every kiss and conversation, even this one. Naomi surprises and delights me in some small way every time we're together. She has no designs on improving me, and this might be the first time I've ever felt wholly accepted, and the fact that right now we're sitting so closely that some of her hair rests on the collar of my shirt is proof. I resist making comparisons between the women I've met, because love isn't math and chemistry exists, but Naomi has never, for example, pathologized my busy schedule, or pressured me into wearing fine jewelry, or sent a devastating text instead of initiating a conversation. Not only do I think about her when we're not together and shiver a little when she smiles at me, not only do I wonder if one day we might be really good at living together—but I love being with her. I look forward to it, relish it when it's happening, and look forward to it again. Anything else that has or will come up feels less significant than this one powerful fact.

Also, when she tells a funny story, she doesn't stop talking like getting the laugh was the only point, like a performer dropping the mic. And I like the way she smells and the way she looks and the way the muscles of her face move when she makes a face at me. I like the way she stops to clear snails from the sidewalk after it rains, and shamelessly dotes on her dog, and buys herself gifts that make life sweeter, like plants and chocolate and fancy bath towels. I'm sure I could make a list of stuff I don't cherish about her, though it would be short and hard fought, but so far I've felt no impulse whatsoever to do so, which is information in itself.

Last weekend, after having sex on her bed, my eye started to itch, and I pulled out one of my contact lenses and looked at it closely. A piece was missing. "A very tiny alligator has taken a bite out of my contact," I told Naomi, who was lying naked with her head on my belly.

"How do you know it wasn't a tiny crocodile?" she said.

Plus, I can stay quiet for too long and she lets me.

"I truly value what we have," I finally say. "And also I feel like I started a project and left it almost finished, but not quite."

She nods thoughtfully in her way. "Like you took a class but missed the final exam."

"Unfinished business," I say, starting to cry.

"Here's what I don't want," says Naomi, rubbing my hair with her palm. She holds up a finger. "Drama addiction. On-again, off-again, back and forth. I've done it, it's a waste of time, and it's a dealbreaker for me."

There's a tone in her voice, compassion mixed with resolve, that I've never heard from her before. There's still so much of her I don't know. So much of us.

I nod and wipe my eyes and cry some more.

She holds up another finger. "And no lying. Not even if you're just lying to yourself and I get in the way. If this ends up being just a bullshit excuse for whatever, I'm going to call you on it."

She's saying I can have what I asked for, but I don't want it anymore. I've lost touch with my own mind.

"And I'm not going to process this with you," she says gently. "You have Amanda for that."

This goes without saying, but I like that she says it.

In the morning, we sit on the back patio with coffee and she tells me in so many words to call her after I work out my shit. When we kiss goodbye, her lips don't part at all.

NO PRE-DATE VIDEO CHAT, no exchange of funny memes, no declaration of nerves or excitement. Just a quick back-and-forth to hash out a time and place, and then two days later I'm in my car, aiming for a bookstore cafe on the far side of town.

I have the oddest feeling inside me. It's not guilt, though by now the guilt has settled arthritically into my bones. It's nothing like excitement. It's the specific melancholy of transition, familiar from the big geographical moves I've undertaken in my life. The feeling of shedding the old to make room for the new. I've loved this twisty, ten-date path I've taken. It's nourished and bruised and pushed and held me. How can it be over? How can it not?

You might point out, not incorrectly, that I'm smack dab in the middle of a win-win. Either Nova Weston and I are on the cusp of launching a plan hatched by the universe almost a year ago, or we're not—phew!—and I can return to building a great relationship with Naomi, assuming that's still possible. Assuming I'm as good at repair as I am at breaking things.

I park on the street and get out of the car. A crisp breeze blows. I spot Nova heading toward me down the sidewalk. She gives a wave and returns her hands to her pockets. We meet in front of the bookstore entrance and she comes in for a quick hug. She smells of lavender. She has freckles and crow's feet, a charming combo.

She opens the door for me, but instead of walking through it, I put my hand on her forearm. "I'm sorry," I say. I'm saying this a lot lately, and it's time to stop. "This might be the latest cancelation ever delivered."

Her handsome chin cocks. "You don't want to go inside?"

I shake my head. "I thought I did, but I—well, I'm in a relationship."

Her eyes narrow. "Why am I here if you're in a relationship?"

"That's a good question," I say. "And the answer is that I just realized it's more serious than I thought."

She shrugs and crosses her arms and steps backward. "If it makes you feel any better, I have another date later."

I have no idea if she's joking or serious, because she's turned around and is walking away.

I'm going to miss my own lesbian adolescence, yes, but any vague ambivalence I feel is gone by the time I settle into my car. Inside me, the melancholy is fizzing away, and in its place is a growing sense of anticipation. The next part? It's going to be so good.

WHEN I GET HOME, intending to give myself a beat before calling Naomi to beg her forgiveness, I find that a letter has arrived in the mail. There's no return address but I recognize the handwriting.

Dear S,

I believe that everyone has the right to change her mind or to end a relationship at any time. Still, when I ended things last year, I owed you more care and attention than I was able to give you. I'm sorry for this, and I'm sorry that I encouraged you to be vulnerable with me when I wasn't sure about my feelings for you. I'm sorry too for the times I disappeared on you. I should have apologized at the time, and I should have said goodbye.

I'm sorry, and goodbye.

Z

But the letter isn't in Z's handwriting. Nothing about it is Z's, in fact. These words are Amanda's, and I love her for them.

FOR MY FORTY-EIGHTH BIRTHDAY, I'm in the mood to celebrate. It's been a murky hash of a year. A clumsy circus of a year, full of high-wire acts and unreliable nets. I've had more fun this year than ever in my adult life, and I have cried more tears.

I send invites to everyone I know to meet at the biergarten on the lake, including most of my first dates. Gretchen of the bloody sheets. Margie, who backed out so sweetly over text. Lucinda, who cried over pizza. Dani, my favorite pickleball partner. Even Joyce, of the earrings.

Gretchen and Lucinda and Margie all ask what they can bring. Dani says she's happy to hear from me and asks if she can bring a date, which warms my heart. Joyce responds to tell me she's blocking my number and has no interest in meeting my "latest victim."

I might have predicted that dating ten women would leave a sour taste or two. People do what they need to do. It's high time I learned to let them.

Naomi is starting a charcoal grill when I arrive, and she wraps a paisley apron around her waist and snaps a pair of tongs in my direction. The air is clear between us. Not a new start, exactly, but a more sure-footed one.

Nadine shows up early with a bouquet of rainbow-colored balloons weighted by a stuffed unicorn. Margie arrives with homemade baba ghanoush. She reports that her girlfriend of nine months dumped her via text last week, but she left the house for this, which I find touching. She lays out a blanket and Nadine joins her on it.

Amanda is not here, though she sent a bottle of non-alcoholic champagne and a cheese platter, which Naomi picked up on her way.

Dani and her new girlfriend arrive with heaps of homemade food and Dani goes around delivering arancini on napkins. Lucinda arrives with her on-again girlfriend. Gretchen shows up with a friend, and it turns out Gretchen knows Dani somehow, and Gretchen's friend knows Dani's new girlfriend somehow. Nadine is stung by a bee and jumps up, flipping her burger into the air. At some point, I turn around and find my old neighbor Lyn and her wife have arrived. They're chatting with Nadine and Margie. Gwen, who last week moved out of the house she shared with her husband, shows up on her bike. Her big year is ahead of her.

Naomi reminds me to eat and refreshes my seltzer and spritzes it with bitters that smell like tangerines. I duck into her side and put an arm around her waist. "Is everything OK?" I ask her.

She kisses my hairline and flips a burger. "Everything is

amazing."

The late afternoon turns chilly and the sun starts to set. I tap a fingernail against my glass and everyone quiets and turns toward me. I feel my face grow hot. I'm wobbly from the moment, all these marvelous women staring at me, but also from what happened two hours ago and is still vibrating through my body like a bad cough. On the way here, I stopped at the co-op grocery to pick up cupcakes and candles, turned down an aisle, and ran into Z. She stood in front of a wall of granola, holding a green basket.

We spotted each other at the same time.

"Hi," I said over the rush of blood to my brain.

"Hi," she said.

She put one hand in her pocket. She rocked a little on her heels.

"How are you?" I asked.

"Good. Thanks."

Her eyes slipped over my shoulder, toward the exit.

"Nice to see you," I said.

I walked past her. In the car, I picked up the phone to call Amanda, then put it down. I sat inside the moment with a box of cupcakes on my lap, then started the car.

Now, I steady my heart and raise my glass. "I would like to sit each of you down and tell you what you've meant to me during this past year of my life. But instead, I'll just say this: This is the greatest club I've ever belonged to, and I adore each of you individually."

I'm beaming and they're all beaming back at me. Nadine's is more of a smirk and Dani's is an all-out grin. Naomi's chin is high, likes she's savoring something tasty. The setting sun coppers the planes of her face. Margie comes to give me a hug and everyone else follows, then Naomi starts to collect trash and pack up the food. Chris Pureka is back in town tonight and Naomi and I have tickets. Everyone wishes me a happy birthday and wanders off to their cars, except for Nadine and Margie, who are still lying on Margie's blanket next to a plate of Dani's homemade cannoli.

It's a strange feeling to leave your own party, even the dregs of it, but Nadine is laughing at something Margie said, and Margie is lying flat on her back with one many-ringed hand on her own belly, as if anything might happen and she's up for it.

Can I see them finding happiness together? What do I know?

I kneel to hug them both. In her ear, I tell Nadine that I will always remember her lying on her stomach on a blanket in the grass, her feet in the air, a cannoli between her fingers.

"What did you say about my feet?" she says, and I tell her I'll call her tomorrow.

Naomi and I head to the show. Chris Pureka starts right on time, just as Naomi returns from the bar with our drinks and pulls my hand into hers.

My brother's not wrong: There's no love without timing. Unromantic, maybe, but true. Maybe I am Nova's bad timing. Maybe Z was mine.

There are choices I regret, but Naomi? What is regret's opposite? What is the word for bumbling clumsily into the right open arms? Luck, yes, but also divinity. She soothed my spirit in those early days, and now our spirits explore the nooks of this too-small world together. We hunt for succor, joy, peace. She dove in with me! We're still diving in.

It's been a year, and it's been a *year*. I still wonder how Z's doing, how heavily her heart beats, how often and heartily she laughs and loves. But I don't think about what we might have made together. Except sometimes, thinly, from a distance.

Chris Pureka isn't big on banter, but now they make a comment about how eighty percent of their songs are about former lovers. "But all breakup songs are, at their heart, love songs," they say into the mic, strumming.

All breakup songs are love songs? Do I believe this? Do you?

It's true that beginnings need endings and vice versa. But whether love leads to pain or pain leads to love or both or neither, there's no question I'll keep casting for it. Who am I to outsmart heartbreak? Let it come for me. Let it do its best.

ACKNOWLEDGEMENTS

I'M GRATEFUL to so many terrific humans. My agent, Emily Forland, who has always believed in my books and fought for them. My editor, Alle Mudrick, who helped me to the finish line. My earliest reader, Shannon Fisher, whose support kept me going when I couldn't see ahead. The best-ever early readers, Michelle Wildgen, Miriam Gershow, Melissa Field, and most of all Curtis Sittenfeld, whose wise counsel in all things creative and otherwise I cherish. I do not believe in asking permission to make creative work, but I do believe in considering the feelings of the humans I partially or fully render on the page. For the time and grace they brought to vetting their parts of this material, I'm very grateful to the real-life women who inspired many of these words. To John Stewart for the same, and also for being my co-conspirator in the life and family we've made together. Bill Daniel, Sidney Daniel, Craig Daniel, Rob Delamater, and the best in-laws ever, John Stewart, Sr., and Jeanne Stewart—everyone should have such supportive and loving people on their team. Missy Orge, for always bringing the gentlest heart and the funniest wit and the tastiest snacks. And my children, August and Lewis, for being exactly themselves.

I love you all. Thank you.